The DESIRE for DEARBORNE

V.B. KILDAIRE

Dreamspinner Press

Published by
Dreamspinner Press
4760 Preston Road
Suite 244-149
Frisco, TX 75034
http://www.dreamspinnerpress.com/

Cover Art by Anne Cain annecain.art@gmail.com
Cover Design by Mara McKennen

ISBN: 978-1-61581-009-3

Printed in the United States of America
First Edition
June, 2009

eBook edition available.
eBook ISBN: 978-1-61581-010-9

For Mom and Dad, with love.

The docks of London were a mass of sights, sounds, and scents. As he stepped off the gangplank, Leander Mayfield fairly reeled under the onslaught. After nearly five weeks aboard the *Persephone*, he was glad to be onto solid land again, although his legs weren't yet accustomed to it. It was preferable to attribute his uneven gait to that than to think the influenza he'd barely recovered from before setting sail had returned.

He did his best to keep out of the way of the other disembarking passengers and then the multitude of workers hauling cargo to and fro. The docks of Boston had seemed crowded and busy, but they were nothing compared to London with her ships and wherries and crates and wagons and people as far as his farm-bred eyes could see.

"Yer box, lad," a stevedore dropped a small trunk at his feet.

"Thank you."

"Get along wit'ye, then," the man ordered briskly.

"Yes, sir." Leander bent to grasp the handle of his trunk, only to be assaulted by waves of nausea. He straightened slowly and closed his eyes, praying both would pass. He shivered; for the past week he had been cold so long that it often seemed he would never feel warm again.

"Move along," said another voice, not nearly as amiably as the first. "Out of the way, there." The owner of the voice, an even larger stevedore, gave him a shove and he nearly fell.

Gripping the trunk handle, he began walking, scanning the area for somewhere to sit and collect his thoughts.

"Beggin' yer pardon, sir." The same stevedore that had jostled Leander sounded much meeker now. "Can I help ye?"

"The Earl of Dearborne was to arrive today on the *Persephone*," came a haughty voice. "Is he still on board?"

Leander didn't hear the stevedore's answer, being lost in his own thoughts. *There was an earl on board? If only I had known that when— oh. I wonder if I'll ever grow used to the fact that I'm the Earl of Dearborne.* Taking a deep breath, he stepped forward. "I'm Leander Mayfield, sir."

Both men turned toward him and Leander suddenly became acutely aware of his clothing. Although he was wearing his Sunday collar and coat, and his overcoat was only a year old, he felt decidedly shabby in comparison to the heavyset man in the fur-lined redingote that was opened to reveal a green silk waistcoat and a fashionably tied fine linen cravat.

"Leander Mayfield?" Cool gray eyes flicked over him and then the man removed his tall beaver hat and gave Leander a slight bow. "Lord Dearborne, I am Morleigh Mayfield. The late earl, as well as your grandfather, were my father's half-brothers."

Leander tried to follow. "That makes us… cousins?"

"Half-cousins, after a fashion." Mayfield didn't sound the slightest bit interested in the fact.

After losing his father and both brothers in the past few years, Leander was glad to find himself with any relations. Standing as straight as possible, he removed his felt hat and imitated Mayfield's half-bow. "I am very glad to meet you, sir."

"The coach is waiting," was all Morleigh said in response. Then he glanced over his shoulder. "Dodds, see to his lordship's trunks."

"There's only one," Leander explained. "I can—"

The stevedore was also eager to make up for his previous error. "Yer lordship, I can—"

"I said the footman will see to it." Mayfield spoke firmly, freezing the stevedore in his tracks. "Come along, Dearborne."

Still a bit dazed, Leander allowed himself to be ushered to an impressive coach with a coat of arms—*his* coat of arms—painted on the door. However, it was the pair of perfectly matched bays drawing the vehicle that made Leander forget his weariness momentarily. He stood admiring them until he realized the footman was holding the coach's

door open and everyone was waiting for him. Quickly he climbed in and sat down, feeling shabbier than ever on the velvet-covered seats.

Mayfield followed, settling himself across from Leander. Silence descended in the coach as it rolled away. Despite the dim interior, Leander could feel Mayfield's eyes on him and searched for something suitable to say. "You have very handsome horses, sir."

"They are your horses, Lord Dearborne, just as this coach is your coach," Morleigh replied, still maintaining his cool, formal tone.

"Oh." Leander fell silent as he tried to absorb that information. His father had owned only two plow horses, and even on the rare occasions he allowed his sons to ride them, Kit and Chance—as the eldest— claimed ownership of them and Leander usually rode sitting behind Kit, hanging onto his brother's coat. The idea of owning such fine animals himself was rather bewildering.

Now that he was seated and no longer had to worry about his immediate surroundings, Leander's body began making its complaints known. His bones ached after the long voyage made in the cold of January and his skin was cold and clammy. There might possibly be a return of his influenza after all, Leander realized with dismay.

Perhaps he should have waited until March to sail, as Daisy, Kit's fiancée, had wanted him to do, but he had been determined to prove he was fit enough to travel. What he didn't tell her was that he was afraid if he didn't sail as soon as possible he would dwell too long on what had happened to Kit and Chance and lose his nerve entirely. All attempts by her and her family to dissuade him had fallen on deaf ears. Now he would have to pay for his stubbornness.

Leander looked out the coach window, deciding he ought to accustom himself to the sights of his new city, but knew almost immediately that it would be impossible to do in a single coach ride— there was simply too much to take in. Buildings lined the streets and Leander tried to guess how old they were and what sort of things they had witnessed. Had they survived the Great Fire or only been built after? How many of them were older than the buildings he'd seen in Boston? How many were older than Boston itself? And— "Is that the Tower of London?"

Mayfield looked out the window. "It is."

Leander stared until the imposing structure was no longer in sight. He'd seen it in several books, but none of the drawings had been able to truly capture the building.

"If you wish to tour the sights of London, I'm sure your man-of-affairs will be more than happy to arrange it."

Leander overlooked the amused disdain in his cousin's voice, more curious about his words. "Man-of-affairs?"

"I believe his name is Marlowe. He was hired by the late earl's man—one last duty before being pensioned off. Of course, he couldn't ride out to meet you in the Dearborne coach, so that duty fell to me."

"I see." Leander didn't want to appear any more foolish in the man's eyes, so he refrained from asking more questions. He had a vague idea what a man-of-affairs did and this Marlowe would probably be able to explain the specifics of his job. "I'm sorry to put you to the trouble."

Instead of saying "not at all," which is how most people in Leander's village of Pelham would have replied, Mayfield said, "There are many things you will have to accustom yourself to."

"Yes, sir." Leander nodded. He didn't want to dwell on those things at the moment, however. Worrying about the enormity of his situation would only bring on the melancholy he was prone to. Better to deal with each concern as it materialized, no matter how difficult it might be.

At the moment his concern was staying alert and not giving in to the dizziness that still lingered. In addition to the chills, he was also feverish and his head was pounding. The sea air that was supposed to improve his health seemed to have had the opposite effect. He tried to concentrate instead on the motion of the coach, grateful for a familiar sensation in the midst of his strange new life. The only difference was that the well-sprung vehicle was far more comfortable than the buckboards or wagons Leander was used to riding in, and the swaying soon lulled him to sleep.

Mayfield roused him just as they were rolling to a halt, and before he was fully awake, the footman had the door open and Leander found himself on the sidewalk staring up at an impressive four-story brick building. "This is where we live?"

"This is where *you* live," Mayfield said, cool amusement still apparent in his tone. "I have my own lodgings in Dorset Square," he added as he descended from the coach.

Having spent most of his twenty-two years in a four-room farmhouse, the idea of so much space was intimidating rather than exciting. He started up the steps when Mayfield motioned for him to do so, wondering if perhaps he was still sleeping after all. The enormous front hall and the line of servants assembled before him seemed unreal. He handed his overcoat, hat, and woolen gloves to the solemn butler as if in a dream.

"His lordship is not well," Mayfield announced once the introductions were finished. "Be sure there is a good fire in his room."

"There is, sir," one of the footmen answered.

"And see to it that he is brought something hot to eat."

Leander's stomach rebelled at the thought. "No." His voice wasn't as strong as he would have liked, so he cleared his throat and tried again. "No food. Thank you."

"Have some negus prepared and brought up," Mayfield amended. "Powell will show you up to your chambers, Lord Dearborne."

"My box," Leander protested, wishing his mind would function well enough that he could speak in proper sentences.

"Dodds has already brought it up," Mayfield said impatiently. "Gibson is no doubt unpacking it as we speak."

Leander vaguely recalled the name of Gibson among all the others, but nothing else about him.

"I must take my leave. I have other matters that require my attention." Mayfield made another slight bow. "Good day, Lord Dearborne."

"Thank you for your kindness, Mr. Mayfield." Leander didn't need Mayfield's condescending look to know that none of his actions sprang from kindness, but Leander felt that he ought to say *something*.

After another polite but cold smile, Mayfield left. Alone but for nearly a dozen servants, Leander looked around at all of them until

Powell, the butler, took pity on him. "If you will walk this way, my lord."

Leander followed the dignified man upstairs and into a room easily twice as large as any in his old home. The dark wooden furniture was so highly polished it gleamed while the curtains and bed hangings were of a heavy, dark blue fabric that Leander guessed might be silk. More important to him was the bed itself, which was large and piled with pillows and blankets.

He jumped slightly when he felt hands on his coat collar and turned to see a tall, wiry young man, not too much older than himself, attempting to remove his coat for him. The man was apparently here to help him undress, which Leander found excessive. "I'm not ill," he assured the man—Gibson, no doubt. "I can do it myself."

"Very good, my lord." Gibson stepped back immediately. "The maid has brought the negus up already." He nodded toward a small, round table.

"Thank you." Leander sat in the deep, well-padded chair next to it and wrapped his hands around the steaming cup. Sipping at the sweet, spicy drink, he watched Gibson lay out his nightshirt.

That finished, Gibson moved next to Leander's chair, standing there in silence until Leander became uneasy and looked up at him questioningly.

"Do you require anything else, my lord?"

"No, thank you."

Gibson bowed—much more deeply than Mayfield had—and left. Leander was relieved to finally have some time alone, even if weariness was pressing too heavily for him to reflect much on the day's events. He was halfway through the cup of negus, which he suspected contained something much more potent than cider, and drowsiness was beginning to overtake him in earnest.

Setting the rest of the drink aside, he rose and began changing into his nightclothes. He caught a glimpse of himself in the mirror over the washstand and paused. Weary blue eyes stared back at him from a pale face. His thick, wavy black hair was in disarray and Leander pushed it

into place even though he was about to turn in and his hair rarely behaved as he wished it to at the best of times. He did look ill, he decided: his face was drawn and his cheekbones more prominent than usual. Hopefully, sleep would help. He didn't want to begin his life in London looking like a consumptive weakling. With a frown, he turned from the mirror and got into bed.

As soon as he was settled, thoughts of the crowded city, the formidable house, or the numerous strangers that shared it with him no longer plagued him. He wasn't concerned with the fact that he didn't know a soul in the country except for a disdainful cousin. All that mattered was that the bed he'd just climbed into was as comfortable as he'd hoped and that the blazing fire and warm drink had managed to chase much of the chill from his bones.

Even the strangeness of resting among so many pillows failed to distract him, and within moments, he was deeply asleep.

I vow, Julien, I am quite annoyed with you."

Julien Sutcliffe arched a dark eyebrow. "I tremble at the prospect of your wrath. Pray tell, what have I done to offend your sensibilities?" He knew himself to be perfectly safe with his teasing. Not only was his aunt unable to remain angry with him for any length of time, her sensibilities were not easily offended.

"I did not see you at Lady Rockingham's soirée last night."

"I should be worried if you had, as I did not attend."

"I trust you have a good reason for your absence. One that does not involve Gabriel Hartley."

Julien favored her with a wry smile. Although his aunt had never shown any disapproval of his preference for male bed partners in general, she also never hesitated to voice her opinion about particular lovers she didn't care for. His latest, Gabriel Hartley, was definitely among that number. Most women in Society would overlook such peccadillos of family members, especially when that family member was also the Earl of Blackstone, but not the Viscountess Carysfort. It was one of the things Julien most admired about his aunt. "Not at all, Aunt Cordelia. In truth, the reason had more to do with a young lady."

"Do not try to fob me off with such fustian." Cordelia's normally warm brown eyes narrowed.

"Upon my honor, such as it is. Did you not see Miss Norville at the ball?"

"Sir Francis Norville's chit?" Cordelia set her cup back in its saucer with a crash. "Never say she is out among Society again."

"It is so. I had it from Lord Archer that she was at the Mountraths' dinner party the evening before."

"That is no reason for you to avoid attending balls."

"It is an excellent reason, Aunt. I have no desire to revive old gossip, and should she encounter me, I'm sure she would take it as an excellent reason to renew some of her complaints."

"Complaints which no one attends to. Not a soul believes her sordid tale."

"No, they made up sordid tales of their own, didn't they?"

"Because you refused to speak of it." Cordelia sounded truly annoyed, and Julien knew this time it was genuine. It never failed to irritate her that he refused to tell her the circumstances surrounding the disappearance of Lavinia Norville's brother.

He'd never told anyone. No one gave any credit to Lavinia's claim that Julien had killed her brother, Tobias, in a duel over her honor. It was common knowledge—even if it was never referred to—that the earl had no interest in women. Instead, the ton chose to believe that it was Tobias whom Julien had been involved with and that he had killed young Norville in a fit of anger or rejection. Since there was never word of a duel and no proof that Tobias had been killed, no one ever spoke of the affair to Julien—at least not directly. There had been whispers and looks and innuendos, however, and Julien had no desire for it all to begin again, two years later. "And I don't intend to ever speak of it," he said firmly.

"Be that as it may." Cordelia sipped her tea, still looking somewhat disgruntled. "If you let it be known that you will not attend any event where Miss Norville is present, she would soon be excluded from every guest list."

No doubt. Lavinia Norville was only the daughter of a baronet, not nearly as desirable a guest as an earl, especially a wealthy earl that flouted the laws of Society just enough to make himself intriguing. "She'd never get herself married that way. Once she has secured a husband, she'll have no more time for old grudges." He didn't add that he felt sorry for Sir Francis and didn't want to cause the older man any further embarrassment. "Besides, you know I'm not fond of such things to begin with."

"It's not good for you to be shut away in this manner."

"I'm hardly a hermit, Aunt Cordelia."

She fixed him with her sternest look yet. "Julien, if you refer to that Hartley creature, you know very well that is not what I—"

"I do not refer to Gabriel," Julien assured her. He found Gabriel stimulating in many ways, but intellectually was not one of them. The man's conversation centered around himself or the most scandalous gossip he could uncover. "I attended a dinner party given by Viscount Seaforth not two days ago."

"Certainly that is preferable." Cordelia wasn't entirely placated. "Even if Seaforth tends to be just as odd as you."

"I believe his fiancée might take issue with that remark." Julien flashed a rare grin.

Cordelia shot him another quelling look despite the fact that her scolding was having no effect. "You know very well that's not what I meant. And for that matter, Lady Penelope is something of an Original herself. Very nearly a bluestocking. I suppose it is a good match, seeing as they're both interested in dusty tombs and crumbling ruins and heathen gods."

"Actually, crumbling ruins and heathen gods are my area of study, Aunt. The Roman Empire, you know. Lady Penelope is concerned with the truth of the legend of King Arthur, while her brother studies the Roman occupation of Britain. Viscount Seaforth enjoys the study of ancient Egypt." Julien didn't continue, knowing his aunt only concerned herself with the here and now.

"And a fine, lively conversation there must be around that table." Cordelia's dry tone rivaled her nephew's. "Speaking of oddities, have you heard of the new American Earl?"

"The what?"

"The new Earl of Dearborne."

"I thought the title was set to go to Morleigh Mayfield."

"Most did," Cordelia said, setting aside her now-empty teacup and warming to the subject. "But it was discovered that Stephen Mayfield's younger son married and had children. He was the younger son of a younger son, so went off to America to make his fortune. Never expected to be in line for the title, I daresay. Thomas is dead now, but one son

survived him. He arrived in London four days ago. It's all quite mysterious; no one has seen him except his cousin and servants. Lord Rockingham had it from Mayfield that the young man is sickly, coarse, and dull-witted."

Julien didn't consider Morleigh Mayfield's opinion reliable.

"I intend to pay a call soon," Cordelia continued. "No one has ventured to do so thus far. I'm sure I would have heard if anyone had. There is a slight connection, you know. The late earl's daughter, Constance, was such a help and comfort when I first entered Society. She made it much easier for Octavius' family to accept me."

Twisting the amber ring he wore on his last finger, the one his mother gave him because it matched his eyes, Julien reflected on what a shame it was that Constance Mayfield hadn't been a part of the family when his parents married. Perhaps she would have been able to ease some of the tension in that marriage as well. His mother, Arabella, along with his Aunt Cordelia and Uncle Carlisle, were the children of Leonard Osgood, a very wealthy merchant. Wealthy enough that all three children married into the aristocracy, despite the fact that their father was in trade. Arabella had married Julien's father at the prompting of both families; her father wanted a connection to the Earl of Blackstone, and his wanted the funds to continuing living in the style he felt was his family's due. The union was not happy. Sebastien Sutcliffe made no secret of the fact that he thought his wife beneath him, and Arabella never let her husband forget that she had been misled. The Earl of Blackstone never thought much of Sebastien's branch of the family and had as little contact with them as possible.

Later, Carlisle married Constance Mayfield, making for a much easier transition when Cordelia wed the Viscount Carysfort. Having often been the pawn or prize in his parents' battles, Julien couldn't help but wonder how much different his childhood would have been had Constance been there to make things easier on his mother.

"I believe I'll issue him an invitation to my ball in a fortnight," Cordelia mused, then fixed her gaze on Julien again. "A ball I expect you to attend, I might add. Certainly you don't make plans with Mr. Hartley so far ahead."

"No, I do not." Julien didn't dare tell her that lately he'd been

considering ending his association with Hartley. If she knew that, she wouldn't give him a moment's peace until she was certain he had. "You have my word that I will be there."

"Excellent." Cordelia rose, shaking out the skirt of her fashionable walking dress. "I must be going. I have to pay a visit to my modiste."

Julien stood as well, seeing her not only to the door, but also handing her up into her coach. She was the only person to whom he extended such a courtesy, leaving it to his staff to show any other guests out.

Walking back inside, he ignored the front parlor and instead walked into his study. He picked up the latest edition of *Roman Antiquities Quarterly*, hoping to find an article that would occupy his mind and take it off the prospect of his aunt's ball.

It was more than a week away, but Julien already felt oppressed by it. It seemed as though there were more balls and entertainments this Season, many of them more elaborate than had ever been seen. It was almost as if the aristocracy was making up for the fact that their new king had chosen to have a very plain coronation and lead a simple lifestyle—an immense contrast to his predecessor, the flamboyant and extravagant George IV.

Completely turning his back on the ton would only make things difficult for his aunt, so Julien contrived to go to just enough balls to keep Society from feeling shunned and thereby shunning him in return. He chose carefully, hoping to avoid too many evenings of tedium. Well-known though his preference for men might be, most mamas saw no reason why that should keep him from making one of their daughters a countess. The rumors of his refusal to marry Lavinia Norville after being purportedly discovered in a somewhat compromising position two years before had made those mamas a bit more cautious about throwing their daughters into his path, but it wasn't enough to put them off completely. There were also adventurous widows who presumed they could change his preference if they tried hard enough.

Most men of the ton, on the other hand, rarely wanted to be seen speaking to him alone for any great length of time for fear of starting rumors. There were other titled men who shared his preference, but most of them wanted to keep it a secret from Society—and their wives.

Julien could never be bothered with that sort of secrecy. He knew what he did with other men was a hanging offense, but he also knew that as a member of the peerage he was perfectly safe as long as he didn't make a spectacle of himself.

And Julien had no desire to make a spectacle of himself. He much preferred being left alone except for people who shared his interests and could satisfy his need for intelligent conversation. When he wished it, there were men of the demimonde who could satisfy his other needs. At times he wondered what it would be like to have one person in his life who fulfilled both needs, but Julien was never one to dwell too long on something that could never be.

"IT'S Parr's understudy, isn't it? That treacherous little slut!" The Angel Gabriel was definitely not living up to his appellation at the moment. "You'd best take care that he doesn't give you a dose. And be sure you don't leave any valuables lying about when you're with him."

Gabriel Hartley had been christened "Angel" by his admirers for his golden-blond curls, silvery blue eyes, and beautiful face and form, Julien reminded himself; not for his temperament, which ranged from self-centered to vicious, or his faulty tenor, which was barely good enough for him to qualify as a singer at all.

Gabriel did not display his bad temper to Julien often, because Julien had made it clear early on that he would not put up with it. At this point, however, Gabriel probably felt there was little to lose.

"I have not taken up with Parr's understudy," Julien assured him. "Or with anyone else."

"Are you becoming a monk?" Gabriel jeered. "Or perhaps you've found yourself some whey-faced miss and are going to make an attempt at being a husband."

"Or perhaps," Julien said coldly, "I've grown tired of second-rate theatrics."

Although not particularly clever, Gabriel was cunning and quickly realized his mistake. "Forgive me, Julien," he said in a much different

tone. "I don't know what came over me. The thought of losing you brought on such madness. Julien, my love, what am I to do if you turn from me?"

It was fortunate indeed that Gabriel didn't have to make his living on the stage, Julien reflected. His style was only suited to the most overwrought of melodramas. Had he once found Gabriel's tempers entertaining? Perhaps he had, at first, but that had been nearly two years ago. "Do not make yourself foolish. We both know you're more concerned with losing your comfortable quarters than my attentions."

Gabriel quickly dropped the pretense of love and became coaxing. "Come now, Julien. What have I done that makes you want to end our association? It has been very pleasurable, don't you think?"

"It has," Julien agreed, watching as Gabriel shrugged off his coat, then began untying his cravat.

"Am I not here and waiting whenever you wish for me?"

"You are." Julien didn't add that Gabriel was paid very well to be so.

"If you've grown bored, I can assure you there are many other things I can do." Gabriel shed his waistcoat next. "Is there anything in particular that intrigues you? There's nothing I wouldn't do to please you."

No doubt. Julien knew that compared to some of Gabriel's previous patrons, he wasn't terribly demanding. Add to that the fine house and generous allowance and it was little wonder the Angel was desperate to keep him on the hook.

Gabriel was removing his shirt with slow, deliberate movements, watching Julien's response the entire time, as he revealed a chest and shoulders Apollo would envy.

Julien wanted to tell him that his well-practiced arts were a large part of the problem, but he wasn't certain Gabriel would truly understand his meaning. Gabriel was by far the most beautiful lover Julien had ever had and initially part of the thrill had been in knowing he was envied by many other men. Just knowing he was envied had been enough for Julien, who had never felt the need to flaunt Gabriel at Madame

Rimbaude's as so many other gentlemen did their companions. He much preferred the comforts of home, whether it was his own or the one he rented for Gabriel. Indeed, Gabriel sometimes had to pester Julien to go out, not because Julien felt the need to hide what he was, but because Julien found most entertainments boring. Perhaps *that* was the key to ending this matter painlessly. "It's been nearly two years, Gabriel. I would think you would be growing bored with me by now," he said, knowing Gabriel would vehemently deny it.

"Never! There is no greater pleasure for me than spending time in your presence. What will my life be without you?"

There was the ring of truth to Gabriel's last protest. Julien hoped that if he settled that matter, Gabriel would cease his histrionics. "I certainly don't intend to throw you into the street. I will pay any outstanding bills you currently have and you may remain in this house until the end of the Season. That should give you plenty of time to find a new patron."

As he'd predicted, that put an end to Gabriel's declarations of love and heartbreak. There was a flash of calculation in the pale blue eyes before Gabriel lowered his gaze. "You're very generous, my lord," he murmured, moving closer. "How shall I ever thank you?" He looked up at Julien through his lashes.

How could one blame Gabriel for constantly employing the same tactics when they always succeeded? Julien was already growing hard before Gabriel brushed a knowing hand across the front of his breeches. Predictable and calculating Gabriel might be, but he was also very talented, and it wasn't as though Julien had plans to begin looking for a new paramour this very night.

Leander's first few days in London were a blur; he'd spent them in bed fighting off the beginnings of another bout of influenza. Once he was well enough to be out of bed, he spent his time exploring his enormous new home and trying to adjust to having a multitude of servants.

He was surprised to learn that Gibson's attempts to help had not been in deference to his illness, but part of a valet's regular duties. Leander couldn't remember a time when he *hadn't* dressed himself, except when illness had left him too weak to do so, and having Gibson there was awkward, to say the least. The valet rarely spoke except to say "yes, my lord" or "no, my lord," but the black eyes were always watchful—no doubt the poor man was just waiting for the opportunity to do his job. As for the rest of the servants, they went about their duties with no direction from Leander whatsoever. Powell had the running of the house well in hand, so Leander had nothing to concern himself with there.

Even after three days, Leander still had no real desire to step outside. Where most young men his age might feel confined, Leander was used to passing the time indoors and often in his bed. The same scarlet fever that had carried off his mother when he was seven had also left him an invalid for much of his childhood.

One of the few things Leander had been allowed to do during his long convalescence was read, and before long, books became his entire world. Although his father couldn't afford many, Grandfather Spencer, a fair scholar in his own right, was always happy to lend Leander as many books as he could read. Leander had shared his grandfather's fascination with the lore of King Arthur. Spencer's copy of *Le Morte d'Arthur* had spent as much time on Leander's shelf as it had on Spencer's.

When he was twelve, another fever brought on—according to the doctor—by excessive study led his father to limit Leander's time

reading, insisting instead that he spend a set amount of time each day outside. This practice did strengthen Leander's body to the point that when looking at him, people rarely suspected he'd been ill much of his life, but it didn't strengthen his constitution to such an extent.

He likely would have begun taking his daily "constitutional" again in London, but on his first day exploring the house, Leander found the magnificent two-story library, with books on every subject filling the shelves. Balconies lined the higher floor along three of the four walls. On the lower floor, a large walnut desk dominated one end of the room, and a fireplace the other. A low sofa with a brown leather seat and two chairs upholstered in dark red velvet made for comfortable places to read, while a large round table provided a place for more study or to take a meal if one didn't care to leave the library.

And Leander never wanted to. For him the outside world had ceased to exist. He barely knew where to start. He'd select one book to read only to find another that looked equally interesting. That was until the second day, when he found a complete translation of Chrétien de Troyes' *Lancelot, Knight of the Cart.* When he was fourteen, his grandfather had managed to get an account of the poem and Leander had read the abbreviated version as often as he could before he'd had to return it. He'd discussed it with his grandfather and father enthusiastically for months afterward, although he'd left out the fact that he felt strangely jealous of Guinevere.

The library of Esmond House, however, contained several of de Troyes' works as well as some works by Malory and Monmouth. Even more fascinating to Leander were a series of essays on Lancelot himself, which made reference to a German poem, *Lanzelet,* from the twelfth century and another in Italian. Painful thoughts of dead family and being alone in a crowded city disappeared as Leander immersed himself in legend, surfacing only when hunger or exhaustion demanded it.

When he finally emerged to take note of his surroundings again, Powell presented him with two silver salvers. One was covered with calling cards and another piled high with invitations. Leander had no idea what to make of either. He had thought his cousin might visit again, but Morleigh apparently had no interest in him now that his duty was done. Nor had Leander seen Marlowe, his man-of-affairs, but the name

alone implied that the man had plenty to keep him occupied. No doubt he would see Leander when he had the time.

Leander had been in London just over a week when Powell walked into the library early one afternoon, interrupting his reading. "I beg your pardon, my lord, but are you home to the Viscount and Viscountess Carysfort?"

It seemed an odd question, when Leander was most obviously at home. "Of course."

"Very good. I will show them to the drawing room. Gibson will be down with your coat immediately."

Leander was briefly confused, but soon caught on. He had spent his time in the house wearing a shirt and trousers, just as he would have in Pelham, but obviously it was not fit for company. "Thank you, Powell."

After a moment, Gibson arrived with his coat and cravat. Thus prepared, Leander walked into the drawing room. Inside was a couple so elegantly dressed that he was immediately self-conscious.

The viscount was a stern-looking man, whose bow and clothing were as stiff and proper as they could be. "Lord Dearborne, I am Viscount Carysfort. May I present my wife, Lady Carysfort?" He gestured to the woman at his side, whom, although she appeared to be well past forty, had a sparkle in her eyes that bespoke a much younger mind-set.

Leander bowed again in response to her curtsey, but after that was at a loss how to proceed. Lord Carysfort did not seem inclined to say anything further and was looking at Leander somewhat askance. Fortunately, Lady Carysfort was more than equal to the situation. "I apologize for intruding so soon after your arrival in London, Lord Dearborne. As an excuse, I claim a distant connection to you."

"A connection?"

"The late earl's daughter was married to my brother. They have both passed on now, but I did feel an interest in the new Earl of Dearborne."

"I'm very glad to meet you," Leander said, meaning it wholeheartedly. Although she was not a blood relation, he already found her infinitely preferable to the haughty Morleigh Mayfield. He glanced

again at Lord Carysfort, who was looking at the Roman sofa. With a start, Leander realized his error and felt his cheeks begin to burn. "I'm so sorry. Please, sit down." There had rarely been visitors to the Mayfield farm in Pelham. Leander had always assumed he would learn more about such niceties when he went to college in Amherst as his brothers had, but first illness—this time pleurisy—and then his father's death prevented him from ever attending.

"How do you find London thus far?" Lady Carysfort asked when they were seated.

"I'm afraid I haven't seen much of it," Leander admitted.

"Yes, we understand you've been ill."

The last thing Leander wanted was for his reputation as an invalid to follow him from Pelham to London. "The voyage did take a toll, but I was well after two days. Since then I've spent nearly all my time in the earl's library."

"Your library," Lady Carysfort corrected gently.

Her words gave Leander pause, as did any direct reminder of his sudden wealth. "Yes, my library."

"I sent you an invitation to my ball," Lady Carysfort continued. "I do hope you will be able to attend."

Leander hadn't noticed her invitation among the piles, but she was the only person who made any effort to meet him, so despite how unsettling he found the idea of attending a ball, he promised, "I will be sure to attend. Thank you."

"We look forward to seeing you there. Hopefully it will improve your regard for London."

"My regard for London?" Realizing he might have given the wrong impression, thereby insulting his guests, Leander hastened to explain. "I have always wanted to travel to London, to England. There are so many things I want to see and I mean to, but... the library here is so splendid and once I started reading...." He felt his face flush again, unsure how much to explain.

Lady Carysfort merely smiled. "You're very fond of reading then?"

"Very. So much that it used to worry my father. I should start going out and about. I know being shut indoors so much is not good for me, but the books—"

"If there is any way we can help, do not hesitate to ask. Indeed, we can recommend several shops that may prove helpful to you."

Leander wasn't about to admit that despite his apparent wealth, he had no actual money. "Thank you, but I—I should probably go over my accounts first. And I will as soon as my man-of-affairs has the time."

That got Lord Carysfort's attention. "Has the time? Never say your man-of-affairs has claimed he hasn't the time to attend you. I would find a new man-of-affairs as soon as may be if that is the case."

"He hasn't refused to call on me," Leander explained. "He just hasn't contacted me yet."

"Why would he present himself to you if you haven't summoned him?" Lord Carysfort frowned. "The only occasion for such would be if there was a problem. Otherwise, he would not presume to disturb you."

"Oh. I—oh." He was a fool. Years spent at studies, and yet he still was a fool. "I suppose the servants here wouldn't mention it if I were mistaken or neglecting something."

Lord Carysfort raised his eyebrows. "Not if they wished to keep their position."

"Of course." Leander pushed his hand through his hair. There was no telling how many things he'd overlooked.

"If there are things you wish to attend to," Lady Carysfort said, "perhaps we should take our leave." Before Leander could protest, they both stood. "If there is any way we can be of assistance, don't hesitate to send word."

"Thank you." Leander nodded, privately vowing to do no such thing. He'd burdened his family with his illness for much of his life, but he was not going to begin his new life here by burdening kindly strangers with his ignorance. Ignorance could be cured easily enough once one was aware of it. "I'm very grateful you decided to visit me." That statement, at least, required no effort.

Lord Carysfort inclined his head in acknowledgment and Lady Carysfort gave him another warm smile. Leander walked them to the front hall, and after more bows all around, Powell was there to show them out. Shoving his hands into his coat pockets, Leander wandered back to the library.

For most of his twenty-two years, all that had ever been required of him was that he live. That he live through the scarlet fever, brain fever, pleurisy, and a multitude of other illnesses. All that had mattered to his family was that he be healthy. He helped on the farm whenever he was well enough, but his father and brothers had been wary of letting him do too much for fear of bringing on another illness. Managing time or money matters had never been an issue; what little money there was to manage his father saw to, and any time Leander was not ill or working had been spent at his studies. Servants were unheard of on a two-horse farm.

His new wealth solved many of the problems that had plagued his family back home, but it had been foolish of him to assume it left him without any duties whatsoever. There were obviously many things for him to see to, and it was his responsibility to learn what they were. Taking a page from the book of his eldest brother, Leander decided not to waste time putting off what needed to be done.

Squaring his shoulders, he stepped out into the hall. "Powell, please come into the library. I need to speak to you." Ordering people about didn't come naturally to him, so he always tried to do it as politely as possible.

A moment later, Powell stood in front of the handsome desk that Leander had seated himself behind. "Yes, my lord?"

"How do I contact Mr. Marlowe if I want to see him?"

"I can send for him at once, my lord. How soon do you wish to see him?"

Curious, Leander asked, "How soon could he get here?"

"Within the half-hour if you wish it."

Leander blinked in surprise, feeling more foolish than ever for having shrugged off the situation for nearly a week. "An hour from now

will be soon enough."

"Yes, my lord. Will that be all?"

It occurred to Leander that even if servants would never correct him, they might answer direct questions. "Did you work for the last Earl of Dearborne, Powell?"

"I did. I was a footman in the household then."

"When did you become the butler?"

"Upon his death, the late earl's butler, housekeeper, and valet all received generous pensions for years of service. Mrs. Cross and I were promoted by his man-of-affairs."

"Mr. Marlowe?"

"No, my lord. Mr. Longheed. He also received a pension after seeing to the household and finding a new man-of-affairs."

"Is that common when an earl passes on?"

If Powell thought Leander's questions strange, he didn't show it. "The late earl was very generous."

Now came something that had been on Leander's mind since he first saw Lord and Lady Carysfort. "Was he extravagant?"

Powell hesitated, obviously unused to voicing opinions on the aristocracy. "With some things, such as books." He glanced around at the library. "But he was a man of taste."

Ever since seeing Lord Carysfort's fine clothes, Leander had become aware of how lacking his own wardrobe was. Once he'd thought about it, he realized that even his servants were better dressed than he was. It was such a bizarre situation that Leander didn't know how to address it. *Best just come out and say it.* "Is his clothing still in the house?"

That gave the butler a moment's pause. "It has been packed away until you decide what you wish to be done with it."

"I would like Gibson to take an inventory of it. All of it. Could you tell him?"

"Yes, my lord."

"I know my clothes are not suitable. How do I go about getting some that are?"

"I believe you would call on your tailor, my lord."

"Wearing this?"

The butler's gray eyes flicked over Leander's clothing. "I can send for some things for you to wear until you pay a visit to a tailor that suits you."

"Do that."

"I'll see to everything at once, my lord." Powell bowed and left the library.

Leander opened one of the desk drawers and pulled out several sheets of paper, then drew the quill and inkwell closer. He would begin by making a list of all the things he could think to ask his man-of-affairs. There were obviously a number of new things he had to learn about, but fortunately, learning had always come naturally to him.

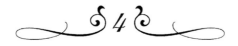

Julien strolled up Bond Street toward Ashworth's, wondering what sort of bill Gabriel had run up there. Ashworth's was very exclusive, only serving the uppermost echelons of Society. One needed a sufficient title or a recommendation from someone with a sufficient title to get an appointment with the tailor. Julien had recommended Gabriel in a moment of weakness and the singer had been taking blatant advantage of it ever since.

Julien intended to make it clear to Ashworth that after this he no longer considered himself responsible for the Angel's accounts. Perhaps that would convince Gabriel that he was serious about ending their association. Of course, if he had stopped seeing Gabriel when he'd said he would, that would have convinced him as well. Instead, Julien had been with Gabriel several times since, even taking him to the opera and theater.

It might have been easier if he'd found someone new before trying to end it with the Angel, but he hadn't yet found anyone who appealed to him. Nor did he care to pay for a mollie from the street or even from Madame Rimbaude's, which catered solely to men of the aristocracy.

There was only one other customer in Ashworth's when Julien entered. At least Julien assumed it was a customer that Ashworth and his three employees were crowded around and all speaking to at once. Julien craned his neck slightly, curious as to who rated such attention. He finally got a glimpse of the young man in the center of the group. It was someone Julien had never set eyes on before in his life, for if he had, he certainly would have remembered.

The youth's—Julien thought he couldn't have been much more than twenty—finely wrought features could have almost served as the model for a young demigod if not for the lost expression. He put the ethereal Angel Gabriel to shame in Julien's opinion, despite—or perhaps because of—the jet black hair and bright blue eyes that gave him a more earthly,

accessible appearance.

The tailors were displaying fabrics and sketches while Ashworth said *yea* or *nay* and the customer merely nodded occasionally. Julien found the behavior odd and wondered if perhaps the young man was someone's new companion, plucked very recently from the country. Then he shook himself. Although the subject of a new companion was at the forefront of *his* mind at the moment, that didn't mean that every handsome young man belonged to someone.

Ashworth ushered the customer off to the fitting rooms, then turned and saw Julien. "Lord Blackstone," he said, bowing. "Forgive me. I did not hear you enter."

"No matter." Julien was tempted to ask the young man's identity, but knew it would be in vain. Unlike most shopkeepers, Ashworth did not brag to all and sundry about who his customers were, and remaining close-lipped had only increased the tailor's cachet. "I'm here to settle the final account of Mr. Hartley."

Ashworth's eyebrows rose, the only sign that Julien had said anything unusual. "Of course, my lord."

Paying a bill of nearly a hundred pounds served to remind Julien that his association with Gabriel was, above all, a business arrangement. He headed to the Pall Mall and his club for lunch. Although he had a membership at White's, Julien usually felt more comfortable at Jupiter's, which was known for members who ignored the strict confines of society. Not only men like himself, but also those who espoused radical philosophies, considered themselves scientific visionaries, or immersed themselves in the outré, as well as many other noted eccentrics.

Both Viscount Seaforth and Lord Archer were members, but they were not present today, so Julien's meal was a solitary one. He was just finishing off with a glass of hock when he heard someone ask if they might join him. Looking up, he saw the plump figure of Baron Vance. The only thing they had in common was their preference for male partners, but Vance wasn't a bad sort, despite being the most flamboyant dandy in town. Julien motioned Vance to a vacant chair and signaled for another glass to be brought.

"I have some news that might interest you, Blackstone," Vance said

as he poured himself a glass.

"Have you?"

"Bit of bad news. About your Angel."

"I wasn't aware I had an angel," Julien replied blandly.

"No need to be coy. You know very well who I mean."

Julien saw no reason to show any interest. Vance was an inveterate gossip and rarely required prompting.

"I ran into Hartley at Mother Madge's last night."

That *was* news, but Julien didn't allow himself to react. "Did you?"

"Didn't see you there."

"That's likely because I haven't been to Mother Madge's for well over a year."

Vance looked vaguely disappointed by Julien's calm. "Thought you ought to know. It almost looked as though he was in the market for a new patron."

"That is probably wise of him."

Vance's eyes widened in understanding. "Who is your new companion? Parr's understudy?"

"I have not met Parr's understudy as of yet," Julien said. But perhaps he should, if so many people were making note of him. For a moment he considered asking Vance if he knew anything about the young man he saw in Ashworth's, but quickly dismissed the idea. He and Vance might share a preference for men, but that's where any similarities in their tastes ended. Julien liked well-proportioned, elegant men, while Vance's tastes ran toward hulking, sometimes brutish types. Besides, if he did ask, it would get around in no time. He finished his glass and nodded to the other man. "If you'll excuse me, Vance."

His coach was waiting outside the club for him, as he'd instructed, and he climbed in after telling his driver to take him home. He gazed idly at the shops as his coach rolled up Albermarle Street and Sutton's Book Shop caught his eye. Instead of the newest, most popular novels, Sutton carried scholarly books on a variety of subjects. Most of his profits came

from the sale of books that were no longer in print, sometimes books that were centuries old. Julien had discovered many unexpected treasures in the shop, but hadn't visited it in months.

Rising from his seat, he opened the trapdoor in the roof of the coach and ordered the coachman to stop. Sutton already had a list of specific books and documents Julien hoped to acquire and was to contact him if any came through the shop, but Julien had also found useful volumes while simply browsing the shelves.

Sutton's was rarely as crowded as other shops; the bookseller made his profits from rare items, not vast quantities. Today was no exception, as there were only three other patrons in the store. Two were passing acquaintances whom Julien nodded to, but the third was the same young man from Ashworth's. The contrast in his demeanor was so great that Julien almost didn't recognize him. No longer seeming even remotely uncertain, the young man looked alert and cheerful as he searched the shelves. He now gave the impression of a very determined, very eager scholar, right down to his clothing, which, although of excellent material, was far too ill-fitting to be the work of Ashworth.

Julien couldn't understand his fascination with the young stranger. Although very handsome, he was not the most handsome man Julien had ever laid eyes on. Indeed, most people would have considered Gabriel's angelic features far superior, but something about the young man intrigued Julien so much that for a moment he even considered striking up a conversation despite the fact that he rarely approached men—especially young men—without having some idea that his advances would be welcome. Before he could decide whether to make the attempt, the young man moved toward the counter, a stack of books in his hands.

Enough, Julien told himself firmly. *You're no longer an uncontrolled pup at the mercy of your urges and a pretty face. You came in here to find a book, not a new paramour.* He tried to concentrate on the book titles, but felt his gaze continually drawn back to the counter.

Sutton himself was waiting on the young man, which was odd. Usually his assistant waited on most customers, because Sutton considered them dabblers or dilettantes and only concerned himself with serious scholars. Then to Julien's surprise, Sutton invited the young man around the counter and into the back where the most prized volumes

were kept. Sutton was notorious when it came to scholarly matters and neither money nor rank could net one an invitation behind the counter if Sutton decided they were unworthy.

Perhaps the stranger was a student from Oxford or Cambridge. That would explain why Julien had never seen him before, but it didn't explain the unnatural interest Julien felt. Allowing himself a wry smile, Julien reflected that there were those who thought most of his interests were unnatural.

Unable to find any books that held his attention, Julien decided it would be better that he leave before temptation got the best of him and he did something foolish. As he climbed back into his coach, Julien thought again about the understudy that everyone was talking about. Perhaps he ought to go to the theater again tonight—this time without Gabriel.

PARR'S understudy was tall and slender with hair a shade darker than Gabriel's, a beautiful face that stopped just short of being feminine, and sly green eyes. After speaking to him for only a few moments, Julien knew that he was likely more clever than Gabriel, but similarly self-interested. It would make for the same situation Julien had with Gabriel, the only difference being the face and form. At least Gabriel already knew Julien's limits, and Julien didn't care to deal with someone new testing his temper and generosity.

If Julien were looking for that sort of novelty, it would be a simple matter to have a different companion every month as so many men did. As long as one had the money, it was possible to have all variety of men provide all variety of pleasure, and in his younger days Julien had done just that. At one-and-thirty, however, he was growing weary of such companionship. There were, of course, other men in Society who shared his inclinations, and many of them would have been more than willing to enter into an association with him, but most of them were unwilling to have their preference known and several were even married. Although Julien preferred to keep his private life private, he did not attempt to hide what he was, and had no intention of entering into the deception of

marriage, either by involvement with a married man or by marrying himself.

Dissatisfied with the understudy, Julien abruptly left the backstage area without engaging anyone else in conversation. Men of wealth and rank were always welcome backstage before and after performances. Theater managers were always eager to meet potential backers. While some of the men who attended were enthusiasts, most—like Julien— were there to meet the actors and actresses.

Julien decided he might as well stay and watch the play. It was a new offering by a playwright whose other work Julien had enjoyed. Hopefully it would take his mind off his current discontent. Fortunately, attending was never a problem, as the Earls of Blackstone had always taken boxes at Covent Garden—as well as at the Theatre Royal—for the Season and Julien had continued the tradition, making the box available to family and a few select friends.

When he arrived at his box, he found that he would not be attending alone, as the Viscount and Viscountess Carysfort were already seated.

"Julien!" his aunt smiled when she saw him. "Wonderful! We weren't at all certain you'd received our note."

"Might have sent a note back," her husband grumbled. "You could have escorted Lady Carysfort and I could have stayed comfortably at home."

"My apologies," Julien said as he bowed over Cordelia's hand. "I did not know you were attending tonight. I only decided to attend myself at the last moment."

Cordelia gave him an arch look as he took his seat, but declined to comment. Julien knew the only thing saving him from some very frank remarks was the presence of Lord Carysfort. The viscount was accepting of his wife's nephew but would definitely not appreciate a discussion about Julien's love life and probably wouldn't have cared for it even if Julien's interest had been in women. Viscount Carysfort had only three passions—his wife, his horses, and his hounds, in that order—and anything he did usually centered around one of the three. He likely never would have bothered with the London Season or the Earl of Blackstone if he was not so thoroughly wrapped around Cordelia's finger.

"Have you any plans after the play?"

Damnation. Julien stifled a sigh. Cordelia was no doubt planning to drag him along to whatever round of balls they were attending. "Only to return home," he said.

"Nonsense," Cordelia said firmly. "You worry me, Julien, spending so much time alone. We are attending the Tracy soirée later. You will join us, of course."

"Of course," Julien replied, knowing there were very few excuses his aunt would accept. Perhaps putting in an appearance at a ball or two tonight and attending her ball would earn him some peace for the rest of the Season.

The play was a sharp satire, and even more entertaining than Julien had expected. Likely it would enjoy a long run. As they made their way out of the theater, Cordelia tried to convince him to send his coach home and join them in theirs, but Julien had no intention of being stranded at a ball until Cordelia decided it was time to go. He managed to placate her by promising to meet them at the entrance.

Once the niceties of greeting the hostess and her two daughters were out of the way, Julien moved to the edge of the ballroom in order to search for certain faces. Primarily for that of Lavinia Norville, because although he wouldn't leave if she was present—his aunt would never forgive him—he did want to be prepared in order to avoid a scene. He didn't see her, but nor did he see anyone else he cared to speak with.

His aunt and Octavius were already in the midst of a conversation with several friends, so Julien took himself off to the card room. If he had to spend several hours at a ball, this was the most painless place to do it.

Fifteen minutes later, he was settled at a table, playing commerce with four other gentlemen. One of them was Lord Belmont's son, who fancied himself a dashing gambler but was too afraid of his father's wrath to ever actually visit a gaming hell. Julien also recognized Morleigh Mayfield, Viscount Ferrand, and Lord Witley, none of whom he liked, but fortunately that wasn't a requirement in a game like commerce. The play was deep and reckless, and Julien knew that it wouldn't require much concentration on his part to win a fair bit of

money—not that he needed it.

He easily won the first two hands, which appeared to bother no one except young Belmont, who, unlike the other men at the table, hadn't yet learned to lose money easily. Or perhaps he was worried about explaining any losses to his father.

"When is the new Earl of Dearborne going to put in an appearance, Mayfield?" Ferrand asked as he made his wager. "My wife has been talking of nothing else for weeks."

"There's no need for her to be anxious to meet him, and you may tell her so. He's a pale, dull creature with nothing of importance to say."

"How old would you say he is? You talk of him as if he were a child." There was an unhealthy interest in Witley's voice that made Julien's stomach turn.

Julien kept his attention focused on the cards, but gritted his teeth. It was just another reminder of the utter hypocrisy in the ton that infuriated him. Because he was wealthy and titled, he was included on every guest list, yet at the same time he had to constantly deal with sideways looks and snide remarks because he lived outside their invisible boundaries and didn't bother to hide it. Mayfield and Witley were both considered excellent gentlemen despite the fact that they visited London's worst hells on a regular basis because they presented the façade that Society wanted to see.

According to what Julien had heard from the workers at Madame Rimbaude's and Mother Madge's over the years, neither man cared much about the gender of the person they paid for. Witley's only requirements were that they be young and innocent, while Mayfield liked them fair and helpless. Both men preferred their victims terrified. Some of the young men who worked at the houses Julien frequented had been subject to the men's attentions themselves before managing to escape the hells for the relatively safer world of male brothels.

"He's not much above twenty, I daresay." Mayfield's voice brought Julien back to his current surroundings. "But he might as well be a child. I've never met a more backward or unworldly fool in my life."

"Then I do hope to see him in Society." Ferrand smirked. "It sounds as though he would be vastly entertaining."

The viscount's words didn't surprise Julien. Most of the ton relied on the mistakes and scandals of others to provide them with entertainment. Julien found it distasteful, but not nearly as despicable as he found Mayfield and Witley.

"I wouldn't anticipate much amusement from him." Mayfield shrugged. "He's such a sickly thing that I doubt he'll even live out the year."

Leander reached up to tug at his collar, but at the last moment he remembered his elaborately tied cravat. Instead, he readjusted his white gloves and tried to relax as the coach rolled toward Cadogan Place. He told himself that Lady Carysfort's ball was just one more thing that he had to adjust to in his new life.

He still hadn't become accustomed to thinking of the enormous London house as his on the day that he first met with his man-of-affairs and learned that he also had two country estates. Douglas Marlowe was earnest and eager to please his new employer, and had tried his best to be helpful. That had made it easier for Leander to get past his embarrassment at some of the questions he'd needed to ask.

Marlowe had been quick to provide him with the names of the various shops he would need to visit and to assure him that accounts would be set up at all of them. Having always gotten his clothing—any not handed down from his brothers—from a general store, Leander had been taken aback to learn that in addition to a tailor for his jackets and trousers, he would also need to visit a shirt-maker, boot-maker, glove-maker, and hatter. Then he'd learned from Gibson how extensive the wardrobe of an earl could be and was glad to have his valet take charge of all his new clothing.

Shopping had been even more of a chore than Leander had expected, but fortunately he'd had the foresight to ask Marlowe for the names of several bookshops as well; they'd served as a reward when he'd finally finished ordering all his clothing. He knew that Sutton's Book Sellers was likely to become one of his favorite shops. Sutton had initially treated him with disdain—as had most of the shopkeepers until they learned he was an earl—but had warmed up once the subject of more obscure Arthurian texts came up. Leander had purchased translations of two more of de Troyes' works as well as a copy of Malory's *Prose Merlin*. In addition, Sutton had promised to contact him if he came across translations of the German or Italian works.

Other than that shopping excursion, Leander still hadn't seen much of London, despite Marlowe's assurances that his coachman would drive him to any of the famous sights he wished to see. There hadn't been any more visitors after the Carysforts, but that didn't concern him. As long as he had a library full of books and now had the funds to buy as many more books as he wanted, Leander was more than content to remain at home.

The coach rolled to a halt, reminding Leander that no matter what he may prefer, always staying at home among his books was not possible. He looked out the window and saw a long line of coaches in front of a large, well-lit townhouse. He'd promised Lady Carysfort he would attend her ball, and so here he was, nerves and all. Although he had no idea how to behave at such a grand affair, he hoped to be able to learn by watching those around him.

The footman opened the coach door and Leander took a deep breath before descending. As he stepped into the cold night air, a disturbing thought occurred to him. "Henry," he said, turning to the footman, "do you and Rand have to wait out in the cold for me all night?"

Leander couldn't see Henry's face, but he knew by the change in the footman's posture that he'd done something unusual—again. It reminded him of the day that he'd wandered down to the kitchen for something to eat and everyone had frozen the moment they saw him. He'd crossed another of those invisible boundaries that he wasn't even aware existed.

Henry glanced up at the coachman, then back at Leander. "Not to worry, my lord. We usually wait in the mews with the other servants. We'll be comfortable enough."

"Good. I'm not sure how long I'll be here."

"They'll send for us when you're ready."

"Oh. Thank you, Henry." Leander nodded and then made himself walk up the steps and into the glittering townhouse. In the crowded entryway, he saw everyone hand their coats and wraps to the footmen and did the same before following the crowd into a room that already seemed impossibly full.

While Leander knew that he had probably seen more people than this at the docks, they hadn't all been pressed into a single room. He

continued to trail behind the couple from the entry, relieved when they led him toward Lord and Lady Carysfort, who were standing at the door to the ballroom and greeting guests as they entered. Lady Carysfort held out her hand when she saw him instead of merely curtseying. "Lord Dearborne, I'm so glad you could come."

Leander was acutely aware of the sudden hush that fell over the people nearest to them, but managed to smile as though he hadn't noticed. "Thank you again for inviting me, Lady Carysfort. Lord Carysfort." He turned to the viscount and bowed.

"Dearborne," Carysfort replied, bowing as well.

"I do hope you'll enjoy yourself," Lady Carysfort smiled.

As much as he would have preferred to stay where his was—with the only familiar face in sight—he knew by observing that he was supposed to move along into the ballroom. There were plenty of whispers and stares as he did so and Leander was at a loss until an older gentleman walked up to him, gave a smart bow, introduced himself as Lord Rockingham and then proceeded to present Leander to his wife and two daughters. That seemed to open the floodgates and man after man introduced themselves and then presented their wives, daughters, sisters, and nieces.

Unfamiliar though he was with ballroom etiquette, Leander couldn't miss all the blatant hints and suggestions that he ask one of the young ladies to dance. Not wanting to admit that he'd never had the opportunity to learn any sort of dance, Leander tried to sidestep the issue as politely as possible. Judging by the frowns he received from the older ladies, he was not very successful.

Everyone now seemed determined to speak to him, generally about things of which he knew nothing. Had he met Lord So-and-so? Would he be attending Lady Such-and-such's soirée the next night? Which clubs did he intend to join? Had he heard about the scandal involving Baron This with the Duchess of That? Leander didn't have answers to most of the questions and much of the time, he hadn't the faintest idea what everyone was talking about.

After the first hour, all the names and titles began to blend together. After the second, Leander was beginning to grow weary of the questions

and gossip. By the end of the third, he was looking for anywhere he could get some peace and quiet. The lights and noise were making his head ache, while the crowded room was suffocating. The rooms off the ballroom were equally full, one with card players and the other with people resting between dances.

Despite the cold February weather, Leander was tempted to venture out to the garden in order to cool off. In the next moment, he decided against it. With his luck, he'd take a chill and end up sick again. He couldn't go wandering through the house, but perhaps he could go out into the hallway.

Seeing a matron approaching—he'd met her earlier but couldn't recall her name—with another young lady in tow, Leander made his way through the crowd as quickly as possible. He spotted a door near the orchestra, half-hidden by carefully arranged plants, and slipped through it. It was a relief to find an empty hallway, with the noise muffled a bit by the closed door. He saw several more doors opposite him, and after a moment's hesitation, ventured to open the nearest one.

The library? Leander wondered, stepping inside. He couldn't help thinking that if this *was* the library, it wasn't terribly impressive compared to the one he'd inherited. There were only two bookshelves filled with books, and in the dim light from a low fire, Leander could make out Egyptian-styled decor. Likely this room was meant to be a showplace rather than a retreat, but it served as the latter for Leander tonight.

As he closed the door behind him, Leander wondered if he was doing something offensive, but couldn't bring himself to leave the room. It was nearly dark, lit only by a low fire in the fireplace, and pleasantly cool after the stuffy ballroom. For the first time since entering the house, Leander was able to breathe deeply. He took another step into the room. What would he say if someone came in? Was there any acceptable excuse he could give for not being with the other guests? He grasped the doorknob again. Perhaps he should go back after all.

"Either come in and sit down or go, but don't keep hovering by the door all night," came a deep voice from somewhere near the fire.

Leander started, looking for the source of the voice. He was finally able to make out someone in one of the chairs before the fire. "I'm sorry.

I didn't mean to disturb anyone. I was just hoping to find somewhere quiet for a little while."

The man in the chair turned and, for a moment, Leander was able to see a bold profile by the light of the fire. "The American Earl." The man sounded surprised.

"Yes, sir. I'm Leander Mayfield. That is, I'm the Earl of Dearborne." Leander doubted he would ever be truly comfortable introducing himself as an earl. To his own ear, it always sounded pompous somehow.

The man stood, his broad-shouldered silhouette blocking much of the light from the fire. "I am Julien Sutcliffe, Earl of Blackstone," he said, and from him the pronouncement was entirely fitting. He gestured to the chair opposite him. "Have a seat, Dearborne."

Leander wasn't sure about someone other than Lord or Lady Carysfort inviting him to do so, but the Earl of Blackstone seemed very sure of himself, so he took the chair. "Thank you. I'm afraid I'm not used to the crowd in the ballroom."

"Crowd?" Blackstone sat again, stretching long legs toward the fire. "This is not a large gathering. You have to wait until May or June for any ball to be considered a true crush."

"More crowded?" Leander couldn't imagine it.

"I suppose this could be considered a crush for February," Blackstone mused. "My aunt is something of a popular hostess."

"Lady Carysfort is your aunt?" Leander finally relaxed completely into his chair. If Lady Carysfort's nephew was present, then no one could object to his being in the library. "She was kind enough to visit me and extend her invitation to this ball."

"And that's why you attended?"

"Yes. I received invitations to other balls, but I couldn't have brought myself to go to a ball where I didn't know a single soul." Leander smiled at his slightly flawed logic. "Although I'm not sure it would be much different than only knowing two people."

"I assume that has changed quickly enough." Blackstone's tone was

languid. He almost sounded bored, but it was difficult to tell without enough light to see his expression clearly.

"Too quickly. I don't know how I'm going to remember everyone I've met."

"I don't know why you would want to."

Leander suspected Blackstone was right, but tried to be fair. "I'm sure there are many people I'll be glad to know."

"Have you met any yet?"

"Well… no." Leander heard Blackstone chuckle and realized what he'd said. "I mean… I didn't mean…."

"I take no offense," Blackstone assured him.

"I'm glad, because truthfully this is the most interesting conversation I've had this evening." Which was rather odd in itself, because they weren't discussing anything significant.

Obviously, Blackstone felt the same way. "Really? My sympathies." He sounded amused, but not scornful as Morleigh had—Leander still remembered his cousin's disdainful tone. "I'm certain you will have the prospect for many more conversations after tonight. Plenty of people will be paying calls to extend personal invitations once it becomes known that is what is required to assure your presence."

"Oh, no." Leander couldn't hold back his dismay. Not only was the prospect of attending more balls daunting, but now he also sounded abominably conceited in requiring a personal invitation. "I hope people don't think I expect such special treatment," he said truthfully. If there was one thing he'd learned growing up, it was that special treatment eventually led to loneliness.

"It sounds like an excellent practice to me," Blackstone said dryly. "Perhaps I'll require it as well. Even better, I may decide I require an ode should anyone wish my presence at their soirée."

Leander knew he was teasing, but couldn't tell if it was mocking. There was a hint of something in Blackstone's voice that led him to believe… "You don't like attending these parties either."

"Why do you think I've sought sanctuary in the library?"

"Why did you attend if you dislike it?"

"Why did you?" Blackstone countered.

"It seemed only polite after Lord and Lady Carysfort made the effort to actually meet me."

"I cannot claim such fastidiousness. I only attended because I'd never hear the end of it from Aunt Cordelia if I didn't."

"So you don't attend other balls?" Leander asked. If he did, it would definitely be incentive to accept other invitations. Leander wasn't sure why he found Blackstone so fascinating. The only thing he could think was that their shared dislike of crowds made him feel an immediate camaraderie.

"Only such events as my aunt manages to drag me to."

Leander couldn't help laughing at the image of the petite Lady Carysfort pulling Blackstone along like a recalcitrant child. He couldn't tell much about Blackstone when they were both seated in near-darkness, but he got the impression of a very imposing man.

Before either of them could speak again, the door to the library opened. "Now this will never do, Julien," Lady Carysfort scolded as she walked inside. "I did not insist you attend my soirée just so you could hide in the library the entire evening. A library which, I might add, you don't consider a proper one because there aren't enough books in— Lord Dearborne." She came to an abrupt halt when she saw Leander.

Leander had stood as soon as Lady Carysfort entered, as had Blackstone. "Forgive me, Lady Carysfort. I just wanted somewhere quiet for a few moments, but then Lord Blackstone and I began talking."

"I see."

"I'm not used to such crowds, I'm afraid," Leander explained.

Lady Carysfort stepped forward and took his arm. Much to Leander's relief, she didn't seem angry. "You certainly aren't going to grow used to them by hiding in my library. Come; there are many more people who wish to meet you." She began leading him toward the door, then glanced back over her shoulder. "Julien?"

"I will be there in a moment."

"I shall be quite annoyed if I have to go in search of you again," Lady Carysfort warned.

"I wouldn't dream of risking your fury."

Leander didn't have time for more than a brief smile before Lady Carysfort swept him out of the library and back to the ballroom. After a few kind but blunt questions, Leander admitted that one of the things he was hiding from was the prospect of having to dance and confessed to his lack of ability.

She drew him toward the door to the card room where a small knot of young men were standing. As introductions were made, Leander noted that they all appeared to be near his age. He was apprehensive, but the men were friendly even after Lady Carysfort left them. Once again, Leander found himself unable to follow the conversation as they spoke of places like Faro's Tomb, Lost Paradise, and Lady Perdition, but was intrigued by the fanciful—if somewhat foreboding—names.

The young bucks were amused by his ignorance and readily invited him to join them later. For a moment Leander was bewildered by the idea of visiting in the dead of night, but as he listened, he soon realized the establishments were gambling dens and brothels. He doubted it was what Lady Carysfort intended when she introduced them.

Leander felt no real temptation to experiment with such vices. He was trying to think of a discreet way to get out of the invitation and conversation when Blackstone strode past on his way into the card room. Leander felt a vague disappointment that his new acquaintance didn't even glance in their direction.

Silence fell over them until Purbeck, who Leander learned was the son of a duke and more or less led the others along, spoke. "Perhaps we should get in some practice here before we go to Lost Paradise."

"At a ball?" Holcombe frowned. "That's always dull. Lord Carysfort will have placed limits on deep play."

"Blackstone just went in," Purbeck countered. "He's Lady Carysfort's nephew. If he raises the wagers, then who is going to object?"

"If you expect to win anything, I wouldn't try it against

Blackstone," Avery, whom Leander thought was the most amiable of the group, warned. "My father says he's no mean player. Everyone else begins gossiping at a ball, even over cards, but Blackstone never allows himself to be distracted."

Talbot was something of a hanger-on, and tried to ingratiate himself by constantly finding fault with others. "Is Blackstone so pinched that he has to take blunt from his aunt's guests?"

Holcombe shook his head. "Blackstone? Man's got a fortune. Mother had hoped to arrange a match between he and my sister, but nothing ever came of it."

"I can't imagine why." Purbeck's tone was sarcastic.

"In any case," Avery continued, "do you really want to begin the evening by losing a packet?"

"Who's to say I would lose?" Purbeck lifted his chin in a mocking pose. "Am I not handsome enough to distract Blackstone?" Several chuckles met his question.

"But you'll be sitting on the feature that interests Blackstone the most," Holcombe said, prompting louder laughter.

"Let's not frighten the lad." Talbot nodded in Leander's direction.

"Lawks, he does look lost, doesn't he? Do you not understand our meaning, Dearborne?"

"Not entirely, I'm afraid," Leander admitted.

"He's a colonial," Holcombe added. "Would you expect him to?"

Leander decided it wasn't worth pointing out that America hadn't been a British colony for well over fifty years.

"Who's to know what they get up to among the savages?" Purbeck's grin was nasty. "But no, our Dearborne is obviously an innocent lamb who should probably be warned about wolves."

"Nonsense, Purbeck," Avery countered. "You know Blackstone keeps himself to the Haymarket and molly-boys."

"Molly-boys?" Leander was often able to guess the meaning of unfamiliar phrases, but this one had him stumped.

"Blackstone takes his pleasure with other men," Avery explained.

"He keeps an actor in Tottenham Court Road," Purbeck added. "No interest in women whatsoever."

Leander couldn't help but notice that for all their sneering about Lord Blackstone, they were careful to keep their voices low.

"Just thought you ought to be aware of it," Holcombe said self-righteously.

"There's no need to frighten him." Avery shook his head. "Dearborne's in no danger from Blackstone. No one is."

"Oh, no?" Purbeck raised his eyebrows. "What about Tobias Norville, then?"

Avery fell silent, but Holcombe stared in disbelief. "Never say you believe the tales that Lavinia Norville puts about? That Blackstone actually fought a duel over a woman? That he killed Norville because of his sister?"

"Of course not," Purbeck scoffed. "I don't believe Blackstone ever had any interest in Lavinia Norville. Many people say it was *Tobias* Norville he truly wanted. It was after Norville disappeared that Blackstone began to pay for his companions."

Talbot's lip curled in distaste. "I still don't see where one would find such companions."

"From the theater," Purbeck replied. "I assume that's where he got the current actor he's keeping. There are molly-houses, as well."

"You seem to know a great deal about it," Leander observed, not realizing the implication of his words until his new acquaintances all froze. It wasn't at all what he'd meant, but he couldn't bring himself to either clarify or apologize. It served Purbeck right for making accusations when Blackstone wasn't present to defend himself, especially since Purbeck would obviously never have the nerve to say such things if Blackstone were around to hear.

"Dearborne." Purbeck's voice was icy. "It just occurred to me that my coach will not carry five. I'm afraid I have to withdraw my invitation."

"I understand," Leander replied, and for once he actually did.

All four men merely nodded instead of bowing when they took their leave, although Avery did send him an apologetic look. Leander wasn't sorry to see them go.

For a brief moment, he considered going into the card room, but he was as unfamiliar with card games as he was with the dances. What he truly wanted to do was return to the quiet of the library in order to think over what he'd learned about the Earl of Blackstone.

Leander considered the rumors about the Norvilles to be just that. Apparently no one knew what had actually happened, but the talk about Blackstone's interest in men sounded like accepted fact. The subject drew Leander like a moth to a flame, despite the fact that he'd never heard anyone speak of such things before in his life. There had been tantalizing hints of it in his Greek and Latin studies, but any details had been glossed over. Leander had always been compelled to discern more about those details.

Perhaps in London he would have a better chance of finding out.

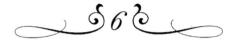

You're just tired."

Of you, Julien thought, but didn't say so. He rolled away from Gabriel and sat up, searching the room for his small clothes.

"Are you leaving? Why not just rest a while and then I'm sure I'll be able to raise your interest."

"I don't think so." Julien stood up to pull on his drawers and then found his trousers. He turned to see Gabriel sitting up in bed.

"But I haven't seen you all week." Gabriel pursed his lips into a pretty pout. "I've been so lonely."

"Lonely? Even at Mother Madge's? I find that difficult to believe."

Gabriel's pout disappeared as his full lips narrowed. "How did you know I've been visiting Mother Madge's?"

That was interesting. Gabriel's words indicated he'd been to Madge's more than the single time Vance had encountered him. Perhaps it was just as well he hadn't been able to perform, Julien decided. It was entirely possible that Gabriel had already shared his talents with other men in the process of finding a new patron. While Julien didn't expect his partners to be as pure as driven snow, he didn't care for tomcats, either.

Julien hadn't planned on seeing Gabriel after Cordelia's ball, but his encounter with the Earl of Dearborne had left him unsettled. When he first saw the stranger from Ashworth's in his aunt's library, he'd thought the dim light was playing tricks on his eyes. Then the young man spoke with an undeniably American accent and Julien knew immediately who he was.

He shouldn't have been surprised to discover that Morleigh Mayfield's description had been utterly misleading, but he was— pleasantly so. While Dearborne was soft-spoken and obviously

unfamiliar with the ways of Society, he was by no means the dull, sickly creature Mayfield claimed. Julien found him engaging and fresh in a way that Americans were often said to be, but rarely were. His careful, reserved judgment about the ton bespoke a sensible and thoughtful nature, and Julien had been sorry when they were interrupted.

He'd stayed behind when Cordelia escorted Dearborne back to the ballroom, not wanting to give anyone reason to gossip about either of them. Cordelia had never mentioned that she'd paid a call on Dearborne, but she had been preoccupied with preparations for her ball, and the few times she had seen Julien, she had been more concerned with lecturing him than anything else.

"Have you had someone spying on me, Julien?" Gabriel's petulant voice brought him back to the present.

"I have not," Julien replied as he buttoned his shirt. "And I have no complaint about you visiting Mother Madge's. I did tell you to begin searching for a new patron, after all."

"Is that so? Then why did you arrive here without sending word first?"

"I see no need to announce my intention to visit a residence that I am renting," Julien said a none-too-casual reminder.

"Are you saying you do not care if I am here when you call?" Gabriel's expression was no longer sulky, but wary.

"It didn't matter much tonight, did it?" Julien tied his cravat loosely around his neck and picked up his jacket, not bothering with his waistcoat.

"Surely you do not blame me for that?!" Gabriel's voice was laced with indignation, but also some fear.

"I do not," Julien assured him. Gabriel almost looked as though he was concerned Julien would spread word of this sorry event, thereby ruining his chances of finding a new sponsor.

"I might have done better if I'd received word before you arrived." The sulky tone was back.

Julien didn't reply as he sat down to pull on his boots. He had the

uncomfortable feeling that the fault in this case was entirely his own. Gabriel had tried every trick in his repertoire and Julien had tried some of his own, even going so far as to imagine Dearborne in Gabriel's place. That was certainly something he'd never had to do before. "Well, you need not concern yourself with my presence any longer. I doubt I will be stopping by this house again until the end of the Season."

Gabriel looked as if he didn't know whether to be relieved or insulted. Julien used the silence to take his leave, striding downstairs without looking back, pausing only to take his things from Gabriel's butler. He climbed into his waiting coach without bothering to speak to his coachman; the driver knew he was to head home.

At least one good thing came out of this night: Julien was now certain that he would not have any desire to see Gabriel again. For the past several months, he had been growing concerned that the Angel had some sort of strange hold on him that he was unable to shake. Gabriel had never been able to engage any emotion other than lust from Julien, but that had been worrisome enough. As for his actual affections, Julien kept them closely guarded and always had. When he was growing up, those very affections had been the prize his doting but warring parents always fought over, so Julien had always doled them out as carefully as possible to ensure that neither felt slighted.

Since the death of his parents, his aunt had been the most important person in his life, but Julien had also been fond of the previous Earl of Blackstone. Algernon had been an enthusiastic scholar who had encouraged Julien in his studies of ancient Rome. It was through Algernon that Julien had met the only non-relations he'd allowed himself to become close to, Viscount Seaforth, Seaforth's fiancée, and her brother. Their parents had also been cronies of Algernon's—a circle of scholars and bluestockings always looked at askance by Society. Their children had grown up surrounded by people more concerned with discussing Socratic philosophy or evolutionism than the latest fashion or scandal, and none of them had concerned themselves greatly over Julien's preference for men. Still, it had taken years for Julien to trust them enough to be honest about it.

Tobias Norville had been one of the few people that had ever succeeded in winning Julien's affections, and Julien always looked upon

that disaster as a lesson well-learned. Ever since then, he had chosen to pay for physical companionship.

As for this infatuation with Dearborne, Julien hoped it would be of a short duration. It made him feel like a lecherous old man, leering after some pretty, young innocent. He knew that for many men of his standing, the solution would be to seduce the young innocent in order to get him or her out of his system, but Julien had no intention of doing that.

His coach rolled to a halt in front of his house, and Julien was surprised when his front door opened to admit him. "I said you didn't have to wait up, Hudson."

"So you did, my lord," Hudson agreed as he took Julien's hat and gloves, then helped him off with his greatcoat.

"I suppose Kay is waiting up as well."

"I believe so."

Julien shook his head in resignation. "Well, here I am, so you may take yourself off to bed."

"Very well. Good night, my lord."

"Good night, Hudson." Julien made his way upstairs where, sure enough, his valet was waiting. "I don't know why I bother leaving instructions," he said as he handed his jacket to the plump, good-natured man and then shrugged out of his waistcoat. "No one on my staff heeds them."

"Yes, my lord," Kay agreed automatically.

Julien stifled a smile as he kicked off his shoes and pulled his cravat from his neck while Kay bustled around the room. He knew that even servants could be judgmental about an employer's habits, and so tried to be as generous with his staff as possible. Although Hudson was not paid any more than most butlers, Julien also paid the tuition and board for his daughter at a respectable school. Kay had been dismissed for marrying, as had the lady's maid carrying his child; Julien hired Kay as his valet and his wife as a laundress, which allowed her to care for their son. The coachman and his wife and brood were allowed to live over Julien's carriage house. The rest of the servants received higher-than-average

wages and more days off than most employees. The result was a staff that would even disobey him if they felt he required their service.

Whether it was out of actual loyalty or just because they didn't want to risk such a good position, Julien didn't know. Either way, his home and person received excellent care with very little sacrifice on his part.

"Will that be all, my lord?" Kay asked after helping Julien into his robe.

"Yes, Kay. Off to bed with you."

After Kay gathered up his discarded clothes and left the room, Julien went to the washstand and splashed some water on his face before removing his robe and climbing into bed. He considered himself a man of intellect, and if he chose, he ought to be able to control or even ignore his baser desires. He *ought* to be able to spend as much time as he liked in the presence of Dearborne—or anyone—without lust clouding his thoughts.

There was only one way to prove it, to himself if no one else.

LEANDER closed the library doors with a relieved sigh and then sank into one of the room's large, deep chairs. Although only about three hours of the day were taken up by calls, they were more taxing than anything else Leander had to do. It seemed that since attending Lady Carysfort's ball, there had been a steady stream of callers, all eager to flatter him, invite him to more balls, and gossip about everyone else in Society. After the first day, Leander learned to take the flattery and gossip with a grain of salt and that it was wiser not to give a definite answer to the invitations.

The only times the calls weren't tedious for him was when the conversation turned to the subject of Lady Carysfort's nephew. Amidst all the salacious innuendo and supercilious whispers, Leander was able to glean a few solid facts about the Earl of Blackstone.

The notion of a man wanting another man instead of a woman was something Leander had never encountered before, yet at the same time it resonated deep inside him. Growing up, he'd never understood his

brothers'—especially Chance's—interest in the fairer sex and had always assumed it was because he was several years younger and he would begin to feel the same things as he got older. When those feelings never developed, Leander decided he was simply not meant to marry—not entirely unheard of, considering his invalid status.

This new knowledge also went a long way in explaining the friendship he'd had with David Palmer when they were both fifteen. A friendship that had surprised many people, including Leander.

The implication from most of his visitors was that Blackstone was doing something wrong or that there was something wrong with him, but Leander couldn't understand how they had come to that conclusion. All he had to judge by was his own conscience and the sermons that had been delivered in the small church in Pelham when he had been well enough to attend. The pastor had never mentioned anything remotely resembling the subject. In a small, struggling farming village, the emphasis in sermons had always been on humility, charity, and hard work. As far as Leander could tell, the people who were so eager to gossip about Blackstone were more sinful than Blackstone himself.

His thoughts were interrupted when the library door opened and Powell entered. "Lord Dearborne, you have another caller."

Leander looked at the clock on the mantel. It was ten minutes past five and he had assumed that his calls were done for the day. He'd learned from Powell that only very close acquaintants called after five, and he didn't have any close acquaintants. Maybe he could simply have Powell say that he was "not at home," a polite lie he had learned of but had yet to use. "Who is it, Powell?"

"Mr. Mayfield, my lord."

"My cousin?" Leander sat up straighter. He hadn't seen Mayfield since his arrival in London. "Tell him I'll be there directly."

Powell bowed and left.

Relieved that he hadn't unfastened his cravat or shed his coat as he was wont to do when alone, Leander made his way back to the drawing room. "Mr. Mayfield," he said, with a smart bow that had become much less awkward for him with practice.

"Dearborne." Mayfield bowed in return. "I'm glad to see you've recovered. I've been much occupied with prior commitments and haven't been able to call before now."

Leander had his doubts about the truth of the last statement, but at least his cousin seemed more amiable. "I'm glad to see you again. Please, have a chair."

Mayfield raised an eyebrow at the phrase, but took a seat. "You certainly aren't wanting for company, from what I understand. Tell me, are the invitations still pouring in?"

"Yes." Leander couldn't help sighing. "So far I've sent my regrets to all of them, but I suppose I'll have to accept some eventually."

"Is it that you don't enjoy balls, or are you trying to cultivate an air of mystery?"

Leander couldn't tell if his cousin was making fun of him or not. "I admit I'm not certain what to do with myself at a ball. I don't know how to dance and—" He didn't want to say that most of the talk at balls held no interest for him. "I am not familiar enough with Society to join in any of the discussions."

"Well, you need not go out in Society if you've no wish to," Mayfield assured him. "You needn't even stay in London. You have two other estates in the country where you can reside. People may think you odd, but that shouldn't be a concern for you."

Leander fell silent as he digested Mayfield's words. He'd thought that attending such functions was a duty, and was relieved to learn otherwise, although he didn't like the idea of being considered odd. "I mean to visit the estates soon."

"Then you don't find the time weighing heavily on you here?"

"Not at all." Leander couldn't help smiling. "Not as long as there is such an excellent library."

"Ah, yes. I've heard that you're a prodigious reader. I don't wonder that such frivolous pastimes as balls seem silly to a great scholar."

Now Leander was certain Mayfield was mocking him, albeit with the utmost politeness. "Nothing of the sort," he replied, aiming for the

cool, almost careless tone he'd heard from so many in Society. He knew he didn't quite accomplish it.

Mayfield didn't seem concerned by Leander's weak attempt to assert himself. "You mentioned wanting to see more of London. Have you had that opportunity?"

Leander wasn't about to admit that he was still somewhat intimidated by the city and didn't know where to begin. "Not yet. That's something else I mean to do." As he spoke, he realized he was saying that far too often and privately vowed to begin *doing* all those things he meant to.

"If you wish to appear in Society but dislike balls, you might consider attending the theater."

A thrum of excitement went through Leander when he heard the phrase "attending the theater." His only experience with live theatrics consisted of a handful of amateur productions he had seen when visiting his grandfather in Amherst, usually old-fashioned fairy tales. The idea of *seeing* Shakespeare's plays instead of merely reading them cheered him as nothing else had since his arrival. "I would like that very much. I suppose Mr. Marlowe will be able to secure tickets. There should be Shakespeare playing somewhere."

"That may not be necessary. The late earl kept a box at the Theatre Royal, where they perform Shakespeare and other classics. If you like, I can check that the box is still in the Dearborne name."

"Thank you." Leander tried to hide his surprise at this unexpected kindness. He couldn't understand why Mayfield was being friendly one moment and scornful the next. Perhaps he was concerned about Leander properly upholding the Dearborne name, or perhaps it simply took a while for the man to warm up to people. Either way, Leander was overjoyed that *this* was one area in which Mayfield decided to be helpful.

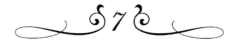

It took a few moments for Leander to recall where he was when the curtain fell on the first act of *Othello*. He'd been worried before the play began that he would by distracted by the audience. It seemed that most of the people attending—especially those in the more expensive boxes—were more concerned with their own performances than anything happening on the stage. He was relieved that once the curtain went up, the audience became quieter, making it easy for Leander to lose himself in the play.

As promised, Mayfield had checked at the Theatre Royal and discovered that a box was held for the Earl of Dearborne, and that *Othello* was the play being performed. They had made plans to attend in two days' time. Just hours before they were to leave, however, Mayfield had sent word that he would not be able to attend. Leander had been apprehensive about attending alone, but the prospect of finally *seeing* Shakespeare performed countered any self-consciousness he felt. The theater's opulent decor had distracted him from the crowds when he'd first entered, and once the performance had begun, the rest of the audience had ceased to exist.

Now he just had to wait for the next act to begin. Leander shifted in his chair and stretched his legs, taking the time to observe the other boxes. People were moving about from one to the other, flirting and gossiping and preening. It took a few minutes for Leander to realize that even as he was observing them, they were observing him, which meant he would likely have several people visiting his box before long. He sighed; despite the constant regrets he sent in response to all the invitations, the number of calls at his home hadn't diminished. It was enough to make Leander wish for his old reputation of an invalid— almost.

The curtain behind his box twitched and Leander hoped that the conversation would center around the play instead of gossip and the balls everyone was attending afterward. When the Earl of Blackstone

emerged, Leander was so surprised that it took him a moment to find his voice. "Lord Blackstone."

"Dearborne." Blackstone inclined his head in greeting. "I see you've decided to venture from your library once again. I trust you're enjoying the play more than you did the ball."

"I am indeed," Leander said, trying not to appear too eager or pleased when Blackstone sat in one of the empty chairs. He couldn't help admiring the casual elegance that Blackstone displayed in something as simple as the act of sitting down.

"You've picked an excellent play to attend. Thus far, this is one of the best performances I've seen in years."

Leander had been trying to decide whether Blackstone's eyes were brown or hazel and nearly missed the man's words. He reminded himself firmly to pay attention to the conversation. The last thing he wanted was to appear foolish in front of Blackstone. "I'm afraid I have nothing to compare the performance to. This is my first time to the theater."

Blackstone raised an eyebrow. "Is that so? I hope you aren't having trouble following the play. Shakespeare can be difficult for those unfamiliar with it."

"I'm not unfamiliar with the play. I've read all of Shakespeare's work."

"Of course." Blackstone nodded with a slight smile.

"Before this I only had the printed words and my imagination to bring the play to life."

"And how does this compare?"

"It doesn't." Leander laughed.

"Well worth the prospect of enduring more gossip, then?" Blackstone asked as he gazed out over the crowd.

The earl seemed to be implying more than he was actually saying, but Leander couldn't tell if it was meant for him. "Gossip is a small price to pay."

"I hope **so**," Blackstone murmured cryptically, then rose. "I believe the second **act is** about to begin. I must return to my seat. No, no need,"

he said when Leander moved to stand. "A pleasure speaking to you again, Dearborne."

"For me as well."

Blackstone left the box and Leander turned to face the stage again, awaiting the next act. When it began, he found that it wasn't as easy to absorb himself in the play. Despite the drama on the stage, Leander's thoughts continually turned to Blackstone.

Unbidden, Purbeck's words came back to him. Was the earl shopping for a new companion among the cast? The idea ruined some of Leander's pleasure at Blackstone's brief visit. Perhaps Blackstone was only here for that purpose and had spoken to Leander, not out of any regard, but merely to pass the time.

Eventually the plotting of Iago drew him in and he didn't think of Blackstone again until the curtain fell between the second and third acts. There wasn't an actual intermission and therefore no visiting between boxes, which left Leander alone with his thoughts. How often did Blackstone search for a new companion? If that's what he was doing. What exactly did Blackstone base his choice of companion on? Looks alone? Leander didn't like to think that of Blackstone and was glad when the third act began, distracting him from his thoughts.

The end of the third act brought another, longer intermission, during which people visited or fetched refreshments. Leander looked out over the crowd again, this time with someone particular in mind. He discovered Blackstone had a box—he assumed it was Blackstone's box—not far from his own. Leander's view of it was actually too clear, for he was able to see the gaudily dressed young man seated next to Blackstone.

Leander had heard enough about dandies and fops to know he was seeing the epitome of the word. The elaborately curled light brown hair was no more natural than the padded shoulders and narrow waist of the bright blue coat. A pink waistcoat was also visible and although Leander couldn't see the peacock's cravat, he suspected it was one of those overly complicated styles worn by those who considered themselves extremely fashionable. Blackstone's simple, stark black and white clothing seemed all the more elegant in comparison.

The peacock kept leaning in—much closer than necessary, in Leander's opinion—to speak to Blackstone. The earl didn't appear to mind; in fact, he seemed amused. Leander couldn't believe that Blackstone would enjoy the company of someone so frivolous. He looked away, reminding himself not to judge based on appearance alone. Perhaps Blackstone wasn't as serious-minded as he'd thought. Perhaps the peacock's feathers hid a fine mind. Perhaps—

"Dearborne."

Leander turned to see who had entered his box. "Avery," he said with some surprise.

"Might I speak to you for a moment?"

"Of course." Leander gestured toward an empty chair.

Avery sat in the same chair Blackstone had occupied. "I feel obliged to talk to you, as I was the one who urged you not to heed the others' warnings about Blackstone."

Leander immediately knew where the conversation was going, but was unsure how to prevent it.

Avery had paused, but when Leander didn't speak, he continued. "Already the entire theater is talking about Blackstone's visit to your box."

"How foolish of me to assume the play was the thing," Leander said.

The paraphrase made Avery pause again, but only for a moment. "You must recall our conversation at Lady Carysfort's ball. Surely you understand why people would speculate if Blackstone shows interest in a newcomer."

"Are you warning me that I am about to become the subject of more gossip?"

"Among other things." Avery lowered his voice.

"You were the one who said I had nothing to fear from Blackstone."

"You probably don't." Avery shifted uneasily. "It just struck me as strange. It's unusual for Blackstone to show such marked attention to someone—especially in so public a place."

Leander tried not to let on how much Avery's words pleased him, but he couldn't help the little thrill that shot through him when he learned that Blackstone's *marked attention* was something out of the ordinary. He looked again toward Blackstone's box, debating whether the attention the peacock was receiving qualified as *marked*.

Avery followed his gaze. "Perhaps his interest is directed elsewhere after all."

Leander's good mood abruptly evaporated.

"I must get back to my parents," Avery said, standing. "I meant no offense, Dearborne. I just thought you should know."

Although he didn't know whether Avery was meddling for his own amusement or was genuinely concerned, Leander decided to give him the benefit of the doubt. "Thank you, but I don't believe I have any cause to worry."

Avery nodded and turned to go, nearly colliding with a couple who were on their way into the box. Leander suppressed a sigh when he recognized the couple. Lord and Lady Moorhouse were untiring busybodies—no doubt they would have something to say about Blackstone.

They did, and so did the rest of the visitors who stopped by his box. Leander was grateful when the curtain finally went up on the fourth act and that the intermission between it and the fifth act was too brief to allow any more visiting.

After the curtain fell on the final scene, even after the applause had died away, Leander remained in his seat, soaking up every last bit of the experience. Finally, he rose and made his way out to the crowded lobby. People were in small groups, making last-minute plans about which balls to attend. Once again, Leander learned how to proceed by watching the people around him. Some were sending theater staff to fetch coaches or hackneys, but usually a gentleman would go out to find the necessary vehicle.

Blackstone was nowhere in sight; likely he had already left with the peacock. Leander was eager to get out of the crowded lobby, and decided to find his coach himself. Rand had dropped him off near the theater doors, so his coach wouldn't be too difficult to find. Fastening his

greatcoat, Leander stepped outside, where the street was crowded with people getting into their vehicles. Not seeing his coach in the immediate vicinity, Leander turned the corner onto Russell Street and began walking toward Drury Lane, keeping an eye out for the Dearborne crest.

The line of coaches stretched along Drury Lane and wound around corners and side streets. Another crowd further up and across the street was made up of people exiting a different theater. Leander hated to think what the congestion would be like if all the theaters on Drury Lane let out at the same time. Once he moved away from the door, the crowd thinned dramatically and Leander gratefully took a deep breath, despite the night's thick fog. He wondered how long it would be before he finally became accustomed to the crowded city.

He walked past two more buildings without seeing his coach. There was barely anyone else nearby so Leander paused to study the line of vehicles. Drury Lane was better lit than most, but even the additional light from the theaters didn't penetrate the fog very far. Leander could see the line of coaches curve around the nearest corner and thought he could see the same thing at the next cross-street.

After a moment, Leander decided to follow the line around the corner, then make his way up to the next block and follow that line of coaches back to Drury Lane. He didn't mind walking alone; he actually enjoyed the solitude—such as it was. In addition to the crowded city, Leander had yet to become accustomed to always having a house full of people. Even when Esmond House was free of callers, there were always servants about. Leander couldn't simply ignore them the way he saw others in Society doing.

The night wasn't too cold, and for Leander, the fog was still more of a novelty than a nuisance. In many ways, it added to the night's dreamlike quality, except that Leander never would have dreamed he'd ever be strolling up a London street after attending the theater and dressed in clothing that cost more than all the clothes he'd ever worn in Pelham.

After he turned the corner and had started down the new street, some of his pleasure evaporated. This street wasn't nearly as well-lit, and the fog began to take on a more ominous appearance. Leander quickened his pace as he looked at the coaches, still not seeing his. Perhaps Rand

had pulled up to the theater again and was looking for him. Torn between turning back or continuing on with his plan, Leander chose the latter.

The shortest path to the next street was a narrow alley. He crossed the street, trying to avoid the worst of the filth on the ground. About halfway down the alley, he thought he heard another set of footsteps, but told himself it was just the echo of his own boots. He walked faster and made a determined effort not to look behind him.

It was a relief to reach the next street, which, although poorly lit, wasn't nearly as dark as the alley. Unfortunately, there was no sign of the coaches he thought he'd seen. Tendrils of fog wound around his legs, only to break when he jumped in response to a coach rattling past. It was the only vehicle visible on the street, so either his eyes had deceived him or the coaches had all been summoned by their owners already.

Eager now to get back to the crowds of Drury Lane, Leander started walking. He'd barely gone a few steps before a hand yanked him into the shadows and slammed him into a rough brick wall with such force that his hat went flying.

"Lose yer way, me fine gentleman?"

Leander tried to catch his breath. "Let go of me!"

The hand around his neck only tightened, holding him firmly against the wall. "I'll be taking any blunt yer carryin'. Yer watch and any bobs y'got too."

"No!" Leander fought to break the man's hold. "I can't—"

"Blood is terrible hard t'clean up." The scent of stale gin wafted across Leander's face as the robber snarled in his ear. "Don't make me spill more'n I 'ave to."

Leander struggled to free himself, terrified of what would happen when the thief discovered he was carrying nothing of value. He nearly squirmed free, only to be caught by the hair and shoved back into the bricks.

"Messy 'tis, then, me—"

"Release him at once!" ordered another voice.

"Bloody hell!" The thief hissed. "Be damned if I'll stretch for this."

With that, he melted back into the alley.

Hardly daring to move, Leander merely leaned against the wall and tried to gather his composure.

"Dearborne?"

There was that voice again, and this time Leander recognized it. *Blackstone*. Shakily, he pushed himself away from the wall and felt a hand grip his upper arm, steadying him.

"Dearborne? Are you hurt?"

Was he? His bones ached a bit, but— "No… no, I'm not hurt." He was still trying to wrap his mind around what had nearly transpired. He'd read about such things, but never imagined it actually happening.

"Lord Dearborne." Blackstone's footman approached, holding Leander's hat out to him.

"Thank you," Leander said, taking it. He had the vague feeling he ought to explain himself. "I was… looking for my coach."

"That's not necessary any longer," Blackstone assured him. "I'll drive you home."

"But what of my coachman? He'll be searching for me."

"Simply send someone to fetch him when you return home. He will be found easily enough."

To Leander it seemed inconsiderate, not only of Rand, but of whomever had to go out and fetch Rand. But since his own plan had proved to be such a dismal failure, Leander decided not to object and allowed himself to be ushered to the waiting coach.

The footman was holding the door open, and Leander climbed in and sat down. Blackstone sat across from him, the footman closed the door, and the coach rolled into the night.

*W*hy in God's name didn't you give him what he was asking?" Julien demanded, and then made an effort to rein in his temper. He really had no right to take the younger man to task for his actions, but he had to vent his emotions somehow.

After dropping off his companion from the theater, Julien had decided to head home—despite the man's suggestions that he stay for the night. His coachman had merely been cutting across some less-traveled streets to save time, and as Julien looked out his window, he'd seen a gentleman being dragged into the alley. Instinct had him jumping from his coach and rushing to the man's aid. It wasn't until he heard the American accent that he realized who the victim was, and suddenly instead of mere concern, icy fear had gripped him.

"He wanted my watch," Dearborne explained, his voice shaky. "And money."

"And you thought it was worth being killed for? Why didn't you hand them over?"

"I don't have a watch. And I only have a few coins in my pocket. He wasn't giving me the chance to say so."

Julien was momentarily thrown by the admission. He'd half-expected some bravado about not giving in to criminals. No wonder the young man seemed so shaken; he'd had no way to prevent the footpad from cutting his throat. "What happened to your coach that you went all the way past Long Acre in search of it?"

"There were plenty of gentlemen who went out looking for their coaches." Dearborne sounded puzzled.

"And I'll wager not one of them left Catherine Street to do it."

"Oh." Dearborne's voice was more subdued than ever.

Julien didn't know when he'd seen anyone so disheartened, not only

by the attack, but by his surroundings as a whole. It made Julien wonder what sort of life Dearborne had lived in America—something he'd never bothered considering about someone of so limited an acquaintance. Inexplicably, he felt the need to cheer the younger man. "I suppose this quite ruins your first evening of theater," he said, hoping the mention of theater would bring a return of the enthusiasm Dearborne had displayed earlier.

"No," Dearborne said immediately. "Not in the least. My own foolishness is nothing compared to how splendid the play was."

"I don't know that you were foolish," Julien countered, surprising himself. It wasn't like him to go to the effort of comforting or consoling someone he barely knew. "You're simply unfamiliar with the city of London."

"Or any city," Dearborne admitted with a self-deprecating laugh. "The first time I was in a city was this January when I sailed for London from Boston."

Little wonder that he was unaware of the dangers of London. "From now on it might be best if you sent for your coach."

"I suppose. I just… feel that I should do such things for myself. If I'm able."

"Too active and independent to be waited upon, are you?"

"Not hardly." A fleeting smile crossed Dearborne's face. "In fact, what happened tonight is probably because I haven't done enough to accustom myself to London."

The enormity of Dearborne's situation was becoming clear to Julien. Not only had he left behind his home, but his entire country and way of life.

"Thank you," Dearborne said.

Julien was briefly startled, and wondered if he had spoken his thoughts aloud. "I beg your pardon?"

"I didn't thank you for coming to my aid. For saving me."

"There are those who would say that sitting in a coach with the Earl of Blackstone is not a particularly safe place for a young man to be."

Even as the words left him, Julien could hardly believe he was saying them. He didn't know what drove him to make certain that Dearborne knew about his reputation. If the young earl hadn't heard already—and he obviously hadn't because he showed no sign of unease—then it wasn't Julien's duty to enlighten him.

Dearborne tilted his head to one side. "I don't put much stock in gossip."

So he had heard *something*, but apparently decided not to believe it. Perhaps Cordelia had told him to disregard rumors about her nephew; Julien wouldn't put it past her. It was no fault of his, then, if Dearborne refused to heed the warnings he had undoubtedly been given. He was spared from trying to formulate a suitable reply by the coach coming to a halt. "Safe and sound," Julien said, amusement at his own words twisting up one corner of his mouth.

Dearborne studied him for a few moments, even after the footman had opened the door. "Thank you again."

There was no mistaking the sincerity in his voice and Julien was astonished to feel his face flushing. "Think nothing of it."

"It will be difficult not to," Dearborne said in that same serious tone. "Good night, Lord Blackstone."

"Good night, Dearborne."

The young earl stepped down and Julien found himself waiting until Dearborne was safely inside before signaling his driver to continue on. He didn't know why Dearborne's gratitude left him so disconcerted, but supposed it was a suitable punishment for tempting fate earlier in the evening.

He should have remained in his own box at the theater when he saw Dearborne, but he'd wanted to prove to himself that he could speak to the American without it having any effect. Instead, Dearborne's obvious enjoyment of the play and friendly regard had captivated him like nothing else seemed to anymore.

After the near miss in the alley, Dearborne's naiveté and vulnerability were more apparent than ever, leaving Julien with the unfamiliar, but overpowering desire to protect him.

Of course, most would say that the only person Dearborne needed protecting from was him.

Powell was waiting at the door to take his things.

"I was driven home by Lord Blackstone," Leander explained. "Someone will have to let Rand know."

"Rand returned over an hour ago, my lord," Powell said. "He received word that you wouldn't be requiring him again this evening."

"What?"

"Do you wish me to summon Rand?"

"No, of course not." The evening's events were pressing down on him and Leander was too tired to worry about Rand receiving someone else's instructions by mistake. "Good night, Powell."

"Good night, my lord."

Leander went up to his room, where, for the first time, Gibson was not waiting to attend him. He wasn't about to call for the valet—it was an enormous relief to have some time alone. Exhaustion made him fumble with his cravat and buttons, but when his head was finally resting on his pillow, Leander found himself wide awake, replaying the night's events over and over.

When he finally fell asleep, it wasn't visions of deadly footpads that invaded his dreams, but a face with features just a shade too stark to be considered handsome, and fiercely intelligent amber eyes.

LEANDER stared at the book he held in disbelief. What was a volume such as this doing on the regular shelves? Someone on Sutton's staff must have made a terrible mistake. Leander knew he was hardly an expert, but the book appeared authentic. A hand-written, beautifully illuminated translation of *The Book of Aneirin*, one of The Four Ancient Books of Wales, was something Sutton would definitely keep behind his counter, not on a shelf with books costing only a few guineas. Perhaps it

was a modern forgery; he had heard that sometimes they sold well.

It made little difference to Leander, as he was more concerned with the story within the pages than the actual book. He went to the counter where Sutton was waiting on another customer.

"Hill will be out as soon as he locates the book for you, Lady Penelope," Sutton said to a woman in a dark-green walking dress.

"Mr. Sutton?"

"Lord Dearborne. I shall be with you in just a—" As Sutton sketched a quick bow, his eye fell on the book in Leander's hand and he froze.

"I found it in the shelves," Leander explained. "I thought it might be an inexpensive copy."

"Oh, dear," said the lady next to him, leaving little doubt as to which book she was waiting for Hill to locate.

"If I may?" Sutton asked, taking the volume for Leander. "I'll only be a moment." He disappeared into the back of the shop.

"I wonder if Mr. Hill will lose his position here," the woman mused.

"I hope not."

"Congratulations on finding it," she said to him, although her politeness seemed a bit forced. She didn't appear much older than him. Her bonnet framed a pretty face that spectacles did little to detract from. "You must be very pleased."

"You were looking for it."

"I have been, yes. Mr. Sutton sent word that he had acquired a volume he believed was authentic. I was hoping to complete my collection."

"You have the other three?"

"I do. Hand-written translations by Richard of Lonsdale. It is believed he did the illuminations as well."

Sutton emerged from the back, his lips pursed in a thin line. He set the book on the counter in front of Leander. "This is indeed a translation by Richard of Lonsdale. Hill placed it on the shelves in error. Shall I

wrap it for you, my lord?"

Leander made up his mind in that moment. "For her," he said, gesturing to the lady.

The woman stared at him and Sutton's eyebrows shot up. Leander willed himself not to blush under their scrutiny.

"Do you wish to inspect it, Lady Penelope?" Sutton asked.

"No need, Mr. Sutton. You've always done well by me in the past. I am quite willing to pay the price we originally agreed on."

Sutton's eyebrows nearly disappeared into his hairline. "That's very gracious of you, my lady. Lord Dearborne, if you would wait another moment, I have some other books that may interest you."

"Sir, I vow, I do not know how to thank you," the lady said when Sutton had returned to the back room.

"I'd rather see the set complete. I wasn't so interested in the workmanship as I was in what the book had to say about King Arthur."

"King Arthur? There's very little of him in *Aneirin*. You want *Taliesin* or *Carmarthen*. Those have the references to Arthur. But truthfully, for historic accounts, you'd be best reading *Historia Britonum* or *Vita Santi Gildae*. And of course, Geoffrey of Monmouth."

The lady obviously had some knowledge of the subject and Leander was eager to ask questions, but before he could, a tall, blond man approached. "Penelope, my dear, are you almost finished? Did you find your fourth book?"

"I did. Sutton is wrapping it now. And it is only thanks to this kind gentleman that I have it at all."

Sutton returned again, this time carrying several books, including Lady Penelope's wrapped volume. "Thank you again for your patronage, Lady Penelope." Then, in almost the same breath, he turned to Leander. "I have not found the specific translations you've requested, but I thought these might interest you as well. One is a copy of *The Birth of Merlin*, and the other is a prose version of *Lancelot of the Laik*. I will, of course, continue to look for translations of *Lanzelet* and the Italian novella."

"Thank you. I'll take them both," Leander said. When it came to his books, Leander was willing to spend as recklessly as any lord in England. When Sutton left to wrap his purchases, Leander turned to find that the lady and her companion were still present, and that none other than the Earl of Blackstone had joined them. "Lord Blackstone."

"Dearborne." Blackstone nodded. "Will you allow me to introduce you to my friends? I understand one of them feels indebted to you."

"There's no need," Leander said quickly.

"To introduce them?" Blackstone quirked his lips.

Leander felt his cheeks burning. "For anyone to feel indebted. I didn't mean to imply—"

"Julien, do stop teasing him," the lady chastised.

Blackstone acquiesced with a slight bow in her direction. "Lady Penelope, may I present the new Earl of Dearborne? Lord Dearborne, these are my good friends, Viscount Seaforth and his fiancée, Lady Penelope Archer."

"I heard Mr. Sutton say you were looking for *Lanzelet*," Lady Penelope said. "Would that be the work by von Zatizikhoven?"

"Yes, of course," Leander replied, impressed by the ease with which she rattled off the name.

"I have a translation I would be glad to lend you until you acquire your own copy."

It took a moment for Leander to find his voice. "Thank you, Lady Penelope."

"It's the least I can do. What was the other work? A novella?"

"It's Italian...." Leander tried to gather his thoughts, not wanting to stammer and appear foolish in front of Blackstone. He hadn't discussed the legends of King Arthur with anyone since his grandfather died and had learned so much more about the legend since his arrival in London that he wanted to plunge into discussion. Instead, he limited himself to answering Lady Penelope's questions. "Umm... *Donna di Scalotta*."

"Of course. There's been a great deal of interest in that lately. There is a regular scramble to translate it nowadays, although I haven't heard

of any that are completed."

"Mr. Sutton said that there are very few copies of the original Italian."

"Very few," Lady Penelope agreed, but she was smiling. "A friend of my father is in possession of one of them. He's having it translated."

"Have a care, Penelope." Seaforth grinned. "He looks as though he's about to fall over."

"Pay him no mind, Lord Dearborne." Lady Penelope shook her head. "Unless it's connected to a pharaoh or the sphinx, my fiancé doesn't believe it's worth his time."

"You'd best be on your guard, Seaforth," Blackstone warned. "It appears your lady has found herself an ally."

"Ignore them both," Lady Penelope instructed. "They have a difficult time of it. One studies Egypt and the other the Roman Empire. They're just jealous that they have to travel hundreds of miles to ever see the places they read about."

"So did Dearborne," Seaforth pointed out.

Leander laughed, surprising himself. For the first time since his arrival he did not want to escape the group of people surrounding him. "I think that may be the best thing about living in England. I'm eager to visit some of those places, although I haven't gone anywhere yet."

"It's not difficult to arrange," Lady Penelope assured him. "All you need to—" She stopped when Sutton returned with Leander's books.

"Thank you," Leander said as he took them.

"Always glad to be of service," Sutton replied.

Once they had left the shop and were on the street, Lady Penelope spoke again. "My mother is giving a ball the day after tomorrow. I do hope you will attend."

"Oh. I—"

"I'm certain she sent you an invitation. It would be from the Marchioness of Lynns."

"Lord Dearborne requires some coaxing before he engages in such

frivolity," Blackstone commented.

Leander was about to protest when he saw the gleam of amusement in the amber eyes.

"Are you like Blackstone, then, who must be practically dragged from his lair?" Lady Penelope asked, shooting a frown in the earl's direction. "I had to make some very dire threats before he promised to attend."

That decided the question for Leander immediately. "I would be happy to attend."

"I'm so glad." Lady Penelope smiled as she took Seaforth's arm.

"Look forward to seeing you there." Seaforth touched his hat brim before leading Lady Penelope to their waiting coach.

"Until Thursday, then, Dearborne." Blackstone's expression was inscrutable. He turned and followed his friends.

"'Til Thursday." Leander hurried to his own coach. He wanted to get home so he could find an invitation from the Marchioness of Lynns and send an affirmative reply.

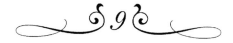

*D*earborne certainly seems to be enjoying this ball more than mine."

"I'm sure it's not a reflection on your abilities as a hostess, Aunt." Julien handed her a glass of champagne.

"So he assured me when we spoke earlier."

It wasn't difficult to spot Dearborne in the crowded ballroom if one knew where to look. He was with a small knot of people, many of whom had been cronies of Julien's great-uncle Algernon. Most people in the group were considered terribly unfashionable and never would have received an invitation from the Marchioness of Lynns had they not shared the marquis' interest in the legends of Arthur. Young bucks generally avoided the group like the plague, but Dearborne had spent most of the evening in their midst. At the moment he was listening to a very plain bluestocking with as much regard as if she had been the most celebrated belle of the Season.

"I'll wager Lady Flora has never had a handsome young man listen to her for so long before in her life," Cordelia commented. "If Dearborne isn't careful, he may find himself engaged."

"To Lady Flora Colchester?" Julien frowned. "Perhaps I shouldn't have brought you any more champagne."

"Don't be impertinent. She's not completely on the shelf, after all."

Julien found it annoying enough that all the mamas in the ton had been trying to marry off Dearborne; for his aunt to try her hand at matchmaking as well was too much to be borne. "Bit too old for him, isn't she?"

"She can't be more than twenty-eight. That's not *so* much older than he is, especially when they share interests in all these old legends and such."

Julien ignored the fact that the woman he considered "too old" for Dearborne was younger than himself. "He also shares those interests with Lady Grenville. Perhaps you think he should ask her to make a run to Gretna Green." Lady Grenville was well into her seventies.

Cordelia looked at him askance and Julien immediately regretted his sarcasm. The last thing he wanted was for her to delve deeper into the subject. Much to his relief, she was more in the mood for lecturing. "No need for that tone, Julien. After all, you were the one who introduced young Dearborne to the Arthurian League."

"Not I," Julien replied, hiding his relief at the change in subject. "Lady Penelope was more than happy to take him under her wing after he handed over a copy of *The Book of Aneirin*."

"The what?"

"*The Book of Aneirin*. It's one of The Four Ancient Books of Wales. They contain some of the first accounts of—" Julien stopped when Cordelia took a large, fortifying swallow of champagne.

"No need to go into all that dusty nonsense. If you want to talk about these ancient books of yours, you'd best take yourself off to the League in the corner."

"I'm not a member of the Arthurian League."

"Yes, yes, you and your Romans," Cordelia waved his protests away. "But heaven knows you spent enough with Algernon that you should be able to hold your own on the subject."

That was true enough. Algernon hadn't cared much for Julien's father, but after Sebastien's death, he readily acknowledged Julien as his heir. Julien had spent most of his school holidays with Algernon at Shadowcross Manor, the family seat in Hampshire. Since no one could be in Algernon's company for long without King Arthur being discussed, by the time he'd reached his late teens, Julien was well-versed in the subject.

He was tempted to join the group, but knew his sudden presence would raise several eyebrows and probably intensify any gossip that might have started at the theater.

"I must have a word with Lady Rockingham," Cordelia said. "I'm

certain I can trust you not to try to escape the ball early."

"I would have to be out of my wits to offend not only you but Lady Penelope as well."

Giving him a not-so-gentle tap with her fan, Cordelia made her way through the crowd.

Julien debated whether he ought to just take himself off to the card room when he sensed someone at his elbow. Turning, he saw the marquis' younger son. "Archer."

"Blackstone." Sidney Archer smiled and nodded. "Deathly bored yet?"

"At your mother's ball? Never."

"You'll have to do better than that," Archer snorted. "Not very believable at all. It could be worse, you know. You could be Penelope and Seaforth. They're still making rounds with Mother and Father." Julien grimaced at the thought, prompting a grin from Archer. "Penny's quite put out about the whole thing. She hoped to spend the evening with the Arthurian League, looking out for her new charge."

"The American earl," Julien said, making certain to sound suitably casual.

"The American earl," Archer repeated. "Penny thinks the world of him since he let her have old *Aneirin*. Seemed a nice enough fellow when I spoke to him."

"He looks to be getting on quite well with members of the League," Julien observed.

"Oh, he is," Archer agreed. "He's eager to soak up as much about Camelot as he possibly can, and most anxious to listen to everyone's views on the subject."

"So naturally they all think him a brilliant conversationalist."

"Naturally."

Julien wondered what had prompted Archer to seek him out—they were not on as intimate terms as he was with Penelope and Seaforth. Most conversations they'd had centered around subjects where their studies converged.

"Have you, by any chance, spoken to Lord Langston recently?"

It was an odd question, but Julien didn't take much note of it. His attention was taken by the fact that Lady Flora's very pretty young sister, Lady Helena, had joined in Dearborne's conversation. "Baron Langston?"

"Yes."

"The man would never risk his everlasting soul by speaking to me," Julien said absently. Lady Helena wasn't the scholar her sister was, but from what Julien had seen, she wasn't a fluff-headed miss, either.

"Oh."

The disappointment in Archer's voice finally registered with Julien. He reminded himself firmly that it was no concern of his who Dearborne spoke with. "Why do you ask?"

"I was speaking with him and some other members of the Antiquaries Club and they mentioned the excavation of a Roman fort— perhaps an entire village—near Worthy Down."

Julien knew the site Archer meant. He'd already visited it, but as it was from late in the Roman occupation, it hadn't interested him as it undoubtedly would Archer. "The one at Wakefield Park? It's but fifteen miles from Shadowcross Manor."

"Indeed."

Normally, this was the time when he would feign disinterest until Archer was at his wit's end, but he was grateful to the younger man for successfully distracting his thoughts from Dearborne and so decided not to toy with him—much. "Wakefield belongs to my neighbor."

"Does it?" Archer's tone was extremely casual, as though he wasn't angling for an invitation to Shadowcross. He was also overlooking the possibility that rumors would abound should he and Julien go off to Shadowcross alone for a few days. And while Archer might not care if people gossiped, his mother would, and the marchioness was perfectly capable of making her son's life hell if she chose.

There was a way to avoid gossip, however. "I haven't seen my cousin for quite some time," Julien mused, apropos of nothing. "I believe

I will invite Bertram and his family to Shadowcross for a visit. Of course, I'd have to invite Aunt Cordelia as well, or I'll never hear the end of it," he continued, acting as though he didn't notice how Archer's expression faded into a puzzled frown. "Seaforth would enjoy the jaunt too, I think, and if I invite him, I ought to invite Penelope. She always enjoys the chance to look through Algernon's library." Finally, he deigned to look at Archer. "I suppose you'll have to come along, to act as your sister's chaperone."

Archer chuckled. "You find your amusement in odd ways, Blackstone."

"You're not the first to say to," Julien replied blandly.

Archer turned red and coughed uncomfortably, reminding Julien that he simply didn't have his sister's aplomb for dealing with such a remark or situation.

"My apologies, Archer."

"Not at all."

"The weekend after next, I believe," Julien said.

"That sounds excellent," Archer agreed, neither his tone nor his expression betraying the excitement Julien knew he was feeling. "I'll tell Penelope, shall I?"

"By all means, if you wish to."

"Perhaps this will cheer her for the rest of the evening."

As Archer went off in search of his sister, Julien abandoned his plan for cards and instead walked toward the doors that led to the gardens, not allowing himself to look in Dearborne's direction as he went. It seemed he now had a house party to plan, though he normally loathed attending such things. To many people it would seem like a great deal of trouble to go to simply to oblige a friend, but Julien had done some quick calculations and decided it would be to his advantage.

Cordelia would be thrilled that he was making the effort, even if his guests were not the most fashionable sort, and perhaps along with a dinner party or two, it would fulfill his social obligations for the Season in her eyes. At least in this case, he could be assured that his guests were

people he could tolerate. Octavius would be glad for the chance to get out of London for a few days, even if there was no hunting to be had. Seaforth and Penelope would be grateful for the opportunity to spend time together, especially since their chaperone would probably be off at Worthy Down most of the time.

The cool night air was refreshing, and Julien felt no desire to go back inside. Instead he strolled deeper into the enormous gardens, keeping an eye out to avoid any couples seeking privacy among the tall hedges and making plans as he went.

He would have to send the invitations out first thing in the morning and even that would be short notice, but he felt certain everyone would accept. He also needed to send word to the butler at Shadowcross immediately to prepare the house. Then, arrangements would have to be made for a coach to carry his cousin's family from Upper Twyford; they might even prefer to spend a few days in London first. If that was the case, he'd need to open the house on Rupert Street for them as well.

It was a bit more trouble than he'd originally thought, but he really ought to visit with Bertram and Augusta, in any case. Although they were only distant cousins, Bertram was next in line for the earldom and he—or more likely his son, Geoffrey—would inherit it one day.

In the far corner of the garden he walked around a hedge and into what he knew was a well-secluded niche, only to find it already occupied. Common sense told Julien he ought to turn back before he was seen, but he hesitated a moment too long.

"Lord Blackstone."

"Dearborne."

"Were you looking for me, sir?"

"No." Julien was able to answer honestly, at least. "I was merely getting some air."

"Oh." Dearborne's voice seemed to hold a note of disappointment.

Julien quickly dismissed that thought. "And you? I thought you would be content to spend the entire evening in the company of the Arthurian League."

"No. I mean, yes, I'm enjoying meeting them, but still… I'm still not accustomed to the crowds—or crush, I suppose."

"I didn't mean to interrupt your solitude. I can leave if you—"

"No." Dearborne took a quick step forward. "No, not at all."

If he had a brain in his head, he would excuse himself at once, but Julien found it as difficult as ever to tear himself away from the American earl and all his earnestness. How strange—and flattering, if Julien were to be completely honest—that although Dearborne appeared uncomfortable with people on the whole, he never sought to escape Julien's company. Surely he'd been warned about Julien several times by this point. "Lady Cordelia is less likely to find us here than in her library." Julien lowered his voice to a conspiratorial tone that should have sent Dearborne running.

Instead the young man smiled. "I spoke to her earlier tonight, but I'm afraid I only bored her with my rambling about Lancelot."

"I wouldn't worry about that. Cordelia is accustomed to listening to me hold forth on my studies."

"Yes, the Roman Empire. Several people I spoke to mentioned that you studied it." Dearborne tilted his head slightly, and in the moonlight, Julien could see the inquisitive expression on his face. "Many of the Arthurian League seem well-acquainted with you."

"Yes, I know."

"Did you study it at one time?" Dearborne's eagerness was unmistakable.

And gratifying. And enthralling. And a dozen other things it shouldn't be. Really, he ought to put a stop to this at once. "Not particularly, no."

"Oh."

Compelled, Julien added, "But I spent well over a decade listening to my uncle discuss it. The former Earl of Blackstone was an avid scholar of Camelot and he acquired quite an extensive library."

"Then the former Earl of Dearborne must have studied it as well."

"I doubt it," Julien said. "I would have heard about him from

Algernon if he was a serious scholar."

"But I found several books about Arthur in his library," Leander explained. "It's enormous."

"Perhaps he was merely a collector of expensive books."

"Perhaps," Leander said with a slight frown. "There are books on nearly every subject. None of them are so old that reading them would cause damage," he mused, almost to himself. "It seems such a waste to have so many books if the subjects don't interest you."

"The former earl may have merely been concerned with having an enviable library." Julien turned away slightly, examining the leaves of a hedge as he spoke. "Surely you've learned by now how important appearance is in Polite Society."

"Of course. I know enough to disregard most of the gossip I hear."

Julien barely stifled a smile. "It may not be wise to disregard all of it."

"I agree. I use my own judgment," Dearborne shot back quickly.

"Ah, yes." Julien faced him again and allowed his lips to twist into a wry smile. "The judgment of the innocent."

Dearborne frowned again. "I am two and twenty. You speak as if I were a child."

"To the ways of the world, you are."

"You've no right to say that." Dearborne took several more steps forward.

"Haven't I?" Julien asked, as if Dearborne's indignation was of no consequence.

"You seem to think me foolish, but I know what gossip you're referring to."

"You *are* foolish if you choose to disregard the danger a young man like yourself might be in by spending time alone with me." Julien's curiosity got the better of him and he wanted to see how Dearborne reacted to the truth.

Dearborne's chin came up and the blue eyes flashed in the

moonlight. "I refuse to believe you would harm me after saving my life barely a fortnight ago. And even if for some reason you chose to, *you* would have to be the fool to do so within shouting distance of a crowded ballroom."

Julien blinked. "Harm you?" Were there some strange new rumors about him that he didn't know about?

"The gossip that you did away with Tobias Norville," Dearborne said. "There's nothing to support it, and I refuse to believe it's true."

The fact that Dearborne—who was really little more than a stranger to him—didn't believe the rumors shouldn't have meant much to Julien, but it did. "You are quite right. You have nothing to fear from me in that regard. But that isn't the sort of danger to which I refer."

Dearborne's posture relaxed. "Then, no, I don't understand."

Julien moved closer and lowered his voice. "You've heard no other rumors about me, then?"

"Oh." Dearborne looked startled, but to Julien's surprise, he didn't move away. "No... I mean, yes, I've heard other rumors."

"And they don't concern you?" Julien moved closer still so that the slightly shorter man would have to raise his head to look him in the eye.

Dearborne did so, swallowing hard. "No."

"You obviously didn't understand their meaning."

Once again, anger flashed across Dearborne's features. "If you think me so innocent, then you should not be trying to intimidate me in this manner."

There was enough truth in the accusation to sting Julien's conscience. "I am merely showing you what happens when you venture places you know nothing about."

"I know something about it."

Julien hid his surprise behind a mocking smile, which only seemed to irritate Dearborne further.

"I know that you... that you...."

"If you can't even say it, there's no reason to continue this

discussion." By all rights, he should stop this conversation immediately, Julien knew. But now something far more intense than his curiosity kept him from ending it.

"Prefer men," Dearborne finally managed, and despite the garden's shadows, Julien got the impression that the fair skin was now flushed with color. "And I've… I've…."

"You've what?" Julien's voice was barely more than a whisper. Suddenly it seemed that he must have somehow known all along.

"I've been with—that is, I haven't…. Well, we were only boys—"

"How old?"

"Fifteen. We didn't—it was only a kiss, and I don't think we even knew what…" Dearborne's words trailed off and he looked down.

Julien put his hand under Dearborne's chin and tilted his face back up. He only intended to ask more about this kiss, but couldn't stop himself from capturing the younger man's mouth with his own.

Dearborne made the smallest sound of surprise before his hands came up to clutch Julien's shoulders as he leaned into the kiss. He readily parted his lips at Julien's urging and tentatively met Julien's questing tongue. Julien slid his fingers through the silky black hair to pull Dearborne even closer, but froze when a high-pitched giggle broke through his lustful haze.

Tearing his mouth away, Julien looked around, but they were still alone in their sheltered corner. The giggle sounded again, and Julien realized with relief that it was coming from another part of the garden. He could hardly believe that he'd allowed himself to get carried away in such a manner somewhere that anyone could have happened upon them.

"What's wrong?"

Julien stared at Dearborne, who was breathing hard, and was barely able to keep from pulling him close again. "Forgive me, Dearborne. I…." *What?* There was no excuse he could give. "Forgive me." He turned to leave, but was stopped by a hand gripping his arm.

"Forgive you for what?"

"For risking your name in such a manner. I, of all people, should

know better. We'd best go back inside—separately." He freed his arm.

"It was worth the risk." Dearborne's low voice followed him, but Dearborne did not.

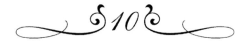

§ 10

It was a relief to get back into his coach and continue his journey when only fifteen minutes earlier Leander had wanted nothing more than to get out of the coach and stretch his legs. Stopping at the inn after four hours of travel seemed like an excellent idea. Leander bought luncheon for himself, Rand, and Gibson, accepting claret from the unctuous innkeeper even though he was certain he would have preferred the cider. It didn't take long for the fawning to make him uncomfortable, though, and he told his staff to finish their meal while he waited in the coach.

The sound of Rand and Gibson climbing back up onto the box distracted him briefly, and then they were under way again, with three more hours before they reached their destination. The big coach was comfortable, but lonely, and Leander wondered again if he shouldn't have ridden his recently purchased horse instead. He had decided against it because he wasn't an accomplished enough rider to travel such a distance and in any case, he would have still needed a vehicle to transport his trunk and his valet.

For he couldn't go without his valet. Although the words were never actually spoken aloud, the entire staff prepared as if it were a foregone conclusion, and Leander didn't argue with their experience. He liked Gibson well enough; if the man was uncommonly quiet, he was always respectful, and if his watchfulness sometimes made Leander nervous, he was always ready with whatever Leander needed.

So here he was, setting forth in a grand coach with his coachman and valet and what seemed to him an unnatural amount of fuss. But Blackstone had invited him to attend a house party, and if a caravan had been required to get him there, then Leander would have found a way to arrange it.

Leander still had no notion how he'd managed to make his way back into the ballroom after a kiss that had left him tingling from head to

foot, or how he got through the rest of the evening. He'd tried to act as though nothing was out of the ordinary when he returned to his friends of the Arthurian League, but found himself constantly searching for Blackstone. He was both thrilled and unnerved to find that more often than not, those amber eyes were fastened on him, as well.

He finally went home to a very restless sleep and rose late with the memory of the kiss still fresh in his mind. He ate breakfast without noticing what was on his plate, distracted by the questions constantly chasing around his brain. Did Blackstone regret the kiss? Was that the real reason he'd been so eager to get away? Had it simply not been a very good kiss? Leander only had one other kiss to compare it to and although David's kiss had given him pleasant butterflies, that was nothing compared to the storm of emotion that crashed through him at the sensation of Blackstone's lips and body against his. Of course, Blackstone had much more experience, so perhaps the kiss hadn't been anything special for him.

By the time he'd finished going through the morning's mail, Leander was convinced that he'd only made himself look like more of a foolish child in Blackstone's eyes. Then Powell brought him a letter that had arrived by messenger. Leander opened it warily—in his experience the extra money paid out for a special delivery was usually warranted by bad news—but it was an invitation from Blackstone to a house party at Shadowcross Manor in a fortnight. Leander sent his acceptance immediately, without the slightest idea where Shadowcross Manor was or how to prepare to attend a house party.

The next ten days were interminable. Suddenly, his books, his library, and his house were no longer enough to pass the time or contain him. He began by taking walks up and down Park Lane, going far enough to see the magnificent Dorchester House and venturing off the lane to walk around Grosvenor Square. Then he crossed Park Lane to begin exploring the enormous Hyde Park. After seeing most of Society on horseback there and hearing from the more fashionable members of the Arthurian League that everyone went riding on Rotten Row in the afternoon, Leander bought himself a pretty, gentle, gray-dappled mare and began riding in the morning to become more accustomed to the saddle.

During a meeting of the Arthurian League, Lady Penelope was more than happy to chat with him about the upcoming house party. From her he learned that she, her fiancé, and brother, as well as Lord and Lady Carysfort and Blackstone's cousin would be attending the same house party. He was vaguely disappointed to hear about that until Lady Penelope commented that it was a rarity for Blackstone to even be giving one. Almost as exciting was hearing about the excellent library at Shadowcross and Winchester Castle, only four miles away, which was said to house the original Round Table.

His cousin Morleigh paid another of his rare calls. Leander told him about the house party, then immediately regretted it, certain that Morleigh was one of those people who would have all sorts of cutting things to say about Blackstone. Instead, Morleigh only commented that it was strange for Leander to be visiting Blackstone's country house when he hadn't been to either of his own. As always it was said with a certain amount of disdain that left Leander assuring him he would visit his other properties soon.

He visited the Tower of London, saw Madam Tussaud's exhibit at the Lyceum Theatre, spent an entire day at the Zoological Gardens and went twice more to the theater. If he hoped to meet up with Blackstone by going out more, he didn't acknowledge it to himself and in any case he wasn't successful, only seeing Blackstone once during those ten days. After a lecture about proof of Lyonesse's existence, Blackstone arrived with Seaforth to collect Lady Penelope. Leander hoped he'd been able to act as though it was just a casual meeting for him, but didn't know how successful he'd been. What he *did* know was that he was nowhere near as successful at it as Blackstone, whose expression revealed nothing. The banked fires Leander thought he saw in the older man's eyes could have merely been more wishful thinking on his part.

Although most members of the Arthurian League spoke well of Blackstone—or at least well of Blackstone's uncle—there were still plenty of people in Society eager to tell him all manner of scandalous things about the earl. Leander knew that not all the gossip could be false, any more than it could all be true, but it didn't lessen his fascination. If he were to be completely honest with himself, that reputation was part of the appeal. David had been sent to Pelham to stay with relatives for the summer after getting into some unknown "trouble" in his hometown.

Most of the young folk had heeded their parents and maintained their distance from the boy who was "too wild," but Leander had been irresistibly drawn to him. Never once did David try to coax him into trouble. The "wildest" thing that had happened between them had been the kiss on the day before David's return to Holyoke and Leander had been equally culpable in that.

The increased activity had been good for him, helping him to fall asleep easily despite constant thoughts of Blackstone. As the day for departure drew closer, he'd had more difficulty, hardly getting any rest for the past two nights. To quell his uncertainty about Blackstone's motives, Leander constantly reminded himself that Blackstone had gone to the effort to invite him. Attractive though Leander found him, he didn't believe Blackstone was so obliging that he would invite someone who bored him out of mere politeness. Leander told himself over and over—and without success—to stop thinking about Blackstone quite so much or risk making an idiot of himself. After all, the house party would be filled with Blackstone's family and friends, so….

That was a bit odd, wasn't it? All the other guests were old friends or family members. Why would Blackstone invite someone he'd only met a handful of times and kissed once? Surely that had to count for something.

Perhaps not. Perhaps the kiss meant nothing to Blackstone. Perhaps he was only being obliging. Perhaps Lady Penelope and Lady Carysfort had taken pity on him and asked Blackstone to issue the invitation.

But could Blackstone be prevailed on in such a manner? To invite someone he had no regard for into his home for five days?

Finally the constant repetition of his thoughts, combined with the motion of his coach, lulled Leander into much-needed sleep.

JULIEN'S friends all knew their way around Shadowcross, as did the servants they brought along, so there wasn't a great need for him to formally play the host. Still, there was his cousin's family, who didn't visit often, as well as Dearborne, so he asked Cordelia to take over the duty of hostess. It also served to console her for having to be out of the

London whirl for five days. As he knew she would, Cordelia threw herself into the role, arriving a day early to plan menus and oversee the preparation of the guestrooms.

The first three arrivals, Seaforth, Penelope, and Archer, were a simple matter for her. They practically settled themselves and were soon ensconced in the Shadowcross Library, while their servants unpacked and easily made their way down to quarters. Bertram and Augusta, along with their seven-year-old son, Geoffrey, required more attention, but Cordelia was more than equal to the task, taking them all into the parlor for tea while the Shadowcross servants assigned to them escorted Geoffrey's nurse up to their rooms.

They were still sitting and chatting when Lennox announced the Earl of Dearborne's arrival. Cordelia bustled off to greet him and Julien followed as soon as he was able to extricate himself from Augusta's report of all the doings in Upper Twyford Society. Twenty minutes in Augusta's presence was enough to remind Julien why he rarely saw his cousin's family. Bertram was a bit more tolerable, but not much.

As he approached the large foyer, he could hear snippets of conversation and what sounded like Dearborne's concern for his coachman and horses, then Cordelia's assurances that room would be found for the night.

"And he is to drive back to London tomorrow, then return in three days' time for me?"

"Of course," Cordelia said. "It's his job to drive the coach, isn't it?"

"You're right, of course," Dearborne nodded. "There are still some things that seem odd to me. For instance, I have no idea what people do at a house party."

"I'm afraid I cannot be of assistance." There was laughter in Cordelia's voice. "I could tell you what goes on at an ordinary house party, but with a houseful of scholars, I've no idea what will be happening here."

"Maligning my abilities as host already, Aunt?" Julien asked.

Cordelia said something suitably witty in reply, of course—she always did—but Julien had no idea what it was. His attention was

entirely focused on the blue eyes that had widened in surprise at his entrance. Julien couldn't say what expression they held or rather there were so many fleeting through them that he couldn't choose only one. There was also a slight flush on Dearborne's cheek and a tentative smile on his lips that Julien wanted to see fully emerge.

"Welcome to Shadowcross Manor, Dearborne," he said easily, despite the fact that the memory of kissing the young man was still fresh in his mind. Although clearly inexperienced, Dearborne's enthusiasm had been unmistakable—and intoxicating. "I hope you'll enjoy your stay."

"Thank you." Dearborne met Julien's eyes, and if his flush deepened, so did his smile. "I'm looking forward to it."

If Cordelia noticed anything amiss, she didn't comment as she ushered Dearborne into the parlor and introduced him to Bertram, Augusta, and Geoffrey. Over tea, Cordelia mentioned the other three guests who were in the library and that they would all meet over dinner at six-thirty. She urged them to take their time with the tea, as they still had two hours to be shown to their rooms and prepare for dinner.

Bertram and Augusta both had a multitude of condescending questions about America which Dearborne readily answered. As Julien listened, he was struck by how vastly different Dearborne's life had been before coming to London and found himself enjoying the conversation.

Even more, he was enjoying the quick, cautious looks that Dearborne kept casting in his direction. Looks that were alternately questioning, shy, or hopeful. Out of long habit, Julien kept his expression neutral whenever he met Dearborne's gaze. It seemed the safest way to deal with the myriad of unfamiliar emotions he had been experiencing since he'd first met Dearborne.

Perhaps he was doing too good a job of hiding his thoughts, because as the conversation wore on, Dearborne began to look chilled and became more subdued.

Julien suspected he wasn't the only one who was relieved when Cordelia rose to show everyone to their rooms. Dearborne was beginning to look decidedly uncomfortable and Geoffrey, although a remarkably well-behaved boy, was growing restless.

As they were walking up the large main staircase, Julien knew he could wait no longer and said, "You appear to have your hands full, Aunt, so I'll show Lord Dearborne to his room." He nodded to Bertram and Augusta. "I look forward to seeing you again at dinner."

Cordelia gave him a sharp look, while Augusta's sour expression was distinctly disapproving. Julien didn't worry much about the latter, knowing it was because he wasn't paying the couple the attention she thought they deserved and stemmed from Augusta's inflated sense of importance. Cordelia, on the other hand, might begin to suspect the truth if he wasn't careful. Julien had no idea what Dearborne's expression might have held, deciding it better not to risk looking in his direction.

They parted at the top of the staircase and Julien led Dearborne down the hall to a large room decorated in cherry wood and green with a large handsome fireplace. Dearborne's valet was already in the room unpacking and Julien barely caught himself before ordering the servant to leave. He leaned close to Dearborne, murmuring, "Will you have your man leave us?" When Dearborne looked at him in surprise, he added, "Unless you wouldn't feel safe alone in the room with me."

That brought a hint of a smile to Dearborne's face. "Gibson, why don't you go downstairs for a while? I'll just ring when you're needed."

"Very good, m'lord."

Julien was briefly distracted by the way Dearborne phrased his orders as a polite request. Then he realized that Dearborne was looking at him questioningly and suddenly found himself at a loss for words. "Dearborne—"

"Lord Blackstone—" Dearborne said at the same time.

This formality was beginning to grate on his nerves, despite the fact that it was nothing out of the ordinary. "My given name is Julien, if you wish to use it," he said, and knew he'd made the right decision when Dearborne smiled.

"And I'm Leander. It would be good to be called by my name again. I haven't heard it since I set sail from Boston."

"Leander," Julien began, and then paused when Leander's smile grew brighter. God help him, the lad was far too transparent about things

that brought him pleasure. It made Julien wonder what other emotions he could bring to that handsome face. He found he'd actually taken a few steps closer before catching himself. "Do you have any notion what would happen should your leanings become known?"

The smile faded. "To whom?"

"To Society."

"No," Leander admitted. "I've wondered, though. That is, I've wondered why I always felt the way I did. I never knew anyone else…." He shrugged helplessly. "I've been trying to learn more about it."

"Ah, yes." Julien gave a low laugh. "Ever the scholar, aren't you? Did our encounter in the marquis' garden prove enlightening?"

Color rose in Leander's cheeks and his eyes dropped to the floor.

The thought that he might have been nothing more than an experiment angered Julien far more than it should have. "And who, pray tell, is next on your lesson plan?"

The dark head snapped up and Leander closed the distance between them. "No one. I never wanted to learn more until I met you in Lady Carysfort's library."

This time when Julien leaned to kiss him, Leander met his lips halfway.

§ 11

The moment he realized Julien was about to kiss him again, Leander grabbed onto the lapels of his coat before the older man could change his mind.

Julien's arms came up around him as the kiss deepened, and Leander moved his hands up to toy with the hair that curled over Julien's collar as he investigated the warm interior of Julien's mouth. He felt a moment's disappointment when Julien broke off the kiss, but sighed when Julien's lips trailed along his jaw.

Leander felt fingers tugging at his cravat and instinctively tilted his head back. After trying for several moments without success, Julien pulled back with a frustrated sound, although he kept one arm around Leander's ribs.

Leander was grateful for the support. He was still dazed. "What *now?*" he asked, startling himself because he sounded perilously close to whining.

Julien's lips curved slightly. "This isn't a good time."

The unsettled feeling in Leander's stomach went from delicious to sour. "You already... you're already attached? To that man I saw you with at the theater?"

Julien seemed briefly puzzled, but then broke into a warm smile. "There is no one else who interests me at this time, I assure you." The low voice seemed to pour over Leander, smoothing away any unpleasant feeling. "But I have a houseful of guests and we will have to be going down to dinner before too long."

That made sense. Leander had been finding it difficult enough to maintain his composure so far. "What should I do at dinner?"

"Do?" Julien released him but didn't step away.

"How should I act?"

"How do you think you should act?"

Leander let out a snort of irritation, making Julien's smile widen. "I don't want to embarrass you."

"Embarrass me? I can't imagine that happening. I've seen nothing wrong with your behavior."

That wasn't helpful. "I try to act properly, but suddenly I'll see people looking at me strangely and I know I've done something odd or wrong, but I don't know *what*." It felt good to finally admit something that had plagued him since his arrival in London. "I don't want to… cause any embarrassment."

"Not to worry. Should it become known that anything has transpired between us, I will most certainly be the one held at fault."

"I don't want that either."

"Is that your only worry?" Julien's look became piercing. "My embarrassment? Are you not concerned that people's opinions of you will likely change should your preference for men become known?"

Leander considered the question. He'd observed how people talked about Julien, but didn't know what would happen in his case. That didn't change the truth of the matter, however. "The people whose opinions truly matter to me are no longer living, and I don't… I don't know what they would have thought."

Julien studied his face so long that Leander began to feel uncomfortable. Just as he was about to break the silence, Julien spoke. "Behave as you always have and there will be no cause for embarrassment." He put a hand under Leander's chin and then bent to brush their lips together lightly. "I'll see you at dinner." He left, closing the door softly behind him.

Several minutes passed before Leander moved, sitting in the comfortable chair near the window with the taste of Julien's lips still fresh on his and more questions fresh in his mind.

What *would* his family have thought if they knew where his feelings truly lay? Would his father have disowned him as many said Lady Carysfort should have done to Julien? Would Kit have thought him sinful and immoral as Lord and Lady Moorhouse did Julien? Would

Chance have mocked him as Leander had heard many young bloods mock Julien? How strange to think of the joy of having his father and brothers back, only to have to live with their scorn.

It was of no real matter to him, however. His family was gone and that was the end of it. Better to concentrate on the present than to dwell on that and risk melancholy overtaking him.

He got up and drew the bellpull to summon Gibson.

"I know the former earl had several essays that attempt to prove and disprove the authenticity of the Round Table at Winchester Castle," Lady Penelope assured him, going through a large stack of papers. "I thought you might want to read them before we went."

Leander looked up from the copy of *Parzival* he'd been scanning, wondering if that would even be possible, as they were going to Winchester Castle tomorrow. During dinner, everyone's plans for the next day had been discussed. Archer was going to the Roman site—Leander was becoming more interested the more he heard about it and now hoped to see it as well—while Lord Carysfort was going fishing with Mr. Sutcliffe and young Geoffrey. The rest of the party was going to Winchester in two coaches. Leander would be stopping at the castle with Lady Penelope, Seaforth, and Julien, and Lady Carysfort would travel on to the town with Mrs. Sutcliffe where they were to go shopping. Listening to the plans had distracted Leander and kept him from mooning over Julien—he hoped—during dinner.

After dinner, Lady Penelope asked Julien that she be allowed to show Leander the former earl's library, and the enormous collection of Arthurian literature fully occupied Leander from the moment he set eyes on it. *Parzival* was the first thing he found and had held his attention ever since, while Lady Penelope prowled through the overflowing shelves in search of the essays.

"Ah! Here are some." Lady Penelope held up a folder. "One of them is by the Countess of Belmanoir. She is one of the few people who claim that the table is not real. The other two claim to prove the table's authenticity. There is one somewhere by Brother Simon of Wexford, or at least a copy of it, written in 1427. He also claims it's real. I do hope I

can find you that one; it's fascinating."

It occurred to Leander that since the essays were for his benefit, he ought to be helping in the search. Reluctantly, he tore himself away from *Parzival* and walked over to the shelves where tomes hundreds of years old sat side by side with books written only twenty years earlier. Where did one begin to look?

"Julien's Uncle Algernon could find anything he wanted in this mess," Lady Penelope said. "I've seen him do so for my father when I was a little girl—it was just as bad then."

"It can't be good for the old books to be kept in such a manner."

"The old earl was more concerned with what was in the books than what anyone was willing to pay for them." Lady Penelope threw him a smile. "It seems you have that in common with him."

Leander smiled back and then looked at the shelves again. "I don't know that I would like my library so disorganized, though."

"Papa told me once that the old earl kept it like this on purpose, so that he was the only one who could find anything. He guarded his books rather jealously, although he loved discussing what was in them."

"I wonder what he'd think of us looking through them now."

"Oh, I think he'd be glad that someone truly sincere about the subject was using them if he couldn't," Lady Penelope assured him cheerfully. "And certainly amused at the difficulty we're having."

Leander laughed. The former earl sounded very odd, but everyone seemed to have been quite fond of him. He continued his search, finding a portfolio filled with papers, which he brought to one of the empty tables. There were essays on all manner of topics, although all Arthurian, and Leander had to make a real effort to remain focused on those that mentioned the Round Table or Winchester Castle. Whenever Lancelot's name caught his eye, sometimes he would pause to read a bit more of the essay, which was how he found one suggesting that Lancelot was actually in love with *Arthur*. The world suddenly narrowed to just words on paper as he read the theory that Arthur was Lancelot's true love and that Guinevere had only been introduced by later authors to hide this.

"—do you say to that, Dearborne?"

Leander was yanked back to the real world and when he looked up, he was astonished to find that Julien and Seaforth had entered the library without his notice. All three were watching him with amusement and he realized that Seaforth had asked him a question. "I'm sorry. You were saying?"

"I was asking if you agreed with Penelope," Seaforth said.

That clarified nothing for Leander. He looked at Julien for some clue as to what was being discussed but could tell by the smirk that there would be no help there. "And what did she say?" he finally asked.

"That if we weren't careful, we might very well lose you in here for a few days."

Leander felt his face growing warm. "It is an excellent collection."

"Of course," Lady Penelope said, her voice quickly going from teasing to chastising as she turned to Julien, "in its present state, one could lose nearly anyone in here. Didn't you say that you were going to have it catalogued?"

Julien seemed amused by the scolding. "I would have enjoyed seeing you rail at Algernon in such a manner."

That gave her pause, but only for a moment. She straightened her spectacles and shot a look at Seaforth when he let out a snort of laughter. "What *do* you plan to do with the collection? It's been years and it's terrible to see it wasting away."

"Why, Lady Penelope, I do believe you're angling for a donation to the Arthurian League."

Seaforth quickly stepped in before she could respond. "My dear, we came to fetch the two of you because everyone else has retired for the evening."

Leander glanced at the clock on the ornately carved mantel, surprised to find that it was nearly midnight.

Lady Penelope checked the small watch pinned to her dress. "Oh, dear. And we want to get an early start tomorrow." She gathered together the essays she had mentioned and gave them to Leander. "You should be able to read most of them before you go to sleep."

"If I may remove them from the library?" Leander looked at Julien, not wanting to appear too presumptive on his first night in the man's home.

"Of course," Julien nodded. "I wouldn't want to be the reason that you fail to complete the task Lady Penelope has assigned you."

Lady Penelope actually looked a bit disconcerted. "Forgive me, Lord Dearborne, I can sometimes be a bit—"

"Dictatorial," Seaforth replied. He obviously enjoyed the sharp looks his fiancée continually gave him.

"Peremptory," she finished.

Leander supposed he must have still appeared uncertain, because Julien took the essays from him. "I will bring these upstairs myself so there can be no doubt about permission."

At the last second, Leander managed to add the essay about Lancelot and Arthur to the pile.

"Don't stay down here too late," Julien said to Seaforth and Lady Penelope.

After exchanging good nights with the couple, Leander followed Julien upstairs.

"Very interesting essay about King Arthur and Lancelot," Julien said when they stopped outside Leander's door.

"You've read it?" Leander made no move to go inside, knowing Gibson was there. The hallway, at least, seemed deserted.

"I haven't read much of Algernon's collection, but that was one essay I found fascinating."

"I probably should read those about the table at Winchester Castle first." Leander smiled. "Seeing as we're going there tomorrow." In truth, he was reluctant to go into his room to read *any* essay if it meant leaving Julien outside. What he wanted to do was reach out and touch Julien, perhaps even be so bold as to pull his head down for a kiss, but he had little idea of how a man and woman with affection for each other conducted themselves, let alone two men. Were there fewer rules to observe, or more? He'd never been good at conversation unless books or

their contents were being discussed and he was reluctant to attempt small talk for fear of appearing foolish. He had to say *something*, however, or Julien would simply—

"I'll bid you good night then, Leander."

"Good night," Leander replied, reluctantly going into his room. He knew sleep was going to be elusive at best, but at least he'd be able to get all the essays read.

"HOW many of those essays did Dearborne have time to read?" Seaforth asked.

"Enough to impress Penelope," Julien said mildly.

The pair in question were in front of the massive round table again, after touring the entire castle. Rather than only being interested in how the castle related to Arthurian legend, Leander wanted to learn everything about the structure. Julien was content to follow along, enjoying the opportunity to watch Leander in his element.

Seaforth, meanwhile, seemed to find the entire outing tiresome— something that was unusual for him. When he commented on the fact that they were viewing things that had nothing to do with King Arthur, Penelope reminded him rather sharply that Leander had never been in an actual castle before and that she thought his interest admirable. That had done nothing to improve Seaforth's mood.

"Penelope has grown fond of him rather quickly." Seaforth's voice was flat.

Julien could think of nothing to say in reply to that, as he was guilty of exactly the same thing.

"Do you think I have cause for jealousy?"

That was simple enough to answer. "No."

"How can you know?"

"I know," Julien said firmly.

Seaforth fell silent and Julien turned his attention back to the pair by the famous Round Table. Julien thought he would never tire of watching the way Leander's diffidence vanished when he was presented with the opportunity to learn. The blue eyes were alight, and one could almost see the clever mind absorbing as much knowledge as possible. A smile hovered near his lips almost the entire time, dispelling his usual expression of melancholy. His sheer joy at learning, at somehow stepping out of his surroundings and into the past was plain for anyone to see.

Such a visible display of one's emotions was terribly unfashionable—in some cases even dangerous—but Julien relished every one of them. Leander's bewilderment at his new life, his shyness in the presence of too many people, even his brief flashes of temper when Julien's teasing touched a nerve, all fed a hunger Julien had never been able to identify.

"Julien." Seaforth's voice interrupted his reverie. "You know I would never presume to intrude upon certain areas of your life—"

"Good," Julien replied shortly.

That was the end of *that* conversation, but Julien felt the weight of Seaforth's gaze several more times during their outing and had to take special care that his own gaze did not remain fixed on Leander for too long.

"Did you enjoy your outing to Winchester Castle, Lord Dearborne?" Mrs. Sutcliffe inquired politely.

Leander looked up from serving himself a lamb cutlet from the platter the footman next to him held. Mrs. Sutcliffe rarely deigned to address him directly. "I did. Very much." He wished he could summon the words to truly express his feelings about the castle, but didn't know where to begin.

"I'll wager you've never seen anything so venerable in America."

"Certainly not." Leander was unable to help smiling. "Considering that Winchester Castle is far older than America itself."

Archer paused with his fork halfway to his mouth. "What a singular

notion. The history of America could likely fit in a single volume."

"It does," Leander agreed, remembering Kit's history book.

"How strange to think of a young country," Lady Penelope mused. "So many things to be done for the first time. Traditions could be *made* instead of followed."

Mrs. Sutcliffe's pursed lips indicated this might not be the way she'd intended the conversation to go. "It all sounds very rough. Little wonder you've had difficulty adapting to Society." Her tone left it open to interpretation whether she meant the ton, or civilization in general.

Leander was about to protest that Massachusetts was one of the oldest states, but Mrs. Sutcliffe had turned to Julien and changed the subject.

"Did Lady Carysfort tell you whom we met in Winchester, Julien?" Mrs. Sutcliffe asked. Leander wondered if she noticed Julien's grimace when she addressed him by his given name. "Mrs. Drummond Wyncham! And quite happy to see me she was." She turned to address the rest of the table. "Daughter of Baron Chatworth, you know. My aunt was married to her brother. She is visiting with Lady Eudora Marling and we are all to take tea with them tomorrow."

"I told Augusta not to promise too rashly," Lady Carysfort broke in. "And informed Mrs. Wyncham that we may not all be able to attend."

"Indeed," Julien agreed coolly. "Other plans have been made."

"Seaforth and I were going to visit the Roman site with Sidney again," Penelope said. She turned to Mrs. Sutcliffe. "I was going to ask if Geoffrey might accompany us. He seemed quite interested and is such an amiable child."

"Of course he may!" The flattery of her son had its intended effect of improving Mrs. Sutcliffe's mood. "And the rest of us shall have a nice visit with Lady Marling."

"I'm afraid not, Augusta," Julien said. "Dearborne and I are going riding tomorrow. I promised him a tour of Shadowcross."

Mrs. Sutcliffe's simper vanished. "Surely that can be done some other time." She looked at Leander as if it was his fault.

It was the first Leander had heard of such a plan, and while his first instinct normally would have been to acquiesce, something—whether Mrs. Sutcliffe's manner or the chance to spend a day with Julien—made him say with every bit of formality he'd learned in England, "The tour is vital to my own holdings. I know so little of such grand estates, you see. We've nothing of the sort in America."

Lady Penelope coughed politely into her napkin.

"Again, something that does not have to be done at once. Julien, Mrs. Wyncham tells me that you've been quite neglectful in your neighborly duties to Lady Marling."

"Augusta," Lady Carysfort tried to interrupt. "Lord Carysfort and I will be glad to attend with you."

"Mr. Sutcliffe," Mrs. Sutcliffe turned to her husband. "Do reason with him."

Mr. Sutcliffe looked alarmed at the thought.

"That is quite enough." Julien's voice could have frozen the claret in his glass. "I've never called upon Lady Marling and have no desire to begin now. We have all made our plans for tomorrow and you shall simply have to make our excuses. I advise you not to make plans on my behalf again."

Mrs. Sutcliffe did not dare another word, but sat fuming in silence. The rest of the evening was rather subdued and Leander took the opportunity to retire shortly after dinner. Although he was gradually growing used to drinking wine with his meals, the many different glasses that accompanied a large dinner could still have an effect on him. That, combined with a busier day than usual and a sleepless night before, made him grateful for an early evening.

After telling Gibson of his plans for the next day and requesting suitable clothes for riding, Leander climbed into bed and—despite his anticipation for the morrow—fell into a deep, comfortable sleep.

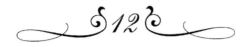

12

"How many acres is your estate?" Leander asked.

"About eighteen thousand."

"Oh."

Julien turned to look at the young man riding next to him. Leander had reined his horse and was surveying the wide green field that lay to the south of the house with a dumbfounded expression.

"I was going to ask why so much land was unused, but I suppose with eighteen thousand, keeping a few hundred acres for pleasure would make little difference."

Having never considered the land "unused," Leander's words gave Julien pause. The acres—it was far more than "a few hundred"—of lawns and patches of woods were there for riding or hunting. Julien had never much concerned himself with the land, other than to make sure his tenants and laborers were content and that his bailiff wasn't cheating him. He wasn't one of those landowners who constantly experimented with "improvements." The estate's income was more than enough to keep him in a comfortable style and he was satisfied with that.

"Do you know if my own estates are so large?"

Julien considered what little he knew about the Dearborne holdings. "I've no doubt at least one is, probably the one in Somerset. The other may just be a country home."

Leander took a deep breath and blew it out slowly.

"May I ask how many acres your father owned?"

"About sixty-five."

You can live on that?! Julien almost blurted, but caught himself. How strange for Leander to have more in common with his tenants and cottagers than with his fellow landowners. "Your knowledge of farming

will no doubt be beneficial."

This only prompted another unhappy sigh. "I was too ill to be of much help on the farm," Leander said, one corner of his mouth tucked downward. "My brothers worked with my father most of the time."

"You have brothers?" Julien said, wondering why they hadn't made the voyage with him.

"Not anymore." Leander's voice was barely a whisper.

Julien winced. This was not the day he'd planned on. The sun and exercise were supposed to put more color in Leander's cheeks and a sparkle in his eyes. It was supposed to be an opportunity for Julien to find out if he could provoke as much enthusiasm from Leander as Winchester Castle and Algernon's library had. The day was not supposed give Julien a pang in his chest when he witnessed Leander's obvious grief. "Shall we continue on?" he suggested. "There's a lake just on the other side of that grove you might enjoy seeing."

"Yes, of course." Leander's smile was forced, but Julien took heart that he at least made the attempt.

Nudging his horse forward, Julien led Leander toward a broad copse of trees, and after a moment's thought, turned toward a trail that went through a part of the grove where the trees weren't so close together. Leander had asked about his horse's temperament while they were still at the stables, admitting that he was not a very experienced rider. The trail through the densest part of the small wood could be difficult even for a seasoned rider, and Julien was not about to risk Leander taking a fall.

Once through the grove, Julien urged his horse to a swift canter down toward the lake. He had gone several yards before he realized Leander was no longer beside him. Looking back, he saw that the younger man had stopped his horse just outside the wood and that his expression had changed from one of misery to one of amazement. "What's the matter?" he asked, trotting back to Leander's side.

"You have a castle."

Julien followed Leander's unwavering gaze to the round stone building on a small rise beyond the lake and smiled. "It's a folly," he said, having never concerned himself much with the structure.

"My eyes are not deceiving me, Julien, truly."

Julien smiled, mostly at hearing his name from Leander's lips. "A folly—built just for pleasure. Blackrock Folly, to be more precise. It was built in the seventeen-forties by the ninth Earl of Blackstone."

"May we visit it?"

As if he could possibly say no to such eyes. "By all means," Julien said with a grand gesture. "Lead the way."

Leander set off at a fast pace, and Julien suspected the only thing preventing him from a full-out gallop was his lack of expertise in the saddle. Grinning, Julien followed him around the lake and up the long slope. By the time he reached the folly, Leander had already ridden around it. "What are the two smaller towers attached to it?"

"One isn't a tower at all, but a chimney. The other is a stairwell."

"A circular stone staircase?" Leander tilted his head back to take in the entire structure. "Like in a real castle?"

"I suppose." Julien shrugged. "It's only three stories, though. I've seen some folly towers as high as seven."

Leander tore his gaze away. "Why? I mean, what is it for?"

"Simply to have it, I suppose. Some are for decoration. Nowadays some people give garden parties from them. Algernon never had much interest in it, and I admit I haven't either."

"Oh." Leander's face fell.

"But I suppose the horses could use a rest after that run," Julien said. "If you'd care to take a look inside."

"You do like to vex people, don't you?" Leander smiled as he dismounted.

"Some are more worth the effort of vexing than others," Julien replied. He led the way to the heavy oak door and pushed it open, then let Leander enter.

Leander turned in a slow circle, twice, and then stopped when he was facing the stairwell. "May I go up?" he asked, his voice hushed.

"Of course."

Before following, Julien looked around the room as well, trying to see what Leander seemed to find so awe-inspiring. About sixteen feet in diameter, the stairwell stood directly opposite the door. A fireplace was in the center of one curved wall, with a window set on each side. Three windows were evenly spaced on the opposite side, with the center one being larger and made of stained glass. The symmetry of the room was admirable, Julien supposed. Each window had the other directly opposite, while the fireplace and stained glass countered one another in the same way as the doors. A heavy table with intricately carved sides and legs, along with four matching chairs, were the only furniture in the room.

The room itself was much cleaner than Julien had expected to find it. Everything was a bit dusty, and the windows were in terrible need of scrubbing, but on the whole it looked very well for a building that hadn't been used in more than fifty years.

He walked up to the next floor, which was empty except for a high-back bench made in the same style as the table. He heard footsteps on the stairs and looked up just in time to see Leander emerge from the stairwell. "Is there anything of note up there?" Julien asked.

"Only a four-poster bed. It's made much heavier than those you see now."

"The bed chamber, I suppose. I recall hearing that this building served as a retreat for the countess. The bed hangings and cushions from this bench would have been taken back to the house long ago," Julien said, wanting to relay as much as he could to the fascinated young man. "There were tapestries commissioned for the two upper floors. They're somewhere in the house as well."

"They lived here?" Leander traced the carving on the side of the settle.

"Certainly not." Julien laughed. "They'd sleep here from time to time, I believe. Thought it a lark. Bit absurd when there's a perfectly comfortable house only two miles away."

"I don't blame them." Leander walked to one of the windows and looked out, then began walking around the room, trailing his hand along the stone wall as he went. He obviously had no idea what an appealing

image he made, with his eyes alight and a smile curving his lips, utterly immune to the gloom cast by the dirty windows. "Imagine sleeping in your very own little castle."

"Not a castle," Julien reminded him. "It's hardly authentic."

"I don't know that I'd sleep well in a *real* castle. It would be too imposing. This is much cozier."

"I could have your things moved out here if you like," Julien offered.

For a moment it looked like Leander was actually considering it, then he smiled and ducked his head. "You think I'm idiotic."

"Not at all," Julien assured him quietly. Leander lifted his head and when their eyes met, color rose in his cheeks. "You're quite correct. It's very cozy." Never breaking eye contact, he closed the distance between them.

Leander's breath hitched and he moistened his bottom lip with his tongue. The action was unconscious, brought on by nervousness, no doubt, but that didn't lessen its effect on Julien. What he *wanted* to do was grab Leander and ravish that tempting mouth, but he forced himself to move slowly, cupping Leander's face in his hand and running his thumb along the reddened cheek. Leander's reaction was immediate. He leaned into Julien's touch and swayed forward slightly.

Such a blatant invitation, however unconscious, was too much for Julien to resist. He slid his hand into the silky black hair and tugged Leander forward for a kiss. Without a moment's hesitation, Leander wound his arms around Julien's neck, returning the kiss eagerly, if somewhat unskillfully. Julien pulled him closer and proceeded to give him a thorough lesson in kissing.

Julien finally tore his mouth away and began pressing soft kisses along Leander's cheek and jaw while the sound of Leander's unsteady breathing echoed in his ears. He caught one end of Leander's cravat and pulled more carefully, but with the same result. "What sort of ridiculous cravats does your valet tie on you?" he finally growled in frustration.

Leander let out a breathless laugh, and added his fingers to the task.

Together they managed to untie it, and Julien quickly unfastened the

top buttons of Leander's shirt, baring the pale column of his neck. When he pressed his lips to the smooth skin, Leander gasped and arched against him as if seeking as much contact as possible. Julien lost no time, pushing Leander's coat off his shoulder and part of the way down his arms. Leander immediately stripped it off the rest of the way to free his arms.

Leander was so receptive to his touch that Julien was impatient to see how he would react when they were skin to skin. Then, to his surprise, he felt Leander's hands fumbling with his own cravat as he smiled against the smooth column of his throat. More proof of what a quick learner the young man was.

Julien quickly shed his own coat and then captured Leander's lips again. He ran his hands down the younger man's back, thinking vaguely that Ashworth's tailoring was excellent as always. He cupped firm buttocks in his hand and moaned into Leander's mouth, then squeezed gently.

Leander startled briefly and then settled again, clutching desperately at Julien's shoulders. When Julien released him, he slumped against the stone wall. Julien nuzzled again at his neck while quickly unfastening his waistcoat and shirt. He shuddered as Julien's hands slid inside his shirt, stroking along his ribs and around to his back. When he pulled Julien's mouth to his own, demanding more kisses, Julien was more than happy to oblige.

While Leander was lost in the kiss, Julien let his hand drift down to the front of his trousers, and was pleased to find a very promising bulge there. He caressed it lightly, prompting a muffled sound, and began unbuttoning the pants.

"Julien…," Leander choked, hanging on as if for dear life.

"Shall I stop?" Julien whispered, although he wasn't sure if he could.

"No, but… dear God…."

When Julien touched his straining erection, Leander cried out as if in pain. Julien froze, but in the next moment Leander was pushing himself desperately into his hand. Bracing Leander with his free arm, Julien began to stroke, his eyes fastened on Leander's face.

Leander's eyes were squeezed shut, his lower lip caught between his teeth, allowing only small whimpers to emerge as he pumped himself into Julien's hand.

Julien could feel Leander's hot breath against his neck; the younger man buried his face there when it was over. He wiped his hand on the hem of his shirt before wrapping both arms around Leander and holding him close. He waited until Leander's breathing returned to a normal pace. "Leander, perhaps we should settle our clothing and return to the house."

"What?" Leander lifted his head, frowning slightly. "No."

"Believe me, I would like nothing more than to stay here with you." Julien kissed Leander's forehead. "But—"

"Not yet." Leander shifted slightly, so he had room to cup the front of Julien's trousers.

Julien drew in a sharp breath. "Leander, you don't have to.... There's no need—"

"I want to," Leander assured him softly, fingers on the buttons. "I don't know if I'll do it properly, but—"

"Anything." Julien felt Leander's hand brush against him and gritted his teeth. He knew Leander was only mimicking what he had done moments earlier, but when curious fingers curled around him, he decided it was an excellent learning technique. "I assure you, anything you do will—" Leander began moving his hand and Julien tightened his embrace, holding Leander's bent head close to his chest.

Leander's touch started out cautious, but quickly grew bold, no doubt encouraged by Julien's groans. Julien tried every trick he knew to hold back his release—such an unpracticed touch *shouldn't* have had such an effect on him—but he finished with embarrassing speed.

With his arms still wrapped tightly around Leander, Julien kept his face buried in the dark hair until his breathing steadied.

"Julien?"

"Mmm?"

"How did you..? Where do I..?"

Julien pulled away and Leander held out one hand. Chuckling, Julien used the other side of his shirt to clean himself off Leander's hand, ignoring any protests. His valet wouldn't think twice about such things if they were noticed, but Leander's might. "There we are," he said, dropping another kiss on Leander's lips. He meant it to be brief, but couldn't resist deepening it. Feeling Leander tremble slightly, he stopped. "All right?"

Leander nodded and gave Julien a shaky smile. "You… you said we should go back to the house."

"We should," Julien agreed, tucking himself back into his breeches.

Leander followed suit and as they set themselves back to rights, Julien kept sneaking in soft kisses, wanting to reassure his new lover. By the time they were ready to leave, Leander wasn't looking quite so uncertain.

"Very cozy indeed," Julien commented as they made their way out to the horses. He grinned. "Are you certain you don't wish your things moved in?"

"And what of yours?" Leander asked and then blushed at his own words. Quickly, he mounted his horse.

Julien chuckled as he settled himself in his saddle. Leander obviously wasn't accustomed to such repartee, but he hoped to remedy that. At the moment, however, he was content to exchange looks and smiles with Leander as they cantered down the slope and through the grove.

If he had been paying more attention to his surroundings instead of Leander, perhaps he would have noticed that they were not alone *before* the shot rang out.

13

The sound of the gunshot was almost immediately drowned out by a piercing squeal that was almost a scream. Even as Leander realized the sound was coming from his horse, he felt himself falling back and countered by lunging forward in the saddle and throwing his arms around the animal's neck. He heard Julien call his name and then another gunshot, but by that point he needed all his energy to maintain his seat as the frantic horse bolted.

Leander cursed himself for losing the reins in his initial attempt to stay on—now all he had were his arms and legs and not nearly enough skill. He felt himself slipping from the saddle and desperately clutched at the horse's mane. There was only the briefest sensation of falling before his body was jarred so violently that it expelled every ounce of air from his lungs. He was unable to stop himself from rolling over and over and when he finally halted, he was left too stunned to move.

There was the sound of hooves galloping toward him, and Leander tried to move before he was trampled. Thankfully, they stopped before reaching him, because his limbs wouldn't cooperate. He was concentrating on breathing normally when he heard his name spoken in a panicked voice. Trying again to move, he managed to open his eyes and move his arms a bit.

"Wait." Julien was kneeling beside him. Leander had no idea when that happened. "Don't move. Were you hit?"

Hit? Hadn't Julien seen his spectacular fall? He felt Julien's hands on him, but in a very different manner than earlier. Some of the fuzziness in his brain cleared and he realized Julien was checking him for injuries. Julien thought he'd been shot. He dragged in a lungful of air. "No," he was able to wheeze.

That was unconvincing, even to his own ears. Cautiously, Leander tried to shift his legs and when they obeyed, he decided it was safe to sit up. His arms weren't quite strong enough for that, and he wobbled badly,

but almost immediately, there was another arm behind his back, bracing him. "Carefully," Julien urged.

Excellent advice. Leander bowed his head as dizziness overtook him. "My horse?" he croaked. His side twinged slightly, so he kept his head down and breaths shallow.

"Probably still running. She should find her way back to the stables."

Leander looked around and was relieved to see they were a fair distance from the grove of trees. "Someone shot at us?"

"We startled a poacher, no doubt." Julien's casual tone was belied by his stark face and burning eyes. "I'll send someone to see to it. If you can move, I think we'd best get back to the house. That is if you don't object to riding behind me."

That made Leander laugh and a sharp pain lanced through his side. Although he managed not to cry out, he couldn't stifle his gasp.

"What is it?" Julien asked, his free hand on Leander's shoulder.

"I'm just a little sore, is all," Leander assured him.

"I'll send for a physician as soon as we return."

Leander was about to protest, but he noticed that Julien kept glancing toward the woods and decided not to delay by arguing. There would be time enough to object once they were safely back at the house. Slowly, he gathered his feet under him and stood. He had to lean heavily on Julien until he was certain his legs would support him, but Julien didn't seem to mind in the least, keeping an arm around him until they'd reached the horse.

When Leander knew he was steady, he nodded to Julien, who vaulted into the saddle. When he held out an arm, Leander grasped it with some confidence, having done the same with Kit countless times. But as he climbed on, simultaneous jolts of pain shot through his shoulder and side, wringing a groan from him.

"Leander?" Julien half-turned in the saddle.

"I'm fine," Leander assured him, reminding himself to breathe carefully.

"Hold on."

They set off at a fair pace and Leander realized immediately that this was *very* different from riding behind Kit. He was acutely aware of the feel and scent of the body in front of him, and if not for the constant twinging of his side, he would have quite enjoyed the trip back to the manor.

"Isis must have returned to the stables," Julien said.

Leander peered around his shoulder and saw half a dozen men and several horses assembled in front of the house.

"M'lord!" One of the men hurried forward to hold the horse when Julien stopped. "We were just about to ride out in search of you."

"No need. Peter, help Lord Dearborne down. Carefully, if you please. Where is Lennox?"

"Here, my lord." The butler hurried down the stone steps.

"Make Lord Dearborne comfortable in the front drawing room."

Before Leander could object, strong hands were helping him down from the saddle and leading him into the house. Behind him, he could hear Julien giving orders and asking about Isis. He was tempted to literally dig his heels in, but as the servants were only following Julien's orders, he resigned himself to being settled on the sofa.

Julien entered the drawing room only moments later. "Lennox, see that Dr. Elliot is fetched here at once. Peter, send for Allen and Mr. Walcott, then tell Ben I wish to see him as soon as he has tended to Isis."

"At once, my lord."

"Aye, m'lord."

Once they were alone in the room, Leander spoke up. "There's no need for a doctor."

Julien moved one of the chairs closer to the sofa and sat. "Humor me."

"People fall off horses all the time," Leander pointed out.

"And are hurt in the process," Julien countered. "I know you are in pain, so allow me to set my mind at ease."

There was little he could say to that, so Leander nodded.

"Thank you." Julien smiled.

"You said someone was tending to Isis," Leander said. "Was she badly hurt?"

"It sounds as though she was hit by one of the bullets."

Leander's stomach abruptly dropped, then twisted almost to the point of pain.

"Leander?" Julien leaned closer. "What is it?"

"What?" Leander said, and his voice sounded weak, even to his own ear.

"You've gone so pale."

"It's nothing," Leander said, but knew there would be no way to avoid seeing a doctor now. Still, it was preferable than to trying to explain to Julien that it just occurred to him that they had truly been shot at.

Julien gave him another of those piercing looks. "I have to meet with my groundskeeper and bailiff. I want to know who fired that gun on my grounds." He caressed Leander's cheek and then stood. "I'll be back after the doctor has seen you," he said and left the room.

Leander closed his eyes and concentrated on the lingering sensation of Julien's fingers against his cheek, which brought back memories of what had happened in the folly. Almost immediately, his cock stirred and he decided it might be best not to think about that encounter until *after* the doctor's visit.

Although he'd pleasured himself many times, it had always been with a sense of embarrassment and even shame. How strange that with Julien there had been little embarrassment and no shame whatsoever. The overwhelming pleasure of Julien's touch had left little room for any other emotions.

Before he came to London, Leander didn't know he was supposed to feel shame for wanting another man, simply because he'd never really realized that wanting another man was even in the realm of possibilities. Since discovering otherwise, he'd been bombarded with information

about the subject. Even if not for having met Julien, Leander was glad to have learned that there were other men like him, that it *wasn't* unheard of or something caused by his years of illness. That alone was worth any remarks or gossip he had to endure.

"Lord Dearborne."

Leander looked up at the sound of the butler's voice.

"Dr. Elliot to see you."

Dr. Elliot was a middle-aged man with spectacles and a slight paunch. He bowed upon entering. "Good day, Lord Dearborne."

"Dr. Elliot." Leander began to rise, but the doctor hurried forward.

"Pray, do not trouble yourself, my lord. I understand you were injured."

"I fell off a horse," Leander explained. "It's nothing serious."

"Ah." Dr. Elliot set his bag on a table, looking uncomfortable. "I received word from Lord Blackstone that you required a doctor. Will you allow me to examine you?"

Leander had seen more than his share of doctors in his life, but had never encountered one with such an obsequious manner. Doctors had always taken the lead in any visits he'd had before. Then again, this was the first time he'd met a doctor as an earl. Elliot was obviously waiting for permission, and for a moment Leander considered refusing. He noticed Elliot seemed worried by his continued silence—no doubt the poor man was torn between obeying Blackstone's instructions and offending Leander. "Yes, of course."

With obvious relief, Elliot proceeded to examine Leander in the most deferential manner and diagnosed sprained ribs. He recommended bed rest for several days in case there were any injuries to Leander's insides.

Leander had no intention of remaining in bed for the rest of his visit, but it seemed that everyone else in the house intended otherwise. Initially, Leander allowed Lennox to escort him up to his bedchamber because he knew the butler was under orders from Julien and even cooperated so far as to take the medicine prescribed by Dr. Elliot.

Medicine that contained laudanum, as Leander discovered when he awoke several hours later. By then, everyone had heard about the shooting and his fall, and he found himself an invalid—again.

Bewildered and still a bit groggy, he didn't object when Gibson helped him into his brocade dressing gown. The reason became apparent when Lord and Lady Carysfort entered his bedchamber. The couple—particularly Lady Carysfort—were quite upset by the day's events, and Leander's insistence that he was not so badly hurt did little to assure them. Then came the Sutcliffes, whose visit was obviously out of duty, with Mrs. Sutcliffe's concern being as plainly false as Lady Carysfort's had been genuine. Their visit was mercifully brief, but was followed by Lady Penelope, Seaforth, and Archer, who stayed until the maid brought up a dinner tray.

Leander sent Gibson down to have his dinner so that there was no one to see him ignoring the classic invalid's meal of lamb's broth and weak tea. He threw back the bedclothes and got up, wincing slightly when his ribs reminded him that he *wasn't* entirely well. Tempted though he was to get dressed and go down to dinner, he knew that such a thing would be beyond the pale, even for an American.

As he looked around the room, his eye fell on the books he had brought up from the library the day before. Taking up *Parzival* again, he settled himself in the chair, and soon enough, the knight's adventures distracted him from his new, unwanted status.

"Aren't you supposed to be in bed?"

Jolted back to reality, Leander looked up and watched Julien close the door behind him.

"I knocked, but there was no answer, so I thought I'd look in. I expected to find you asleep."

"I slept most of the afternoon."

"You should be in bed. The doctor ordered bed rest for you."

It was bad enough to have Julien's guests consider him an invalid, to have Julien do so as well was unbearable. "I don't need bed rest," he said firmly. "And if I'd known that medicine would make me sleepy, I never would have taken it."

Julien's eyes widened. "After your injury, the doctor felt you needed rest."

"Confining me to my bed is taking things to ridiculous lengths."

"You took a fall—"

Leander gritted his teeth. "Do you have any notion how many people take falls like mine—worse than mine—and go right back to work? I'm not the strongest of men, but I'm no weakling, either."

"I assure you, no one considers you a weakling." Julien looked a bit pole-axed by Leander's outburst.

"Then stop treating me like one." Leander's side twinged, and he forced himself to calm down. "It's truly not necessary."

"Very well." Julien gave a stiff nod. "You may do as you please, of course. My only concern was for your well-being."

Leander's irritation subsided at his words. "I know, but—that is, I'm grateful for it, but—"

"But what?" Julien's tone was decidedly cool.

Leander wished he had another explanation, but he really didn't want to lie to Julien of all people. "I was bedridden most of my childhood—most of my life. Right up until a few months before I set sail for England. I vowed to myself that I would not be an invalid here."

Julien's expression softened. "I hardly think of you as an invalid," he said as he moved closer and looked down at Leander. "But I can't have anything happen to you, can I?"

Determined not to let the teasing fluster him, Leander countered, "It's very tedious, you know. How would you like to go visiting only to find that you had to spend most of your time in bed?"

Julien arched an eyebrow. "I suppose that would depend on who else was in the bed with me."

That brought several interesting images to mind. Leander's face must have betrayed his thoughts, because Julien let out a low laugh.

"Do not tempt me. Let us make a bargain. Do me the favor of resting tomorrow and if you feel well enough, you can join us at dinner."

One day, Leander was determined, he would learn how to phrase things so as to make refusal practically impossible. "Very well." In truth, normally such an arrangement would be no chore for him when he had several new books to read, but he didn't want to lose any time with Julien.

"I suppose asking you to take another dosage of medicine would be a waste of time." Julien smiled. "So I will bid you good night."

When Julien bent to give him a soft kiss, Leander rose slightly and parted his lips. He only got a brief, tantalizing taste of Julien's tongue before the older man pulled back.

"Too tempting by half," Julien murmured and then quietly left the room.

Leander gave up on *Parzival* for the rest of the night.

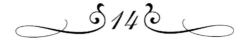

Julien eyed the single letter left on the salver with distaste. He'd opened and read everything else that came in the post, and could put it off no longer. Finally, he broke the seal and began to read Gabriel's carefully ornate handwriting. He had to wade through nearly two pages of flowery phrases and poor spelling before he found the object of the letter, which was Gabriel's news that he had found someone new and would be vacating the house on Windmill Street within a few days.

With enormous relief, Julien folded the letter back up and tossed it aside. That saved him the trouble of asking Gabriel to vacate the house—something he'd been intending to do that day or the next. It also meant Cordelia's suggestion that Gabriel might have somehow been behind the shooting had no merit. Not that Julien ever seriously considered it. Gabriel wasn't about to kill his source of income, and Julien hadn't yet asked him to leave the house, thereby completely severing ties.

Some of his other guests had ideas as well. Seaforth casually reminded him that Bertram was next in line and that Augusta was always keen to increase her social standing. Lady Penelope had been the only one with the courage to suggest it might somehow be tied to the Norvilles—belated revenge for Tobias's disappearance.

Although Julien didn't believe any of those theories, nor was he convinced that it was the work of a poacher. He'd told his guests it was likely a poacher, however, and most of them seemed to accept it. After the shooting, the rest of the house party was very subdued. There had been no more trips to see local sights and everyone stayed close to the house, mostly out of deference to Leander's injury.

Despite his insistence that he was fine, it had been apparent that Leander's injury was still causing him discomfort the next day. But another night and day of rest had done the trick, and when the time had come for the journey back to London, Leander seemed quite recovered.

Perhaps Julien had been overly cautious in summoning the doctor and insisting on bed rest. Leander had certainly thought so, surprising Julien with his anger until the reason behind it became clear.

It was very different from the upbringing Julien had expected for an American, but did fit in well with what he'd seen of Leander's personality. In many ways, Leander was not only adapting to English Society, but to society in general. His shyness and uncertainty made much more sense, and so perhaps did the protectiveness Julien felt toward him.

Julien wished he had a reason for his recent behavior, for his insistence on moving slowly with Leander despite the younger man's obvious eagerness. It made him glad that no one—especially those who shared his preference—knew of what was happening between them. Half of them would find it very amusing to watch how carefully he was proceeding, and the other half would be trying to seduce Leander themselves. While Leander had said that Julien was the only one who interested him, and while Julien sensed a core of integrity in him, he had no way of knowing for certain how susceptible Leander would be to the charms of another. Just the thought was enough to make his blood simmer, which was very unsettling, as jealousy had never been a problem for him.

Even more unsettling had been the way his insides froze sickeningly as he watched Leander fall from his horse. Julien knew it should alarm him that Leander's well-being had become so important to him so quickly. It bespoke a power that he hadn't allowed anyone since Tobias Norville, and despite his vow never to be so foolishly led by his emotions again, Julien found himself inexorably drawn to the American.

Julien tried to keep himself occupied for the rest of the day. He wrote letters, including one to his bailiff telling him to continue searching for the shooter. He went out to pay some bills, stopping to check that Gabriel had truly vacated Windmill Street and pick up the key. When he returned home, he tried reading the latest journals, but by afternoon, he gave up trying to distract himself and ordered Kay to fix him a fresh cravat and fetch his favorite coat. Leander had enjoyed the theater so much that an invitation to the opera seemed like an excellent idea.

It had only been a day since their return to London, and by rights Julien should probably just send him a note inquiring about his health and issuing the invitation, but he doubted Leander would notice the faux pas, or care if he did. After sending a footman to have his horse saddled—it was only a short distance to Park Lane—Julien took up his gloves and hat and went downstairs. He reached the foyer just as Hudson was opening the door to someone and skidded to a halt. For a moment he considered dodging into the drawing room to avoid the caller, but knew there wasn't enough time. Hopefully whoever it was would notice that he was on his way out and make the call a brief one.

Then Julien saw who it was and completely changed his opinion about unexpected callers.

"The Earl of Dearborne, my lord," Hudson said, out of habit rather than necessity.

Standing just inside the door, Leander did indeed notice Julien's appearance. "I'm sorry. You were going out. I can call back later."

"Not at all. Please, come in."

Leander still looked uncertain, but Hudson had closed the door behind him and was holding out his hand for Leander's hat and overcoat.

Julien handed his hat and gloves to the butler as well. "Tell Thomas to unsaddle Spartan. I won't be needing him." He gestured for Leander to follow him into the drawing room and closed the door behind them.

"I don't mean to keep you," Leander said once they were alone. "I knew I probably shouldn't have called like this... today, but—if you have other plans I can—"

"Leander," Julien said, stopping the tumble of apologies. "I was going to pay a call on you."

"Oh." A smile tugged at Leander's lips. "You were?"

"I was. I wanted to make certain you had fully recovered."

"I barely notice it anymore," Leander assured him.

"And since your visit to Shadowcross Manor was somewhat of a disappointment—"

"No, it wasn't." Leander stepped closer, all earnestness.

Julien smiled. "Then let's say not everything went as planned."

Leander tilted his head briefly and then nodded.

"I thought to make it up to you, I could ask you to accompany me to my box at the opera tomorrow evening," Julien said, and waited for the keen response he'd come to expect from the American.

Instead, Leander's smile faded somewhat. He opened his mouth as if to speak, and then closed it with a slight frown.

Julien watched as Leander struggled for words. Was he trying to think of a suitable excuse to decline? Despite his brave words about not caring for the opinions of Society, perhaps Leander was having second thoughts about being seen in public with him. Julien tried to remain in a generous mood. *He* had decided they should move slowly, so what did it matter that Leander was being cautious as well? There was absolutely no reason for the sudden pang in his chest. Determined not to let Leander see the effect his reluctance had, Julien kept his tone neutral. "Do you not care for the opera?"

"I have no idea. They're usually in Italian, aren't they? I don't know anything about—of course, I'll be happy to attend with you." Leander bit his lower lip thoughtfully. "There must be all sorts of books about opera."

The sudden lightening of his mood made Julien laugh out loud. He should have known better. "If you prefer, we could attend the theater again."

"No, I… no. It would be good for me to see something new and different."

"Are you certain? We could wait until you've had time to sufficiently research the subject—or learned to speak Italian."

"Julien…."

Delighted by the chiding tone, Julien closed the distance between them and slid an arm around Leander's waist. Without a moment's hesitation, Leander put his arms around Julien's neck. "Ah, so now we come to the real reason for your call." Julien grinned.

"Not only for—" A flush hit Leander across his cheeks. "I wanted to

see you."

"And that's all?"

"I didn't know if—I couldn't very well walk in and throw my arms around you, could I?"

"Is that what you wanted to do?" Julien asked.

Leander's flush deepened, but he didn't look away. "What would you have done if I had?"

"This." Julien lowered his head.

The small, contented murmur Leander made when their lips met was the most captivating sound Julien had ever heard. He felt Leander's fingers in his hair and pulled the younger man even closer.

"Julien, I just received a note from—"

At the sound of the familiar voice, Julien broke off the kiss and turned to look at Cordelia, who was frozen in the doorway. Hudson was behind her, looking worried; no doubt he'd tried unsuccessfully to announce her.

Leander hadn't broken the embrace, but was staring intently at Julien's cravat, not daring to look in Cordelia's direction.

Julien could hardly blame him.

"Julien." Cordelia's voice was icy—a tone she'd never used with him. "I wish to speak to you in the salon."

"I'll be there in a moment."

Cordelia swept from the room, and Hudson closed the door.

"I'm so sorry," Leander whispered when they were alone.

"For what?"

Leander finally lifted his head. "For being here?"

"I hope you're never sorry for that." Julien laid a hand against Leander's neck and brushed a thumb against his cheek. "Not to worry. It's not you she's angry with."

"She's angry with you but not me?" Leander frowned. "That doesn't

make sense. We were both—that is, I was just as—" Embarrassment brought him to a halt.

"I'll talk to Cordelia," Julien assured him. "But I think it would be best if you went home."

"I should go in with you," Leander protested.

"How gallant of you," Julien teased, not wanting to let on how touched he was. "But she's my aunt, after all. I'll send a note to let you know when I'll arrive to collect you for the opera."

"But—"

"Trust me." Julien bent to give him the softest of kisses. "She's my aunt and I know how to deal with her." That wasn't entirely true, since he wasn't sure how Cordelia was going to react to this situation.

"Are you certain?"

"I am." Julien ushered him to the front door. "As much as I appreciate your concern, this is something I'd best deal with alone."

Leander slipped on his coat and took his hat from Hudson, obviously reluctant, but unwilling to say anything in front of the butler.

Julien walked with him to his waiting coach. "I'll see you tomorrow."

Leander nodded, but didn't look reassured as his climbed in.

Julien waited until the coach rolled away before going back inside.

"Lord Blackstone," Hudson said. "I wish to apologize. I know it is my duty to announce any callers—especially unexpected ones."

"Not to worry, Hudson. You know as well as I do that my aunt has always treated this house as her own. Is she in the salon?"

"Yes, my lord."

Bracing himself, Julien walked in. Cordelia had not seated herself, which did not bode well. Julien took a deep breath. "I believe you said something about a note that—"

"Don't. Julien, don't you dare."

Julien wasn't sure how to proceed. This was very different from her

usual disapproval of the men whose company he kept, but he didn't know *what* exactly had angered her to such a degree.

"How *could* you, Julien?"

"I know we could have been more discreet, but we—"

"Discreet? You know very well that I'm not about to faint at the sight of you kissing someone." She began pacing. "I thought better of you than this, Julien."

Julien considered remarking that whatever she thought of the kiss, Leander had liked it well enough, but knew she would not take kindly to such a jest. "You've known for years that I prefer—"

"I'm not talking about that. I'm talking about Dearborne."

"What is your objection to Dearborne?"

"Do not make light of this, young man!" Cordelia glared at him. "It's one thing to amuse yourself with that Hartley creature or Baron Vance—"

Now that was going too far. "*Vance?!* For God's sake, Aunt Cordelia! Just because we are similarly inclined doesn't mean I would *ever*—"

"But Dearborne?" she continued as if he hadn't spoken. "He's just a boy, Julien. What are you thinking, seducing a young innocent?"

"You've been reading too many horrid novels, Aunt."

"Julien!"

She was not going to be easily appeased, but Julien was reluctant to discuss Leander when things were still so new and uncertain.

"Is that why you invited him to Shadowcross?" Cordelia demanded. "I admit I wondered, but I never thought you would stoop to taking advantage of the poor boy. It's not like you, Julien."

"That *poor boy* is two and twenty, as he told me most decidedly."

Cordelia's eyes narrowed. "Do you mean to say that Dearborne seduced you?"

Why must it be one seducing the other? Julien wondered. "No, of

course not."

"But you're saying he is similarly inclined. That you didn't influence him?"

"I didn't influence him," Julien repeated firmly. "He is inexperienced, but not uncertain."

Finally she stopped pacing and fixed him with a stern look. "Not uncertain?"

This was very possibly the most uncomfortable conversation he had ever had with his aunt—which was saying something—and Julien just wanted it over. "I assure you, I never would have proceeded unless I thought Lean—Dearborne was certain."

Her furious expression fading, Cordelia settled herself on one of the delicate Rococo chairs that furnished the salon. Julien didn't know whether to be relieved that her anger had subsided, or alarmed to see her looking so thoughtful. "It sounds as if you are rather fond of him."

Under no circumstances was Julien about to be drawn into *that* conversation. "If you're satisfied that Dearborne is not a victim of my unnatural lusts, perhaps you could tell me why you called."

"Oh, Julien." Cordelia patted the chair next to her invitingly, as if she hadn't been railing at him only moments before. "Come sit and tell me about—"

"Absolutely not."

"Very well." Cordelia sighed with a more familiar moue of irritation. "I came to ask if I might have the box at the Haymarket tomorrow night."

Julien froze. The woman was truly frightening at times. "You have a sudden overwhelming desire to attend the opera?"

"Not myself, but Lady Rockingham. It was she who sent me the note."

"Surely Lord Rockingham has his own box at the theater."

"Of course he does. That's why Marianne wishes to use another one."

He didn't want to know. Truly he didn't, but he had to ask. "Why can't Lady Rockingham use their own box?"

"Why, because she doesn't want Rockingham to know she's attending, of course."

"Of course." Julien rubbed his eyes.

"Marianne believes that Rockingham has taken up with one of the sopranos. She wants to see the woman. Then when Rockingham—"

"Good God, I don't want to know the details." Julien held up his hand. It would be little trouble for him to send a note and arrange to go to the opera the following day. Or tonight. Julien glanced at the clock. There was still plenty of time for them to prepare to attend tonight. He was quite certain that Leander would be glad as he to meet again sooner rather than later. "You may have the box and are welcome to it."

"Excellent." Cordelia smiled, fully restored to her usual cheerful self. "Now that that's settled, about Dearborne—does this mean you've ended your association with that dreadful Hartley?"

"If I say yes, will you be satisfied and drop the subject?" While he normally enjoyed having Cordelia around—even when she decided to pry—at the moment he had a very time-sensitive note to write.

"Oh, very well. But this is not the last we'll speak of it."

"I know."

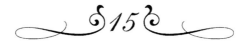

§ 15

Leander shrugged out of his coat as he walked into his library and draped it over the back of the chair nearest the door. After a moment, he also loosened his cravat; he wasn't likely to have any callers now and even if he did, this would be the perfect time to use the polite "not at home" lie. He dropped into his favorite chair, for once without a book in his hands.

He'd known, logically, that there would be many problems to face once the truth about him became known, but he hadn't expected it quite this soon, and certainly not from Lady Carysfort. Julien seemed to believe her anger was directed at him, not Leander, but that made no sense. Surely she'd already known about her nephew—Julien never seemed terribly concerned with hiding what he was.

The door to the library opened, interrupting his thoughts. "Are you at home to Mr. Mayfield, my lord?" Powell asked.

Leander groaned inwardly. Although not eager to see Mayfield, he couldn't bring himself to give the lie to a relative. "I'll be there in a moment," he said.

Powell nodded and closed the door.

With a sigh, Leander got up and put his coat back on. He entered the drawing room where Mayfield was waiting. "I trust you are well, cousin," he said. Somehow speaking first helped him feel as though he were in control of the conversation.

Mayfield didn't seem to notice. "I am, thank you." He paused briefly, his eyes on Leander's neck.

Leander remembered his ruined cravat, and just like that he was reduced to the foolish foreigner Mayfield so obviously thought him. He started to reach for his collar, but caught himself at the last moment.

"I trust you enjoyed your visit to Shadowcross Manor," Mayfield

said with as much courtesy and condescension as ever.

"Very much," Leander replied, cursing himself for being so pathetic at polite small talk. It was even more difficult because he doubted Mayfield cared in the least what he thought of his visit. "The former earl's library is excellent."

"Ah, you spent your visit in the library, I take it?"

Strange how he could make that sound like a flaw, when most of Julien's friends found it amusing, but quite understandable. "Of course not. I visited Winchester Castle and toured the grounds of Shadowcross Manor."

"Blackstone's grounds?" There was some snideness in Mayfield's tone, but not enough that one could truly take offense.

Leander decided to ignore it. "Blackstone was kind enough to take me on a tour."

"Perhaps you can return the favor once you've seen your estates. Your tenants are likely curious about their new landlord."

The last thing Leander wanted to do now was leave London, even for a short time. Even if it was his duty. "Surely I have a bailiff or steward running things on my behalf. I understand that there are many who rarely visit their estates and barely concern themselves with the running of them." He didn't intend to be one of those people, but he wanted Mayfield to know he wasn't *completely* ignorant of the ways of Society. "I shall merely write to the bailiff for a report, or perhaps have my man-of-affairs do so."

"You certainly are adapting to your new life," Mayfield said, and even though the words were complimentary, it was obvious Mayfield was not impressed.

Leander hated that he couldn't come up with a suitable response. It wasn't as if he hadn't dealt with difficult people before. When he was well enough to go to school, he'd endured plenty of jeers for his bookishness and illness from those who were willing to risk the wrath of his older brothers. It had been simple enough to respond in kind to the rude schoolboy taunts, although he never had the same knack for it that Chance did. But how to respond when the words were quite polite, the

tone *nearly* polite, but something in the manner suggested an insult?

He was saved from trying when Powell entered the drawing room. "Excuse me, my lord, but this just arrived for you. The messenger was instructed to wait for any reply."

"Oh." Leander took the note from the silver tray Powell held out. "Thank you." He recognized Julien's handwriting immediately, but wasn't about to open it in front of Mayfield.

"I'll let you see to your message," Mayfield said as if he were doing Leander a favor. "Good day, Dearborne."

"Good day," Leander said absently. The moment the door closed behind Mayfield he broke the wax seal and unfolded the letter.

> *Leander,*
>
> *Rest assured that all is well between myself and my aunt. She is not angry with either of us now that the situation has been sufficiently explained.*
>
> *She has asked for the use of my box at the Haymarket tomorrow evening, and under the circumstances, I felt it would be prudent to grant her request. As I would rather we not attend with her and her friend, our plans must be changed. Would tonight or the evening after next be preferable to you? If neither, then any evening that is convenient.*
>
> *I await your reply,*
>
> *J.*

Leander refolded the letter and hurried back to the library where he dashed off a reply. He handed it to Powell for the messenger on his way upstairs to decide which coat and waistcoat would be best. He also made a mental note to tell Gibson to try a simple style of cravat.

JULIEN took a moment to check Leander's appearance by the lights outside the theater, and was glad to see it was as pristine as it had been

when he first climbed into the Blackstone coach. The ride to the theater had been passed in the most enjoyable manner, and even though they had limited themselves to kisses, Julien wanted to be sure there was nothing that might cause any extra gossip. Arriving together and sharing a box would merely be discussed by the most rampant busybodies, but arriving with clothing in the slightest disarray would set everyone talking.

Once inside, they left their hats and greatcoats to the care of Julien's footman and began making their way through the crowd.

"Good evening, Julien," said a decidedly smug voice.

Julien turned to see Gabriel Hartley standing with the Marquis of Steane. So this was Gabriel's new patron, and judging from Gabriel's tone and smirk, the Angel thought he'd moved up in the world. Perhaps he had, but from what Julien knew of Steane, he would require much more of Gabriel to earn his keep than Julien had. "Mr. Hartley," he said coldly, so that Gabriel knew he'd overstepped his bounds.

"Blackstone." Steane nodded, but his glittering eyes were fastened on Leander. Gabriel was also looking at Leander, but with a mixture of contempt and superiority that set Julien's teeth on edge.

"Steane. Allow me to introduce the Earl of Dearborne." Gabriel's smirk vanished, but Steane looked even more interested. "Dearborne, this is the Marquis of Steane and Mr. Hartley."

"The American Earl," Steane said after the niceties had been exchanged. "And how do you find London thus far?"

"I… it's—" Leander paused. "I don't believe there is enough time before the performance to describe how completely it has exceeded any expectations I had."

Steane inclined his head in surprise and Gabriel frowned in disappointment, which further irritated Julien. Were they expecting him to sound like an uneducated buffoon? Fortunately, Leander's words were also the perfect excuse to take their leave. "Quite right. We'd best get to our seats." He nodded to the pair and steered Leander toward the stairs that would take them to his box. Leander was silent the entire time, obviously preoccupied. "Is there something you wish to ask?" Julien inquired, although he already knew what the question would be.

Leander hesitated briefly. "They… they're together, aren't they? Like us?"

That wasn't the question Julien expected. "Not exactly like us. Their association is based on money and nothing more."

The blue eyes widened. "You mean Mr. Hartley is…?" Leander obviously didn't know which word to use, so Julien nodded to spare him. "Oh." He turned to watch the crowd assembling in the pit.

"Are you shocked?"

"Only that it never occurred to me that men as well as women could be paid companions." Leander was doing a reasonable job of maintaining his aplomb. "That, and it seemed as if you and Mr. Hartley…."

"We did."

Leander turned and gave him a searching look. "You paid."

Looks like that one are the reason everyone still thinks of him as an innocent boy, Julien thought. "After a fashion, yes."

"Why?"

It took Julien a moment to absorb the single word. "What?"

"Why? I can't believe you *had* to."

"It's not uncommon," Julien said, knowing full well it wasn't an actual answer. "It's simpler," he added. "Less trouble."

"Less trouble… than this?" Leander indicated the both of them.

"To say the least," Julien muttered. Suddenly those guileless blue eyes seemed able to see all his past transgressions and excesses.

Leander still heard. "Then why?"

"Some people are worth the trouble," Julien said shortly, wanting the subject dropped.

Thankfully, Leander did just that, and contented himself with watching the patrons take their seats. He appeared thoughtful, but not resentful. Now Julien wanted desperately to know whether Leander's opinion of him had changed, but wasn't about to ask. Instead, he also

focused his attention on the crowd, taking note of those who were taking note of them.

Finally, the house lights went down and the curtain rose on *Semiramide*. During their brief conversation in the coach, Julien had asked Leander if he was familiar with the legend of Semiramis of Babylon. Leander had admitted to having only the vaguest knowledge, so Julien had relayed it as it related to the opera.

Julien was much more interested in watching Leander watch the opera than the performance itself. He'd attended many in his lifetime, including other performances of *Semiramide*, but didn't possess the ear for music required to truly appreciate it or to know the difference between mediocre and superb interpretations.

Neither did Leander, Julien guessed, if the younger man's slightly perplexed expression was anything to judge by. During the intermission this was confirmed when Julien asked him how he liked it so far.

"I'm enjoying it," Leander replied, but without the fire Julien had seen when discussing *Othello*. "I'd probably enjoy it more if I understood Italian."

"And if it was spoken instead of sung," Julien added.

"The music is beautiful, but not the sort I'm familiar with. I suppose I will become accustomed to it, though."

"But you prefer plays."

"Of course," Leander said, as if there could be no doubt. "I mean to see all sorts of plays, but I really want to see as many of Shakespeare's as I possibly can."

"This season? That will be quite a feat."

Leander's put-upon sigh made Julien grin, as did any sign of exasperation from the normally reticent American.

The second half passed slowly for Julien, who was anticipating the ride back, among other things. He passed some of the time when he wasn't watching Leander by wondering which of the sopranos was Rockingham's new mistress and what in God's name Lady Rockingham and his aunt intended by attending the next night.

When they made their way through the crowd after the performance was over, no one attempted to speak with them, but there were more looks and Julien knew there would be speculation. That didn't bother him. As long as Leander didn't care, he certainly didn't.

Julien's staff was as attentive as ever. A footman was waiting in the lobby, holding their greatcoats, and the coach was only a few yards from the theater doors. Soon they were settled inside the coach, and Julien was glad it would take some time to drive through the mass of vehicles. Leander's attention was focused out the window. "Whatever is outside appears much more interesting than anything you saw on stage," Julien commented.

Leander turned from the window and let the small curtain fall. "Sometimes I wonder if I'm ever going to get used to how crowded London is. I don't know how anyone can get through all that traffic."

"It will take some time," Julien agreed. "Right now everyone is in their coaches debating which ball to attend first."

"Balls? After the opera?" Leander shook his head when Julien nodded. "The crowd at the opera would be enough for me for one night. I'd much rather just go home afterward."

"I'm sorry to hear that," Julien said. "I was about to invite you to my home. I can assure you there will be no crowds." Perhaps he'd been conceited to assume Leander would agree immediately, but as the silence stretched on, Julien began to feel disappointed. Finally, Leander began stammering without actually saying anything. "Speak freely, Leander. You aren't likely to shock me."

"I'm not certain what… how long would I be there?"

An odd question. "As long as you like," Julien replied, which prompted an impatient exhalation. "Why do you ask?"

"My butler and valet will be waiting up for me."

Of course. He would have to accustom himself to Leander's unusual consideration for staff. "We can stop at your home and you can tell your staff not to wait up for you. I'm sure somewhere could be found for you in my home for the night, if that is acceptable." It was a simple statement, and awaiting Leander's reply shouldn't have unsettled his

nerves to such a degree.

"I suppose this is what you meant by my being troublesome." Leander sounded apologetic.

"I don't believe that's exactly what I said." Julien smiled.

"Of course I wish to go with you," Leander said with a matter-of-factness that warmed Julien.

"Very well." Julien stood and opened the trapdoor to give his coachman instructions. "A simple problem to solve," he said as he sat back down.

"They'll know, though, won't they?" Leander's voice was hesitant. "Or at least they'll suspect."

"Who? Your staff?" Julien was more puzzled than disappointed by Leander's concern. It was decidedly strange that the opinion of his staff should matter when he hadn't cared who saw them at the opera. "I suppose they might. Does that disturb you?"

"Well… once I knew there were other people like me—like us—I tried to learn more about it."

"Yes, I remember." Julien grinned.

"I learned that it's considered wrong by a great deal of people," Leander continued, apparently having decided it was best to ignore such asides. "It's against the law in most places."

"It is," Julien agreed. "You were aware of all this before the house party."

"Yes, of course. And from what I can see, there are consequences from three different areas I'll have to deal with for breaking this… rule. Society's, God's, and the law of the land. I see no reason to trouble myself with Society's opinions. I don't know most of their rules and those I do know seem ridiculous. And for breaking their rules I would be gossiped about and shunned by some. Hardly a calamity for me."

Julien intended to spend the trip home from the opera in the same way they had spent the one there, but found himself becoming interested in the subject and Leander's opinions. It was certainly no hardship to listen to the light, clear tenor.

"The laws of God are generally quite clear, as is the punishment for breaking them. Except that it's impossible to be certain of punishment in the afterlife, especially since no one has ever returned with confirmation of it."

That startled a laugh out of Julien. "I did not expect to hear that sentiment from you."

"No? Father always told us to take sermons with a grain of salt, for how could mere mortals hope to interpret God's true will? Besides, God gave us the power to think and reason and decide. One should make proper use of those gifts."

Considering Leander's fascination with Camelot, Julien hadn't expected him to be quite such a progressive thinker. "And that leaves the law of the land," he prompted.

"Which is the only one I must truly concern myself with." Leander sighed. "I certainly never imagined myself breaking the law, but we aren't either of us doing harm to anyone. Yet if we are caught, the punishment is hanging."

"And how does all of this involve your staff?" Julien asked.

"Aren't they the most likely to discover it? To know enough to report or accuse?"

Julien smiled. For all his intelligence and thoughtfulness, there were some things Leander tended to overlook. "It's not likely they would. If I may ask, what do you pay your staff on average?"

"Pay?" Leander sounded bewildered. "I believe anywhere from twenty-five to sixty pounds a year, depending on their duties."

"Then you have little reason to worry. Even your lowest amount is quite generous. No servant is going to risk losing such a place by sending their employer to jail, especially when that employer is also as kind to them as you are." Julien paused for Leander to absorb this. "And even should someone accuse us, our title and wealth would protect us from the worst punishment, and probably allow us to escape it altogether."

The coach began to move with some speed. They were finally through the worst of the traffic.

"We shall be at your house soon and you can decide what you want to do."

"I decided that the moment you asked me," Leander replied.

16

Powell didn't bat an eye when Leander told him he would not be needed again that night, so Leander had no way of knowing what the man actually thought. The butler was a master at maintaining a blank countenance. Leander could only hope that Julien was correct in his assessment of the servants and of Leander's supposed generosity toward them.

As he climbed back into the coach, Leander resolved not to waste any more time thinking about problems that might occur. He certainly hadn't accepted Julien's invitation because he wanted to discuss rules or laws. While it was true that he enjoyed his conversations with Julien, even those that left him bewildered, more than anything he wanted to experience again those sensations Julien had stirred in him at the folly.

"And how soon do you suppose your butler will be making a run for the magistrate?" Julien asked when they were under way.

Leander wondered what Julien expected of him when he made such jests. No matter how he responded to them, Julien seemed amused. It did make him worry that all he was for Julien was an amusement. He tried to respond in kind. "I can't imagine Powell running anywhere. He's far too dignified."

Julien chuckled. "That is a requirement of the job. Would you have hired a butler who *wasn't* dignified-looking?"

"I don't know. I haven't had to hire anyone yet."

"You kept all the staff you inherited?"

"More or less. The house was fully staffed when I arrived, and I've had no reason to replace anyone. Maybe I'll have to hire staff at my estate," he said, the idea just occurring to him. "I suppose I'll find out when I visit."

"Are you planning to visit soon?"

"I should, shouldn't I?" Leander asked, wondering what Julien's opinion on the matter was. "It's my duty, really. My cousin certainly thinks I should."

"Your cousin?" Julien said flatly. "Morleigh Mayfield."

"Yes. He mentions it every time he visits. I'm sure he thinks I'm shunning my responsibilities."

"I wouldn't bother with Morleigh Mayfield's opinion, if I were you."

"He's not the most pleasant of men," Leander admitted. "But he's the only relation I have left."

"You'd probably be better off without that particular relation." Julien's voice had cooled considerably. "There are very nasty rumors that follow him around."

Leander had heard plenty of rumors about Julien as well, but he didn't say so. Society seemed to thrive on gossip and innuendo. Likely not even half of such rumors were true.

It was only a short distance from his house to Julien's in Grosnevor Square and soon the coach rolled to a halt. Anticipation curled in Leander's stomach as he followed Julien and watched the older man tell his butler that they would not be needing staff again that night without any apparent concern. Julien, of course, noticed. "I can assure you that my staff has no intention of turning us over to the authorities," he said as they walked to the study. "Hudson has been with me for years and is well aware of my preferences." He lifted a decanter. "Port?"

"No, thank you."

Julien poured himself a glass. "Are you afraid that I want you foxed so I can have my wicked way with you?"

Leander laughed. "I think by now you'd know there's hardly any need for me to be foxed."

When Julien turned toward him, Leander could see the slight smile on his face, despite the dim light provided by the dying fire and a single lamp. Leander immediately regretted his words, knowing that members of the ton prided themselves on restraint. Julien probably thought him

hopelessly backward.

Julien set down his glass and stalked toward him. Before Leander had time to wonder about his intentions, Julien pulled him close and brought his lips crushing down.

It had only been a few days since their encounter in the folly, but Leander had been impatient for Julien's touch ever since. Eagerly, he pressed close, plunging his fingers into the dark chestnut locks and opening his mouth to admit Julien's questing tongue.

It wasn't enough. Leander grabbed the lapels of Julien's coat, crushing the expensive fabric as he dragged it off Julien's shoulders. Julien finished taking it off, then returned the favor, removing Leander's coat. When Leander reached for his cravat, Julien grabbed his shoulders and gently eased him back.

"No need to rush," he whispered. "We have all the time in the world."

Leander tried to calm his racing heart, but without success. He looked up to see Julien smiling that enigmatic smile again.

"What do you want?" Julien asked.

"I don't know. You," Leander suddenly blurted. "I want—I just… more…."

Julien's smile widened, but it was pleased and not the least bit mocking. He held Leander's head still and kissed him again, but softly, coaxing Leander's mouth open instead of demanding.

Every touch of Julien's tongue to his sent a tingling jolt straight to Leander's groin. He didn't realize he was arching desperately against Julien until he felt hands on his hips, moving him back slightly again.

"I believe it may be time to take this up to my bedchamber," Julien murmured, his lips brushing Leander's hair.

Just like that, Leander's pleasant haze of desire vanished as if someone had thrown freezing water on him. Up until that moment, nothing had seemed entirely real. The opera, the shooting, the folly, the house party—all felt as if they could have been his imaginings. He half-expected to wake up in his family's small farmhouse to find that his

entire voyage to London had been nothing more than a fever dream. Somehow the idea of being together in Julien's bedchamber made it all too real.

That confused Leander even further, because didn't he *want* this to be real? Hadn't he longed to feel *any* sort of emotional connection since losing his father and brothers? Hadn't he *wanted* to know why he'd always felt so different from those very same brothers? Hadn't he always secretly wished for someone to want him the way Julien did?

"Leander?"

Leander forced himself to meet eyes that gleamed almost golden in the near-darkness.

"Leander, if you're having doubts—"

"No," Leander said quickly. "Not doubts. It's just—I don't... I just...."

Julien's hand came up to cup his cheek and as Leander leaned into the warm palm, he made his decision.

"I'm sorry." Leander tried to smile, but suspected it was a little shaky. "For a moment I just—" He stopped himself before he began stammering stupidly again. "I'm ready, but you'll have to lead the way."

"My pleasure," Julien replied with another smile and feather-light kiss. He slid an arm around Leander's waist and ushered him out of the study and up the stairs. As they went down the hall, Leander's nervousness began to increase, despite his desperate attempts to suppress it.

Once inside, Julien released him and stepped away. He unbuttoned his waistcoat and tossed it onto a curule chair, then untied his cravat and stripped it off as well. Next he pulled off his shirt and threw it after his waistcoat. Naked from the waist up, he moved closer.

Leander swallowed hard, unable to tear his eyes away, entranced by the way the lamplight played over the broad planes of Julien's chest. Julien remained still when Leander placed his hands on either side of his ribs. After several moments more of internal debate, Leander gave in to his instincts and leaned forward, pressing his face to Julien's chest and inhaling deeply.

He heard Julien's sharp intake of breath seconds before strong arms came up to encircle him. Leander let his own arms slide more fully around Julien and held on. He had no idea how long they stood like that, but when Julien began unbuttoning his waistcoat, Leander found that the worst of his nervousness had subsided.

Julien divested Leander of his waistcoat then reached for his cravat, unraveling the knot with ease. "Thank God," he muttered. "I thought I'd have to fight with your damnable cravat again."

"I told my valet I'd prefer a simpler style," Leander admitted without thinking.

"You… what?" There was a note of incredulity in Julien's voice.

Leander's face felt as if it were on fire.

Julien was laughing softly, but he sounded delighted. "Why would you do such a thing?" He bent slightly to kiss Leander's burning cheek. "Hmm?"

When Julien unfastened the top button of his shirt and nuzzled his throat, Leander forgot he ever owned a cravat. Lost in the sensation of Julien's lips and tongue against his skin, he was barely aware of the rest of his clothing—even his boots—being shed. Then they were skin to skin and the only thing solid in the entire world was Julien, so Leander held on as tightly as he could. Even so, he suddenly found himself falling back, Julien with him, until they landed on something soft. After a moment, Leander realized it must have been Julien's bed.

Julien was on top of him, a wonderfully heavy weight, and Leander could feel the older man's hard length pressing against him. Instinctively he moved his legs apart so their hips fit together more snugly.

Insinuating one hand between them, Julien adjusted their cocks so they were fitted more firmly together, which forced a moan of pleasure from Leander, and once he started, it seemed he couldn't stop. The tightness of their bodies together provided the most exquisite friction and Leander's hips began moving of their own accord.

One of Julien's hands was on his hip, the other in his hair, and Julien's lips were pressed to his ear, whispering encouragement as he matched Leander's movements.

Leander felt his release upon him and wasn't able to prolong it. All he was capable of doing was holding on for dear life and chanting Julien's name as he pumped himself upward. A moment later, Julien bore down even harder and added to the warm wetness between them.

Julien's weight was pressing him into the mattress, an unfamiliar position that made it difficult to breathe. Still, Leander had no desire to move, content to keep his arms around Julien's sweat-dampened body.

Eventually, Julien stirred, dispelling the pleasant fog that had enveloped Leander. When Julien rolled off him and got off the bed, Leander went from being warm and sated to messy and embarrassed. Julien retrieved a towel from the washstand and began cleaning him off. Immediately, Leander sat up. "I can do that."

"No matter." Julien leaned down for a quick kiss. "I'd say that was worth a little trouble, wouldn't you?"

Julien said it in such a relaxed and untroubled manner that Leander couldn't help laughing a little. "Yes," he said. "It was… yes."

Grinning, Julien stole another kiss before tossing the towel back to the stand and pulling back the blankets on the bed. "Come; let's get some sleep."

Leander had never shared a bed with anyone except his brothers and that had been more than ten years ago because he'd been having nightmares. He wasn't about to tell Julien that, however, so he climbed under the covers Julien held up for him. He was unsure what to do next; surely he wouldn't be able to sleep after *that*.

Yet as he settled himself back against the pillows Leander felt drowsiness begin to overtake him. When Julien lay down next to him and threw an arm across his waist, it seemed the most natural thing in the world.

Leander meant to say something else, anything else, but before he could, his eyes drifted shut and sleep overtook him.

JULIEN awoke at an ungodly hour feeling better than he had in months.

He was briefly confused to find another body in his bed—it had been nearly two years since he'd shared it with anyone—but then he realized who it was and smiled.

Leander was slumbering peacefully and at some point had shifted closer. That he was able to sleep so deeply his first night in a strange bed implied a level of trust that Julien wouldn't normally have believed. So many times during the previous evening, Leander had been uncertain, even frightened, but had always been willing to follow Julien's lead.

There was a part of Julien that was suspicious of his good fortune, that wondered if Leander had other motives, but for the life of him Julien couldn't imagine what they could possibly be. As the Earl of Dearborne, Leander lacked for neither wealth nor importance.

If it was an act, it was a masterful one, but the more time he spent in Leander's company, the less inclined he was to believe it an act at all. It was impossible to look into those clear blue eyes, to hear that earnest voice, and think the young man anything but genuine.

Julien drank in the beauty of the form next to him. He'd always thought of farm boys as solid, even burly, but Leander certainly didn't fit that mold. That might have been due to the illness he'd mentioned, which would have kept him from hard work, although it hadn't left any other traces on him expect the paleness of his skin. Just as Leander's face could serve as the model for a Roman statue, so could his body, slender but beautifully formed.

As Julien watched, Leander's eyelids fluttered and he let out a soft sigh. Julien remained silent and still, curious to see how Leander would react to waking up in his bed. Leander rubbed his eyes and then opened them and stared at the bed hangings with a perplexed frown. Julien could tell the exact moment realization set in, because color flooded the fair skin. "Good morning." He smiled.

Leander turned toward him and his color deepened. "Good morning," he managed. Then there was silence as Leander looked everywhere but at him. "This is… I've never—this has never happened to me before."

Had it been anyone else, Julien would have responded with a dry "*a likely story*," but instead he said, "I know."

"I don't know what to do next."

"What would you like to do next?" Julien asked, prompting a frown.

"Whatever I'm supposed to do."

Considering the laws of society Leander had flouted with little apparent fear, he chose the strangest times to concern himself with etiquette. "You're a young man of considerable wealth and rank. I imagine that you can do whatever you like."

Leander made a frustrated sound. "Even if it includes doing you bodily harm? Do you ever mean to answer my questions seriously?"

"My, but you are grumpy in the morning," Julien said mildly.

Leander gaped at him and then grabbed the pillow behind his head. Julien was certain he was about to be pummeled and was rather looking forward to it when Leander's expression suddenly changed to one of alarm. "Julien, the door...."

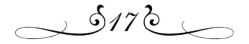

§ 17

Julien turned toward the door, not knowing what he would see, but it was only Kay entering.

"Good morning, my lord," Kay said, hanging both their coats on the clothes press.

"Good morning." Julien glanced at Leander, who had hidden himself as much as possible without actually burrowing under the covers.

"Will you be requiring anything this morning, my lord?"

So Kay had noticed Leander's reaction as well; otherwise he would have simply walked in and begun gathering their discarded clothes. "See that breakfast is ready in an hour or so."

"Very good, sir," Kay said, and retreated.

"The coast is clear," Julien said once the door was shut again.

"I'd rather stay here if it's all the same to you." Leander's voice was muffled.

"Perhaps you could tell me why you're willing to be seen with me in public when you know people will talk, but insist on hiding from my servants when I've already told you they know about me."

"That's not what this is about," Leander said, moving the blankets back slightly.

"No? Then what?"

"I… It's just that I don't know the man. I've never seen him before in my life."

"That was Kay, my valet."

"I don't care who he is. I'm not wearing any clothes."

Julien wasn't certain he'd heard correctly. "Not…? I assure you that

my valet would not be offended by that. It rather goes with the job."

"I'm still not entirely comfortable with my own valet," Leander muttered. "Let alone someone else's."

Such modesty didn't surprise Julien, once he thought about it a little. Still, he couldn't resist pointing out, "I'm here and you're not wearing any clothes. In the same bed."

"That's different."

"How so?"

Leander was quiet for so long that Julien thought he wasn't going to answer, but finally he said, "Because you aren't wearing any clothes either."

Julien bit his lip, not daring to speak for fear of laughing.

Leander obviously sensed his amusement, though, "I know there's no logic to it, but I can't help it."

"Perhaps if your valet didn't wear anythi—" A pillow hit him full in the face. When he could see again, Leander was sitting up and trying to frown, but his eyes were sparkling.

"My, but you are especially aggravating in the morning," he said, mimicking Julien's tone.

"So I've been told," Julien agreed, not adding that he'd never enjoyed the telling half so much.

"I know it makes no sense." Leander sighed. "I suppose you can just attribute it to colonial prudery."

"Prudery is the last thing I'd accuse you of."

"This is all very… new to me."

"I know," Julien said, sobering. "Forgive my teasing."

"I don't mind most of the time, but occasionally a serious answer could be useful."

"You mean when you asked about what we do in the morning? It truly does depend on the person," Julien said, then nearly lost his train of thought when Leander sighed again. The sight of his bare chest rising

and falling brought back memories of the previous evening that were most distracting. "I, myself, would be perfectly content to spend most of the morning in bed with you." He saw Leander's eyes widen and smiled. "And I suppose that has shocked you? Let me guess: you find the notion of lazing about in bed a sacrilege. You believe we ought to be up and hard at work by six."

"Not hardly. I'd be the last one to disparage someone for staying in bed."

"I'm glad to hear it." Julien rearranged his pillow so he could half-sit comfortably. "Now what shall we do while we're here?"

To his delight, Leander's color rose again.

"What do you normally do in the morning?"

He was teasing again, of course, but Leander, being Leander, took the question seriously. "Well, I'm awake by seven or eight and I take a walk before breakfast. I try to take at least one good walk a day, two if possible, and—"

"Why is that?" Julien wondered at the importance he placed on them.

"Father believed walking would help strengthen my constitution as I grew older. I suppose it did, because I was sick much more often when I was young. I've been very fortunate since coming to London, despite the fact that I didn't go out for the first month or so. And," he broke into a smile, "I've purchased a mare for myself and have been riding many mornings as well."

"You seem to enjoy it."

"I do. Although I'm not very good at it." He looked at Julien with some embarrassment. "As you've seen."

"You didn't have many chances to ride in America?" Julien queried.

"No. Even when I was well enough, we only had two work horses, so pleasure riding was rare. And then, there were three brothers and only two horses. I had to ride behind Kit."

"You were the youngest brother," Julien guessed.

"Yes. Kit was the oldest, so—" Leander's bright expression

vanished as if someone had snuffed a flame inside him. "Kit would have been the Earl of Dearborne." His gaze turned distant. "He would have made a splendid earl. He'd know how to take charge of the estates. Chance would have known too, but he would have preferred London—or at least Tattersall's. He would have been there to buy a horse every week if he could."

The longing in Leander's voice was painful to hear. To Julien it sounded as if he hadn't even begun to recover from the loss. "The three of you were very close, then."

"Yes, but Kit and Chance were the closest, being only a year apart. I was four years younger, so they always looked after me. More than they should have sometimes, I think."

"The way you speak makes it sound as though you lost them at the same time." The moment the words left his mouth, Julien cursed himself for getting so involved in the story that he forgot who he was speaking to.

Leander wasn't thrown by the question. In fact, he seemed to be somewhere else entirely. "Yes, I did."

"What happened?" Julien couldn't help asking.

Leander blinked, as if suddenly realizing where he was. "I'm sorry. I shouldn't be—" He tried to smile. "I'm not very good company, talking about such things."

"Forgive me for prying."

"It's not that," Leander assured him. "It's just that it's a long story."

Somehow it seemed important that the story be told. "We've plenty of time."

Leander stared at him and then took a deep breath. "It actually began when I was almost eighteen. There was an outbreak of cholera. Both Father and I caught it, and I had pneumonia as well, but he was the one who died. Even though I survived, it was months and months before I actually recovered. Kit and Chance came home from college to take care of me."

"College? How—?" Julien stopped himself before he asked the

question.

"Our grandfather had left enough to pay for the three of us to go to college."

"Stephen Mayfield?" Julien had always heard that Mayfield had disowned his youngest son for journeying to America.

"Granville Spencer. He wasn't extremely wealthy, but Mother was his only child."

"And your mother…?"

"Died in the yellow-fever epidemic when I was four. I had it as well, and I believe I was nearly seven before my family finally stopped worrying I would die in my sleep. I still caught everything that came through, though. That's why Kit and Chance had to come home and run the farm." The blue eyes looked into the distance again, seeing something far beyond Julien's bedchamber. "Crops had been poor the year before and Father had taken out a mortgage on the farm. Hail ruined the next crop, so Kit and Chance had to use their tuition to pay the note and support us. Two more years of drought and terrible crops, and by then we weren't the only farmers in trouble. Many of the farmers were using what little money they had left to equip a ship—the *Atlantic Maiden*—to sail for India. I convinced my brothers to use half of my tuition for us to invest as well. I didn't see why I should go to college when they couldn't."

"Ships to India usually do well."

"It was supposed to, but after a year and a half, there was no word from it. We had better crops, but they weren't good enough for anyone to get out of debt. We all needed the profits from that ship, so everyone scraped together what little they had left for a second, smaller ship. None of the other farmers wanted to sail, so they offered part of the money as payment for representatives. Kit and Chance agreed to go so they wouldn't have to use any more of the tuition. That… was the last I heard from them."

Julien couldn't think of a word to say.

After drawing a shaky breath, Leander continued. "Fifteen months later, the letter came from England, so I gave the Reades the deed to our

farm and what was left of the money after booking passage."

It must have been horrible to have to board a ship after losing his brothers to one, so Julien didn't dwell on that. "Who were the Reades?"

"A family in Pelham. Their oldest daughter, Margaret, was betrothed to Kit. They took me in after I fell ill *again* last fall. They wanted me to wait until I was healthier before I set sail, but I finally decided I'd imposed long enough."

There was a note of self-loathing in his voice that Julien didn't like to hear. "I'm sure they didn't consider you an imposition."

"No, they were kind people and they never so much as hinted that I was a burden, but that doesn't change the fact. My brothers and father never treated me like one either, although I see now that I must have been."

"Leander—"

"They wouldn't touch my tuition; that's why they agreed to sail. What did I want with college if they couldn't finish? And now, now that there's no need for money or work. *Now* I'm healthy. I haven't been ill since my arrival. Why couldn't it have been this way when I tried to help on the farm? If only—" Leander's voice thickened and he cleared his throat. "I'm sorry. I've never spoken of this to anyone before and...." His voice failed him and he looked away.

His grief was a palpable thing that made Julien's throat tighten. He caught Leander's arm and tugged slightly.

That was all it took. Leander turned and pressed his face against Julien's shoulder. Instinctively, Julien wrapped him in a tight embrace. He didn't feel any tears against his skin, but could hear the hitches in Leander's breathing.

When Leander curled closer, so obviously finding comfort with him, Julien knew he was lost.

He could only hope that this didn't end as disastrously as it had the last time someone managed to steal his heart.

WHAT Leander wanted to do when Julien's coach brought him home was crawl into his bed and never emerge again, but he refused to let himself be that cowardly. Instead, he decided he would go out for a walk. A very long walk. A walk so long that it left him too tired to think about anything.

After changing his clothes, he set out, prepared to walk all afternoon if he had to. The weather suited his mood—cloudy and gray—and the fog was unnaturally thick for the daytime. Or perhaps it only seemed that way because he'd been in the country and away from London's murky air for a few days.

When he got to Oxford Street, he turned east, walking at a fair pace. He was still turning over the morning's events in his mind when he reached Marylebone Street nearly a mile away, so he kept on walking.

If only he had gone home the night before, then none of this would have happened. Next time—if there was a next time, which he doubted—he would take his own coach and save them both such a ridiculous scene. Leander knew he would never be able to recall the pleasure of the previous evening without it being overshadowed by his humiliating display the next morning.

He realized he was hunching his shoulders, practically cringing at the memory, so he straightened his back and walked even faster. It did no good, however, as he couldn't outpace his embarrassment. How could he have allowed himself to lose control to such a degree? Leander knew he would probably never be as self-possessed as most people in Society, let alone equal to Julien, but that was no excuse for turning into a blubbering mess and hiding against Julien's shoulder like a child.

Julien, of course, had been wonderful, holding Leander until he'd recovered himself and even insisting Leander have breakfast instead of sending him on his way. He had spoken to Leander softly, kindly, no doubt fearful of provoking another outburst. If he was disgusted by Leander's behavior, he didn't show it. But then, Julien was a master at maintaining a calm facade no matter what he might be thinking or feeling.

Leander's side twinged suddenly, reminding him that despite his brave words to everyone, his ribs still weren't completely healed. He

stopped for a moment and as he waited for the stitch to subside, he looked around to get his bearings. It was an unfamiliar area, but he could see another large street farther up and could hear a great racket from street peddlers crying their wares. Leander thought it might be Tottenham Court Road, which, if he followed it, should take him down to the Strand.

That was only *if* he was correct about which street it was. If he was wrong, he would likely get himself hopelessly lost with no way home. Still unaccustomed to carrying much money, he didn't have enough to hire a hackney if he had to. Better to return the same way he'd arrived— straight along Oxford until he reached Park Lane.

People on the street were beginning to look at him askance. A busy thoroughfare like Oxford was not the place to stand aimlessly looking about. The ache in his side had subsided, so Leander started back the way he came.

He hadn't gone more than a few steps before he felt the first drops of rain on his face.

Of course.

It was just what he needed to complete his miserable afternoon. He pulled his hat down lower, turned his collar up, and quickened his pace even more. It did little good, however, and by the time he reached his house, he was soaked to the skin and chilled to the bone.

Powell was waiting by the door and helped him off with his dripping things. "Rand was about to prepare the coach to go in search of you, my lord."

"No need. I'm home." Leander's teeth were chattering. "How long would it take to warm up water for a bath?"

"It can be done at once, sir. It's laundry day and there will be water boiling," Powell assured him as he accompanied him to the staircase. "I'll see that it is ready as soon as Gibson has seen to your clothing."

"Thank you."

"Shall I have some coffee and brandy prepared for you, my lord?"

Just the idea of it warmed him. "Thank you, Powell. That would be

just the thing."

Whether the walk did the trick, or whether it was the warm bath—more likely it was the two cups of coffee well-laced with brandy; whatever it was, within an hour, Leander was too sleepy to worry about Julien any longer or to realize that he'd ended up in bed despite his brave plan.

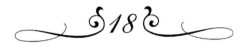

"I'm sorry to find you ill," Morleigh said, taking the chair opposite Leander without being asked. "I called earlier, but you were still asleep."

"I'm not ill," Leander said. "I was merely caught in the rain." Conveniently, he ignored the fact that he'd awoken after several hours of sleep feeling weak-limbed and still chilled. Powell had brought him soup and more coffee and then Leander had gone back to bed and slept until only an hour ago. He also did his best to ignore his aching head and his side, which hurt whenever he took a deep breath.

"Very well. But you should know that the air in London can affect those unused to it."

"I've been in London nearly five months."

"That means little. Many people who have lived in London for years have succumbed to its miasma."

It seemed to Leander that Morleigh wasn't using his usual, mocking tone. Either that or he was just too tired to notice it.

"I know you are tired of hearing this from me, but perhaps a trip to the country would be beneficial to you. Not necessarily your estate—the long journey would be too taxing—but Afton Manor is only forty miles away."

"I'm not so ill I need to be bundled off to the country," Leander retorted, the pounding in his head making him snappish.

It actually worked to his advantage, because Morleigh also dropped his condescending manner. "Many people visit the country simply to recuperate from Town life. It doesn't have to mean anything more than that."

"I just returned from a visit to the country."

"Forgive me, but it doesn't appear to have been very restful."

Leander smiled in spite of himself. "Perhaps it wasn't, but I enjoyed it greatly."

"I see." Morleigh frowned. "It was at Blackstone's invitation that you went, was it not?"

"It was." Leander braced himself for any cutting remarks, although he wasn't sure what he would say in reply.

"I understand you have been much in his company."

"I have."

"I admit that concerns me."

This wasn't what Leander had expected. Morleigh wasn't really being snide at all. "There is no need for concern." Some part of Leander was enjoying giving short, useless replies. He was glad to finally be on the other end of one of these conversations.

"I find it difficult not to be," Morleigh said as he toyed with one of his watch fobs. "You certainly understand what I am referring to. I know you are not so naive as I thought at one time."

Leander had no doubt that Morleigh was merely trying to stay on his good side with such words, but it *was* nice to finally be treated as something other than a country bumpkin or wide-eyed innocent. "Yes, of course I know what you mean. And I hope *you* know that Jul— Blackstone is in no way responsible for… certain aspects of my character."

Morleigh nodded slowly, almost respectfully. "Very well. Quite frankly, that is not my concern. You are of age and it is little matter to me if you are with one man or twenty, provided you are discreet." He held up his hand before Leander could protest that he had no intention of being with twenty men. "My concern is specifically with Blackstone. He is a dangerous man."

That was something Leander had heard often enough, but it usually referred to his preference. The other rumors he had long since dismissed as untrue. Surely Morleigh wasn't about to bring *that* up.

"Perhaps you've heard the name Tobias Norville in connection with Blackstone."

He *was* going to bring that up. "I've heard that his sister continually spreads rumors about Blackstone." Leander tried to imitate the cool tone he'd heard others use when they wanted to discourage a specific topic of conversation.

It had no effect on Morleigh. "And which rumors are you familiar with?"

"That Blackstone killed Norville in a duel over his sister."

"We both know it's highly unlikely Blackstone ever had any interest in Miss Norville," Morleigh said. "Surely you've heard that his true interest lay elsewhere."

"I have," Leander admitted reluctantly. He rubbed his forehead in an attempt to alleviate the painful drumming behind his eyes. "But I don't believe it."

"I took the liberty of investigating that rumor as closely as possible for your sake."

Whether it was for his sake or not, Leander had no intention of asking what he'd found.

Morleigh needed no encouragement, however. "There's a great deal of secretiveness surrounding the whole thing, of course. Most people tend to believe that Tobias Norville refused Blackstone's advances and Blackstone became enraged and did away with him."

"I don't believe that," Leander said firmly.

"Nor do I, after speaking to several men who share Blackstone's— and your—tastes. It was known in certain circles that Blackstone and Norville were indeed involved. In fact, they were as inseparable as two could be while maintaining such secrecy."

It became painful to breathe, but in a way that had nothing to do with chills or sprained ribs.

"No one knows exactly what became of him," Morleigh continued. "Opinion seems divided between Norville coming to harm at Blackstone's hand or Norville fleeing England to escape him. One thing that is almost certain is that Tobias Norville was very much like you."

"No one you've spoken to could know me well enough to say that,"

Leander said, his temper rising at the assumption.

"No, *I* say that," Morleigh replied in a conciliatory tone. "From what I've heard of Norville and seen of you. Norville was also very… refreshing and unfamiliar with the ways of Society."

That sounded like a very polite way of calling someone a bumpkin, and Leander wasn't about to reply to it.

"So you must see why I am concerned for you."

Leander ignored the tiny but persistent sense of unease that was beginning to develop. "There's no need for concern," he said again. "I'm in absolutely no danger from Blackstone."

"That may very well be," Morleigh said, although he looked dubious. "But I wouldn't be comfortable unless I'd said my piece and urged caution."

"I do appreciate it," Leander said. He agreed with Morleigh up to a point. It might be wise to move more carefully. Not that he thought for a moment that his life was in danger from Julien, but his heart certainly was. As for Morleigh's concern, Leander had his doubts to its authenticity. Despite his cousin's words to the contrary, Leander suspected this visit had been based on Julien's interest in men. Perhaps Morleigh's real concern was for the reputation of the Dearborne title. "I'll do my best to be careful."

"I can see I shall have to be satisfied with that," Morleigh said, looking anything but. He stood up. "I'll go now and allow you to rest. No, no," he said when Leander moved to rise as well. "I know my way out. I hope you recover soon."

Leander wanted to protest that there was nothing to recover from, but was too tired to belabor the point. Once Morleigh was gone, Leander got to his feet and headed for his library, wanting nothing more than to curl up in his favorite chair with a good book.

Powell was in the hall and walked with him to the library. "Can I get you anything, my lord?"

"Tea would be fine," Leander said. Something hot to drink would help him shake off the last of this chill.

"Yes, sir. I'll send Betsy in to lay a fire."

It was a bit late in the year to have a fire going during the day, but it sounded so appealing that Leander didn't object. "Thank you."

In no time at all, Leander was settled in front of a comfortable fire with a cup of tea beside him and de Troyes' *Yvain* open on his lap. The next thing he knew, the book was sliding off and he clutched at it involuntarily, startling himself awake.

Blinking, he found that the fire had nearly died away, which would explain why he felt chilled again. He reached for his tea only to find that it, too, was cold. Setting his book and tea aside, Leander got up to check the clock on the mantel and was dismayed to find that he'd slept another afternoon away. Sighing in frustration, he started to leave the library and collided with Powell.

"I beg your pardon, my lord," the butler said, stepping back. "I was about to check if you were awake."

"I am, as you see," Leander replied, then shivered.

"Dinner will be served soon. Would you like to take it in the library?"

His stomach became queasy at the thought of food, even though the cook had learned that Leander preferred simple meals and had stopped preparing several courses each night. "I hope Cook hasn't gone to too much trouble. I'm not very hungry."

"Is there anything in particular you would like?" Powell asked.

"Soup, if there's any. *Not* broth—something heartier than that."

"I will see to it at once, my lord," Powell assured him. "The Earl of Blackstone called earlier and left a note for you."

"Blackstone was here?" To his embarrassment, Leander's voice nearly cracked as it hadn't done in almost a decade.

"Yes, but when I informed him you were asleep he told me not to disturb you. The note is on the mantel in the drawing room."

"Thank you." Leander didn't have any specific rules for his staff— he'd never needed any—but now he had reason. "From now on, if Blackstone calls, please wake me."

"Of course, my lord."

Leander managed to keep to a walk as he proceeded to the drawing room where he saw a folded paper bearing his name on the mantel. He unfolded it and read Julien's now-familiar scrawl.

My dear Leander,

> *I am very sorry to hear you are unwell. I hope it is not serious and that you will be able to attend the ball being given by the Dowager Viscountess Seaforth the evening after tomorrow. I know that Seaforth and Lady Penelope are both looking forward to seeing you again, although not nearly as much as I.*

Yours,

J.

Warmed by the last words of the letter, Leander sat at the room's well-stocked desk to write his reply. He would have liked to repay the call in person, but decided it might be better to rest one more day, just to be certain he *didn't* become sick.

Dear Julien,

> *I am sorry to have missed your call. I am not ill; I merely got caught in the rain and took a slight chill. I will most certainly be at Lady Seaforth's ball and look forward to seeing you there.*

L.

Julien refolded the note and tucked it back in his pocket, telling himself he was turning into a lovesick fool. How many times had he reread the note since receiving it late yesterday afternoon? And it wasn't particularly flowery or profound. For someone with such a love of the written word, Leander was surprisingly succinct when putting pen to paper. He seemed more concerned with stressing that he was not ill than anything else. Julien wondered if Leander's definition of "a slight chill" was similar to that of "a little sore" when nearly breaking his ribs.

Having decided against calling, Julien found the time weighing heavily on him, which was utterly ridiculous. He'd never had any trouble passing the time before meeting Leander, so it should be a simple matter to pass a day or two until Lady Seaforth's ball.

It took some effort, but Julien sat down at his desk to see to his other correspondence. Among the invitations and introductions—most of which he ignored—was a letter from Bertram. At least, the handwriting was Bertram's; Julien suspected it had been dictated by Augusta. It had to have been mailed the moment they arrived home. No doubt Augusta had spent the coach ride composing it. Apparently their brief time in London hadn't been enough for her, because now Bertram wrote that they were considering another visit in order to enjoy the Season.

It was no trouble for Julien to give them the use of the house in Rupert Street or a healthy allowance, but he dreaded the idea of Augusta using him to further her constant—and often ridiculous—attempts at social climbing. Julien wrote a reply inviting them to stay at Rupert Street, but emphasized that any calls or invitations were to be at his convenience. He knew subtle hints would be lost on Augusta, so he wrote very plainly that she was not to impose on Cordelia or any of his friends. She was to limit herself to *her* previous acquaintances and those who called on her. From what Julien knew of Society, the connection to an earldom would ensure enough callers to keep Augusta busy.

He was addressing the envelope when Hudson entered. "Lord Seaforth and Lady Penelope to see you, my lord."

"Thank you, Hudson." That was a pleasant surprise, especially today when he needed all the distraction he could get. "See that these are posted," he said, handing his letters to the butler on his way to the drawing room. "And what brings you out this afternoon?" he asked his friends.

"We are going to visit Fromme's collection of antiquities," Penelope said. "And thought you might wish to join us."

Louis Fromme was a noted eccentric who had a passion for collecting all manner of manuscripts and artifacts. After his death, his son opened the collection to the public—no doubt hoping to sell some of the pieces. Julien had been meaning to visit it at some point, and today was perfect timing. "I believe I will." He nodded to the footman. "My

coat."

"Excellent." Seaforth nodded. "Penelope wants to call on Dearborne as well. She believes this would suit him perfectly."

Julien looked at Penelope only to find her watching him intently. It seemed he had just walked into a trap, but he wasn't entirely certain what kind. "I don't believe he will be able to join us. He was unwell when I called yesterday." He knew that would only pique Penelope's curiosity further, but there was no way around it.

"I thought he was injured more severely than he let on." Seaforth frowned. "His ribs?"

The more Julien thought about the ribs, the worse he felt. What had he been thinking, taking Leander to his bed when he *knew* that the sprained ribs weren't the minor injury Leander had made them out to be? Of course, Leander hadn't seemed to be in any pain, but Julien was learning that the one thing Leander was adept at hiding was physical discomfort.

"Strange," Penelope said casually. "He was well enough to attend the opera on Monday."

God help him, he was in for it now. First Cordelia and now Penelope. "He said he was caught in the rain and took a chill," he replied with equal sangfroid.

"I hope he'll be able to attend Mother's ball," Seaforth said, while Penelope looked more speculative than ever.

"He assured me he would," Julien said, relieved when the footman arrived with his things. "Shall we go?"

Penelope waited until he had coat and gloves on and then took his arm. "I trust *you* enjoyed the opera, Julien," she said as they left the drawing room.

Julien sighed. So much for a welcome distraction.

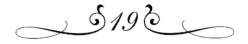

Do you see Dearborne anywhere?"

Julien glanced around the crowded ballroom. "I do not."

"I hope he's recovered enough to attend." Cordelia took a healthy swallow of champagne. "Don't you?"

"Of course." Julien was careful to keep his tone bland. He sometimes thought that an angry Cordelia might be preferable to an interested one. "Did Lady Rockingham enjoy the opera when you attended?"

"Hmm… changing the subject already? Very well. Of course she didn't enjoy the opera, but she is condoling herself with an excellent new set of emeralds."

"So Lord Rockingham has to pay for his pleasure twice."

"Julien, what a terrible thing to say." Cordelia finished off her glass. "Serves Rockingham right, anyway. Why, if Octavius ever—Julien! Do try to behave."

Julien had begun laughing, both at the notion of Carysfort seeking anyone other than Cordelia and at what Cordelia might do if she ever caught him. "Forgive me." Surreptitiously, he looked around again but only saw a formidable woman approaching them. "Ah, here is Lady Rockingham. No doubt she is eager to plan your next spying mission. If you'll excuse me, Aunt." He bowed to Cordelia and then to Lady Rockingham. "Lovely emeralds, madam."

"Impudent pup." Lady Rockingham had been calling him the same thing for two decades.

Julien grinned and made his escape. He scanned the ballroom again, but still saw no sign of Leander. For a moment he considered checking Lady Seaforth's library, but decided against it. That had been Leander's first ball when he hadn't known anyone. Surely he wouldn't go into

hiding tonight.

Seaforth and Penelope were dancing, and had been for most of the evening, which Julien thought might be deliberate on Seaforth's part. He suspected his friend had taken pity on him after Penelope spent the previous afternoon interrogating him.

Both she and Cordelia were exceedingly protective of Leander and Leander's heart. Strange that neither woman seemed too concerned about his, but then he'd always gone to great lengths to prove that was unnecessary.

"Look alive, Blackstone," a voice said.

"I beg your pardon," Julien said to Baron Vance, having nearly stepped on the rotund little dandy.

"You're going to have to be more awake than that if you don't want to lose that pretty little American of yours."

"I beg your pardon," Julien said again, but this time his tone made Vance's eyes go wide.

"I only meant that since word is out about Dearborne...." Vance cleared his throat. "Well, there's no denying what a handsome—you know I have no designs on him myself, but—"

"Spit it out, man," Julien ordered in a low voice.

"When Dearborne arrived barely ten minutes ago, Creighton was waiting for him. They went into the garden."

Julien's insides turned to ice, but it was quickly melted away when his anger began to smolder. Viscount Creighton was one of those men whose preference wasn't known by most of Society. He married the reigning belle of her Season who happened to be an heiress as well. Cool and dignified, if Lady Creighton knew the truth about her husband, she never let on, which made it all the easier for Creighton to maintain his position as a proper gentleman of the ton.

Among the circle he shared with Julien—a circle Society never acknowledged—Creighton had a very different reputation. Although well into his fifties, he only pursued men in their twenties. While not as cruel as some, he wasn't particularly kind, either, especially once he tired

of a young lover. He had tried with Julien years ago, but even then Julien hadn't cared for excessive secretiveness or for men who chose to marry. There was little stigma to remaining a bachelor, despite the fuss about heirs.

Creighton could be charming when he chose, however, and Leander was still unfamiliar with Society in general and men like Creighton in particular.

All this simmered in Julien's mind as he strode through the ballroom and out to the garden. This early in the evening there were few couples out among the shrubbery and soon enough Julien heard a familiar voice coming from the other side of a row of tall hedges.

"—that Julien wanted to meet me out here. I haven't even said hello to Lady Carysfort yet."

"Blackstone doesn't care whether you speak to his aunt." Creighton sounded politely surprised and a bit condescending. That would not go well for him.

"Whether he does or not, Lady Carysfort has been very kind to me since my arrival in London. I want to talk to her." Leander's voice was mild, but Julien heard the firmness underneath.

Creighton did not. "I believe I should speak to you about Blackstone."

That was his cue. "This should prove fascinating," Julien said as he stepped around the hedge, enjoying the contrasting reactions. Creighton's face fell while Leander's lit up with a smile.

"There you are." Leander glanced in Creighton's direction. "I was beginning to think you were mistaken, sir."

Julien grinned, wondering if Leander had begun to suspect Creighton's true purpose. "Creighton."

"Blackstone." Creighton cleared his throat. "Well, I'll leave you now," he said, making a hasty exit.

Julien's temper had begun to cool from the moment he'd found them and now that he was alone with Leander in a secluded corner, his mood improved considerably. "I'm glad you were able to attend."

"I said I would," Leander replied, frowning slightly. "I'd never met Lord Creighton before. I didn't know you were acquainted with him."

"I know him a little."

Leander's eyes widened. "Oh. Is that why you had him give me the message?"

"I left no message with him."

Leander stared blankly at him for a moment and then shook his head in a self-deprecating manner. "I wondered about it when he told me, but I didn't want to call him a liar. After all, he had no reason to make up such a thing."

"He had a very good reason," Julien replied. "He wanted to speak to you alone."

"But why—oh. *Oh.*"

Julien couldn't tell in the dim light, but he would wager any amount that Leander was blushing. He could, however, see when a shudder went through Leander's body. "Not to worry," he said, seeking to give the younger man some reassurance. "He wouldn't have done anything more than talk."

"What? No, of course not." Leander didn't seem concerned.

So that wasn't the reason for the shiver. It wasn't that cool of an evening, but if Leander had been ill, he could still be feeling the effects of it. As much as he would have liked to spend more time alone with Leander, he said, "My aunt will be glad to see you. Shall we go in search of her?"

"How much of our conversation did you hear?" Leander smiled as they headed back into the ballroom.

"Not much more than that," Julien admitted, wondering now why he'd been so angry. He should have known that Leander would not succumb to Creighton's charms.

"*Do* you care whether I speak to your aunt?"

"Seeing as Aunt Cordelia is the reason we met, I'm glad the two of you are friendly. What's more, if my aunt does not have the opportunity to speak to you, I'm the one who will hear about it, so yes, I care very

much."

It was good to hear Leander's laughter as they entered the ballroom where they were immediately accosted by Cordelia, who still had Lady Rockingham in tow. A few moments later, Lord Carysfort joined them to commiserate with Leander and Julien about having to attend at all.

Seaforth and Penelope were there as soon as their waltz ended, and then the Dowager Viscountess appeared for an introduction. Several members of the Arthurian League stopped to talk to Leander as well.

Standing about for several hours discussing King Arthur or the differences between England and America was not the way Julien would have chosen to spend an evening with Leander, but he was glad there were many diverse people speaking to them. They were mostly intellectuals and bluestockings, but were also of excellent family, which meant that although Society might wonder and gossip about what might be between Blackstone and the American Earl, the American Earl was now accepted enough that they would do little more than that.

Leander seemed to be enjoying himself, but after the first hour, he began to lose some of his color. The blue eyes, which had only seemed slightly shadowed when Leander first arrived, now had dark smudges underneath them.

Cordelia noticed the difference when she met up with them again after circulating through the room and herding Carysfort onto the dance floor a few times. "This really is a monstrous crush, isn't it? Have you had any refreshment, Dearborne? Champagne?"

"No, thank you." Leander smiled, but it wasn't as bright as before.

"He doesn't partake, Aunt," Julien explained.

"Lemonade, then," Cordelia said, stopping a passing footman who was carrying a tray. "Here you are."

Leander obediently took a glass, but only had a small sip.

"Are you well, Dearborne?"

Julien knew what had prompted her to ask the question. Leander's face was now quite pale and was also covered with a fine sheen of moisture.

"I'm fine, thank you."

"It really is almost suffocating in here," Cordelia continued, waving her fan vigorously. "Some fresh air would do me wonders." She linked her arm through Leander's. "Shall we?"

Leander barely had time to set his glass down before Cordelia swept him out to the garden.

Julien waited some time before following at a leisurely pace, reminding himself that if he started being too blatantly obvious, Society would no longer be able to conveniently overlook his actions. He found Cordelia and Leander seated on a stone bench near the back of the garden.

"Ah, Julien," Cordelia said. She stood up, and Leander immediately did as well. "Do come and keep Dearborne company. I really ought to find Carysfort."

Julien did as instructed, taking a seat next to Leander as Cordelia glided back into the house.

"I take it your aunt is no longer displeased with us," Leander said.

"She never was displeased with you," Julien corrected.

"She seemed to think I was ill," Leander added, giving him a pointed look.

"Well, your color is off and she knows that you aren't fond of crowds."

Leander nodded. "It's no longer a matter of getting accustomed to them. I suppose I'm never going to be comfortable around so many people."

"You've stayed long enough that leaving now would not be an insult to the viscountess."

"Truly?" Leander's voice held a hopeful note.

"Truly. You are quite free to return home." Julien lowered his voice, "Unless, of course, you would like to accompany me again." This time when Leander gave him a quizzical look, Julien didn't let it worry him— much. "What is it?"

"I can't help feeling that I should be inviting you to my home."

"As I've said before, you don't *have* to do anything you don't want to."

"I only meant that I've been to your home here in London and to Shadowcross but I've yet to return the favor."

Julien smiled. "As happy as I would be to accept the invitation, I thought my home would be preferable because my staff is already accustomed to such things. Your staff may need more time."

Leander nodded slowly. "And by returning home with you, they would begin to catch on."

"I should think so." Julien felt Leander stiffen next to him and was confused until he realized Leander had only done so in order to keep from shivering. He wondered if he should simply allow Leander to go home and rest, but knew that he couldn't very well retract his invitation now—nor did he want to. Still, it would probably be a good idea to get him out of the night air. "We can say good night to my aunt and then have a footman summon our coaches. You can send yours home with a message for your staff and we can leave in mine."

Leander clasped his hands between his knees and kept his eyes on them. "Perhaps it would be best if I took my own coach."

"If you prefer."

"It would be less troublesome for you."

Julien thought back, but could recall nothing he would change, except perhaps—"Surely you don't regret our conversation about your brothers."

Leander's head ducked even lower.

"I certainly do not consider your grief troublesome," Julien said truthfully. A strange truth—normally he did not like his lovers bringing their life's problems to bed. He leaned close to the younger man so their shoulders were touching, "And even if I did, I believe we've already established that I thought you were worth the trouble."

Leander didn't raise his head, but he did press himself closer.

"Shall we go with my plan, then?" Julien asked quietly. Leander

nodded and they both rose. When they reached the door, he added, "I'll summon both coaches while you find Lady Carysfort." Now that they were in the light, Julien could see that Leander's color had become very hectic. He might have just been flushed from his earlier embarrassment, but that seemed doubtful. "Or you could sit somewhere quiet until the coaches arrive at the door."

"There's no need for that."

Fortunately everything went smoothly and the coaches were waiting when they'd taken their leave of Cordelia and Lady Seaforth. Julien climbed into his coach and a few moments later, Leander followed.

With no apparent concern for propriety, Leander slumped into the seat next to Julien instead of across from him. Pleased, Julien drew Leander into an embrace and smiled when the younger man shifted to be as close as possible. He was about to comment that this was an excellent way to pass the drive home when he realized there was nothing particularly sensual about Leander's actions.

Then he heard a mumbled, "You're so warm."

Julien wasn't *too* disappointed to discover that Leander was only interested in absorbing body heat. It was surprisingly pleasant to just sit with Leander nestled against him. The coach had just begun moving with some speed when Leander lifted his head to murmur an apology. Julien silenced him with his lips and the rest of the ride was passed in the exchange of long, slow kisses.

"I trust you are considerably warmer now," Julien murmured when the coach rolled to a halt.

"Yes, thank you." Leander snuck in another soft kiss and then disentangled himself before the footman opened the door.

By the time they got inside the house, however, Leander was shivering again.

"Tell Kay to see that there is a good fire in my room," Julien instructed Hudson as the butler took their things. "After that he may retire for the evening, as may you."

"Very good, my lord. Lord Dearborne." He gave Leander a small bow as well before going upstairs.

Julien put his hand on Leander's back and guided him into the drawing room and a warm fire. "Are you certain you're quite well, Leander?"

Letting out a growl, Leander grabbed Julien's cravat and pulled him down into a deep kiss.

Julien was startled by both the sound and the kiss, but happily went along. "If that was incentive for me to stop asking after your health," he said when they finally broke apart, "it's failed miserably."

"Julien, I swear—"

"No rash promises, please. Take heart, once we're in my bedchamber, I won't have time to ask, will I?"

Leander stared at him, lips pressed together, then grabbed Julien's hand, dragging him out of the drawing room and up the stairs. As they went, Julien made a mental note to provoke Leander to the point of exasperation more often. It made him forget any shyness or uncertainty and was most stimulating.

"And now?" he asked once they were inside.

Leander's angry expression dissolved into one of surprise, and then he laughed. "Do I need to apologize?"

"Not in the least," Julien assured him, and began unbuttoning his waistcoat.

Leander responded by reaching for Julien's cravat. There was no real hesitancy in removing their clothing this time; Leander was obviously eager to be skin to skin, clutching at Julien's shoulders and lifting his face for more kisses.

Julien was more than happy to oblige. He didn't know what had prompted Leander to give up his inhibitions so completely, but the result was intoxicating. When he pressed Leander back onto the bed, Leander parted his legs and lifted one knee. The movement brought other things to Julien's mind—things he hadn't intended to attempt so soon.

He ran his fingers along the back of Leander's raised thigh while kissing his way down the smooth neck and chest. Moaning, Leander arched up toward Julien's lips and Julien took the opportunity to cup one

of the firm cheeks, giving it a gentle squeeze. Then he slid one finger into the cleft, making Leander jump.

"I want this," he murmured, pressing his lips to Leander's ear. "I want to be inside you. Will you let me?"

"I don't—oh, God," Leander panted desperately. "I want—I don't know what…."

"It will hurt a little at first." Julien kissed Leander's ear and stroked the entrance to his body. "But if you trust me, it should prove even more pleasurable than anything before."

"More…?" The lamp on the bedside table made it easy to see Leander's dazed look. "Julien, that's—yes, *please*…."

Julien captured Leander's lips again and removed his hand, reaching for the small container of oil that he kept tucked under one corner of his mattress. With slick fingers, he began to massage the puckered opening, while his lips roamed over Leander's chest. As he teased Leander's nipples with his tongue, he felt fingers thread through his hair, then clench when he slid his own finger inside the tight passage.

He kept moving his finger until Leander was begging, then added a second. Now he could reach deep enough to prod the sensitive spot that would bring the most pleasure. He knew he had found it when Leander bucked his hips off the bed, then pushed hard against his hand. After a few more strokes, Julien removed his hand, prompting a desperate whimper from Leander.

Raising Leander's other knee, Julien positioned himself, pushing in as slowly as possible and trying to think about anything except the silky heat surrounding him in order to maintain control. "Leander," he whispered, "am I hurting you?"

Leander had his bottom lip between his teeth, but now released it. "Not… not really. It's just…." He drew a deep breath, as if trying to drag air into his lungs. "Strange… I couldn't even have imagined…."

Julien began to move, watching Leander's expression for any sign of pain. Seeing none, he leaned forward and drove deeper, changing the angle slightly. Leander let out a choked cry and grabbed his shoulders hard enough to leave bruises. Julien made sure to brush against that same

spot with every thrust and grasped Leander's straining erection, stroking it in time.

By concentrating on Leander's reactions, Julien was able to hold back until he felt Leander's seed coat his hand and Leander's body tighten around him as the younger man convulsed beneath him. Finally he could give up his control and frantically pumped himself into the welcoming body.

It took much longer than usual for Julien to regain his senses, but eventually he rolled off Leander and reached for a towel. He cleaned them both off, and not once throughout his ministrations did Leander move. "Leander?" he murmured, wondering if he'd hurt his young lover after all.

"Mmm?" Leander's only response was that and a dreamy smile.

Julien smiled as well and, tossing the towel aside, curled himself around the beautifully sated body.

Leander snuggled in to the warm body next to him and tried to escape back into sleep, but it was no use. He was awake and feeling miserable.

It was truly frustrating, because if not for the blinding headache and the cold that had seeped into his very bones, this could have easily been the best morning of his life. He remained still, thinking only about the night before and the incredible pleasure he'd received and—hopefully—given.

Part of him still found it difficult to believe that this was happening. To him. With Julien. That it seemed so unreal had made it easier for him to act the way he had. To stop questioning how to proceed and simply follow his instincts. To say he'd enjoyed the result was an understatement.

"Leander?" Julien's voice was barely more than a whisper.

"Yes," Leander said reluctantly.

"So you are awake." Julien hadn't moved the arm that was curled around Leander's back. "I wondered."

"I don't want to be," Leander admitted. "I'd much rather stay exactly as I am."

"Have you need of the chamber pot?"

Leander willed himself not to blush. Julien's tone was so matter-of-fact. "No."

"Then there's no need for you to move, is there?" Julien began stroking his hair.

The caress soothed his headache somewhat and Leander sighed happily. He lay in contented silence despite the congestion he could feel tightening in his chest. If he moved too abruptly or breathed too deeply he would start coughing and Julien would undoubtedly begin to worry

again. He sighed once more, this time not so happily, and then had to hold his breath to keep from coughing.

As always, Julien noticed immediately. "What's the matter?"

"I suppose it's time for me to make plans to visit my estates."

Julien didn't say anything for some time, then, "Which will you visit first?"

"The one closest. The other is some one hundred thirty miles away. That's what Mayfield suggested, anyway."

"Mayfield." Julien's tone went from neutral to flat. "Your cousin."

"Yes. He thinks it an excellent idea. He even offered to accompany me." Leander tried not to hope that Julien would offer the same thing.

"I wouldn't be eager to travel with him if I were you."

"I'm not, exactly," Leander admitted. "He's not the most amiable of men, but it was kind of him to offer."

"Visit your estates if you must, but not with Mayfield."

"Why not? I should think it's better than traveling alone." Leander knew he couldn't hint any more blatantly than that and he wasn't going to try. He wasn't.

"It's not."

No longer comfortable, Leander sat up. "I understand you may not like him, but—"

Julien sat up as well. "I don't want to hear any more about him."

Leander hadn't known there was such bad blood between them. "Very well. I won't speak of him again."

"You will not associate with him again."

Leander was certain he couldn't possibly have heard correctly. "He's my cousin. He's the only living relation I have left."

"I don't care. You will cease contact." Julien's voice held a note of finality that clanged disagreeably with everything Leander had experienced with him up until now.

"Cease contact? I can't do that."

"Of course you can."

"I suppose I could," Leander conceded. "But that doesn't mean I will or even that I *should*." Although in truth, it would be no hardship if he never saw Morleigh Mayfield again, except that he would feel guilty for shunning the man without good reason. "I'm sorry you don't like him, but that's not reason enough for me to cut him out of my life."

Julien's face became more and more impassive until Leander didn't have the slightest idea what he was thinking.

"If I didn't like someone in your family, would you cut them off?"

"That is hardly a logical comparison."

"Perhaps, but only because I've never had any objections to your family. But what if I did? Would you cut them off?"

"Of course not. There is no reason to."

"And except for your objection I've no reason to cut off my cousin."

"My objection is not reason enough?" Julien's eyes narrowed.

Leander wished Julien could see how grossly illogical his argument was. "Julien, I want—" He had to stop when a cough threatened, and perhaps it was for the best. What would he have said? *I want to please you*, but that made for a very poor beginning. What else did Julien expect to dictate about his life? "I'm sorry, but no."

"I'm not jesting, Leander."

No one had taken *that* tone with Leander since his brothers had been lost at sea, and even before then, it had been a rarity. As far as he was concerned, no one except his father and brothers ever had that right.

"Do you hear me?" Julien demanded.

Leander met the fierce amber eyes that were also demanding his acquiescence. The truly frightening thing was that he *wanted* to agree just so that could go back to that warm closeness they had shared upon awakening. It seemed like a dangerous precedent to set. "I hear you, and I've been glad to let you guide me in many things, but I can't follow blindly about something like this. I can't let you dictate whom I can and

cannot see." The morning was turning out even worse than their last one together. Leander swung his legs to the side of the bed and looked around. Kay had obviously been in while they were still asleep, because their clothes were neatly arranged on the press.

"Where are you going?"

"Home," Leander replied, but hesitated. Despite everything that had transpired between them, Leander felt himself flush at the thought of walking across the room without his clothing. After a moment, he threw back the covers and stood. A slight twinge in his lower body—not painful, but unexpected—distracted him from his embarrassment.

Julien got out of bed as well, and grabbed his dressing robe that was laid out at the foot. "Come now, Leander. There's no need for theatrics."

Leander looked up from buttoning his trousers. "Theatrics? I'm not the one giving orders."

"It's for your own good."

As he pulled on his shirt, Leander wondered if Julien meant that to sound as threatening as it had come out. "*What* exactly is for my own good? Avoiding my cousin or obeying you?" More than anything, he wanted to get out of there. The spacious room suddenly seemed constrictive and an ache began in his chest to match the one in his head.

"Leander." Julien's voice was much calmer now. "Mayfield is not the best of men. There are rumors about him."

Leander closed his eyes, willing his head to stop pounding. "Rumors, Julien? You ought to know better."

"I beg your pardon," Julien said icily.

"There are rumors about everyone. About you. By now, there are probably some about me as well."

"The rumors about Mayfield are… quite unpleasant. Leander, stop."

Leander moved away when Julien tried to take his arm and continued fastening his waistcoat. He didn't want to sit down to pull his boots on, but his head was beginning to spin. Taking a seat, he got them on as quickly as possible. "I think it's best if I go home before this becomes even worse." He reached for his coat, not certain whether he

was referring to their disagreement or his head.

Julien stood in front of the door, blocking his way. "Did you hear what I said?"

"I did." Did Julien truly expect him to judge someone based on *gossip*? If Leander was the sort of person who did that, he never would have visited Julien's country home, let alone gone to his bed. Julien had been accused—however indirectly—of murder, among other things. "There have been unpleasant *rumors* about Mayfield. There have been unpleasant rumors about you as well. Would you have me believe those?"

"This is entirely different. I'm telling you."

There was a definite warning in Julien's voice, but again Leander couldn't tell if the warning was about Mayfield or about disobeying him in general. One thing he did realize in that moment was how much he hated being *ordered* to do something. He didn't mind following when he didn't know about something—and there was a great deal in London he didn't know about—nor did he mind acquiescing to a request when it pleased someone, but being expected to obey without question brought out a stubborn streak he thought only Chance had possessed. "Julien, please let me by," he said, trying to sound as calm as possible. "This discussion is over and I'd like to go home."

"Stop acting like a fool," Julien snapped.

Stung, Leander struck back. "Not agreeing with you doesn't make me a fool. *You* need to learn that I'm not one of your paid companions who is obligated to obey you." He regretted the words as soon as they left his mouth even though they made Julien step out of the way. Leander walked past as quickly as he could without breaking into a run.

Not surprisingly, Hudson was in the foyer when Leander reached the bottom of the stairs. "Good morning, Lord Dearborne."

"Good morning, Hudson. May I have my coat and hat, please?"

The only sign of the butler's surprise was his slight hesitation before retrieving the requested items. "Shall I summon the coach, sir?" he asked as he helped Leander with his greatcoat.

"No, thank you. I'll walk." Leander didn't want to risk seeing Julien

again. He'd walked greater distances many times before, albeit never when he was feeling so miserable both physically and emotionally. He finished pulling on his gloves and took his hat from the butler. "Thank you, Hudson."

"Good day, my lord." Hudson held the door open for him.

Leander took a deep breath when he was finally outside and was immediately seized by a coughing fit. He set out for home as quickly as possible, considering his dizziness. Perhaps if he went straight to bed and stayed there for several days, he wouldn't have to send for the doctor.

"I'M sorry, sir. Lord Dearborne is not at home."

Years of habit kept Julien from revealing his surprise and disappointment at the butler's words. He nodded sharply to the man and returned to his waiting coach. "My club," he said to his coachman before getting in.

So Leander was still angry, was he? Well, perhaps he had been somewhat dictatorial, but Leander's immediate refusal had thrown him off balance. After following Julien's lead with hardly a murmur of protest, Leander had inexplicably decided to dig his heels in. Over Morleigh Mayfield, of all people.

He'd definitely struck a nerve somehow. One that he hadn't been aware existed. That much was evident from Leander's remark about paid companions.

Unless Leander felt as though Julien was treating him as a paid companion. Julien shook his head. Surely that couldn't be it. How would Leander even know how one treated a paid companion? Likely he'd only said it in his fit of temper.

When his coach stopped in front of Jupiter's, Julien realized he didn't particularly want to go inside. He was here, though, so he decided he might as well have a drink. With any luck there would be something inside to distract him.

He walked in and glanced around, but saw no one he knew or cared

to talk to. Ordering a glass of hock, he found his favorite chair unoccupied and gladly took it. It was one of the more secluded spots and from it he could see the newest selection of books and journals that the club made available. He found nothing to interest him and so just sat and sipped his drink.

Obviously, he had approached the Mayfield subject in the wrong way. Perhaps if he hadn't been so adamant and had taken more time to convince Leander, he would have been successful. He never should have mentioned rumors, either. Leander apparently disregarded any information that came through gossip. To a certain extent Julien agreed it was a sound policy, but one also had to consider who relayed the information.

Would Leander see this disagreement as reason enough to end their association? No, Julien decided, knowing Leander had far more depth than that. And if he was willing to end it over such a trifling, then Julien was well rid of him. Although Julien had been glad to move slowly and carefully with the young man, he wasn't about to tolerate a lover with whom he had to watch his every word.

"Blackstone." The Marquis of Steane sat down in the chair opposite him uninvited and set his glass on the small table between them.

"Steane." Julien wished he'd picked up a journal after all so he'd have a reason to ignore the man.

"And where is young Dearborne?"

"I haven't seen him today," Julien replied coolly.

"He seems a very amiable and charming young man," Steane observed.

"That he is," Julien agreed. He was tempted to ask after Gabriel, but decided such tactics were beneath him.

"One would think you'd be eager to spend as much time in his company as possible."

Julien ground his teeth as unobtrusively as possible. "He has obligations that must be attended to. As do I."

"Naturally." Steane took a sip of his port. "But if I were you, I

would keep a close eye on him. From what I hear, he's caught the interest of many people. There are many who would like to make him the focus of their attentions."

Julien didn't have to see the glint in Steane's eye to know the marquis was one of those men. "They could try," he said with as much arrogance as he possessed, which according to others, was considerable.

Some of Steane's supercilious expression faded.

"If you'll excuse me," Julien finished his glass in a single gulp, "I have other appointments to attend to." He stood before Steane had the chance to reply and left. "Home," he ordered, climbing back into his carriage. He could feel blood pounding at his temples and took several deep breaths, forcing himself to calm down.

Of course other men would be interested in Leander once the young man's leanings became known. Hadn't he wanted Leander from the first moment he'd set eyes on the American? And while it was considered bad form to poach another man's paid companion, such an unwritten rule wouldn't apply to Leander. There were plenty of men who would do anything Leander asked for the chance to be with him. Certainly they wouldn't dream of insisting Leander cut off a relation.

Leander had made it clear he had no interest in anyone except Julien, but things could change. For all he knew, someone had already made Leander a more appealing proposition. For all he knew, that's where Leander was at this very moment. If that was the case, perhaps Julien would be better off considering other options for himself.

But he knew that wasn't a possibility. Just the thought of someone else seeing Leander's body—touching it, kissing it—made Julien's stomach turn and his very blood seethe with jealousy.

Again, he was doing Leander a disservice. Leander was naive, yes—as much as he hated to be called that—but he was not fickle. Likely if Julien wrote a note explaining himself and withdrawing his demand, things would settle themselves soon enough. Then he could find another, more subtle approach to keeping Mayfield at a distance.

When he arrived home, Julien went straight to his study and

wrote out a letter, which he immediately had delivered to Leander.

Now there was nothing to do but wait.

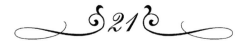

Julien sighed when Hudson announced Lord Seaforth and Lady Penelope, wishing he'd told the butler he wasn't at home to anyone. His friends were likely just concerned about him, but he wasn't in the mood for sympathy or company and hadn't been for the past five days. That was when he'd sent Leander a note of almost-apology.

There had been no reply.

The day after sending the note, he'd called again, and again he'd been told Leander was not at home. Furious with Leander for the humiliating experience of being turned away *twice* and furious with himself for allowing it, he'd returned home vowing that he would not call on, or even think of, the American again.

That proved much easier said than done.

Not sure how he'd react to meeting up with Leander, Julien avoided places he might encounter the younger man. It was no great hardship, as Julien had never been very social to begin with. Not thinking of Leander, however, proved much more difficult. Every time he lay in his own bed, his mind was filled with memories of the last time he'd shared it with Leander, of Leander's eagerness and responsiveness.

With a determined effort, Julien pushed those thought to the back of his mind before greeting Seaforth and Penelope. They already suspected an attachment between he and Leander, and it would never do to have them think he was in any way affected by the severing of that attachment.

"There he is," Penelope said when he walked into the drawing room. "I vow it's been an age since we saw you last."

"It's been little more than a week," Seaforth pointed out.

Penelope's sharp eyes narrowed behind her spectacles. "Are you well, Julien?" she asked with a little frown. "You look quite poorly."

"Thank you, Penelope. I'm so glad you could call and brighten my day."

"Forgive me. It's only that many people of our acquaintance seem to be ill lately."

"The grippe is going about several families," Seaforth added.

"The meeting of the Arthurian League yesterday was very small. I was hoping to see Dearborne there since he seemed so enthusiastic about them, but he did not put in an appearance."

She would have to bring up Leander. "And did the meeting grind to a halt without him?"

Seaforth's eyebrows rose at Julien's biting tone, but Penelope ignored it as she always did. "I was concerned he was still suffering the effects of his fall, so we called on him before coming here."

"Did you?" Julien managed to keep his tone bland despite the sudden lurch of his heart as it stuttered to a stop.

"Apparently he's well enough to travel, as he's off visiting his estate."

Julien's heart began beating again.

"I'm surprised you didn't know." Seaforth gave him a piercing look.

"He mentioned seeing to his holdings," Julien replied, resisting the urge to shift his shoulders now that a massive weight had disappeared from them. "He just didn't say when he was going." Even the fact that he'd been a fool, brooding about it for five days, no longer bothered him. Of course Leander wouldn't use Society's polite "not at home" excuse to avoid *him*.

One week ago, Leander going off to the country without a word would have aggravated him, but today Julien was able to shrug it off. Likely Leander wanted to make a point about his independence, which wasn't surprising. Once Julien had more time to think about it, he'd been able to admit that if anyone had dared to speak to him the way he had spoken to Leander, he would have immediately done the exact opposite.

"Julien?" Seaforth's voice brought him back to the present.

"I beg your pardon. I was wool-gathering."

"Are you going to join us at Lady Grenville's salon today?" Penelope asked.

The last thing Julien wanted to do at the moment was sit and discuss the merits of Plato's teachings, Sappho's poetry, Cicero's speeches, or whatever subject had taken Lady Grenville's fancy this month. "I'm afraid I'll have to decline, but I would be happy to meet you later to go riding."

His offer was enough to placate Penelope, as he knew it would be. "That's an excellent notion. The air would do you a world of good."

He probably should have expected that, Julien thought, exchanging a wry smile with Seaforth.

After a little more conversation about the Egyptian tablets that had recently been acquired by the London Museum, Seaforth suggested he and Penelope be on their way. Julien wondered if Seaforth might have noticed his inattention and suspected the reason. He saw his friends to the door and gave his promise to meet them in Hyde Park at four-thirty.

It was difficult to begin the letter to Leander, but once Julien swallowed some of his pride, he was able to find the words.

PARR'S understudy, unsurprisingly, had found himself a patron, but Julien didn't regret that loss. He hadn't wanted the actor when he'd had the opportunity and certainly didn't want him now. In fact, none of the available actors appealed to him.

He'd been hoping to find someone relatively new, but the actors backstage at the Haymarket were jaded and all too familiar with the game. Try though he might, Julien couldn't help comparing them to Leander. That they all were lacking only darkened his mood further.

It had been nearly two weeks since he'd sent Leander a letter and there had been no reply. Every time Julien thought of it, his skin crawled with humiliation. He had humbled himself—to a certain extent—in that letter, and Leander had ignored him.

"No one who appeals to you?"

Julien turned to see Roderick Fleming, the youngest son of the Earl of Yarford. "Not tonight."

"I'm surprised to see you here," Fleming continued. "I was under the impression you had an understanding with Dearborne."

Not deigning to reply, Julien let his look speak for him.

"Yes, well, none of my concern, of course." The younger man swallowed nervously. "Didn't mean to pry. No offense intended."

"None taken." Julien's tone was mild. He had no quarrel with Roderick Fleming, a broad-shouldered, snub-nosed man in his late twenties. With no duties to a title and a sizable fortune left to him by a doting aunt, Fleming never had reason to hide his preference and was a good-natured, kindhearted fellow with a fancy for men who were as feminine as possible without actually being women. Julien never quite understood the appeal of that, but knew there were many men who shared Fleming's tastes. "And you? Have you met anyone of interest?"

"No, nothing," Fleming replied, obviously relieved by Julien's bland tone. "I was about to take myself off to Madame Rimbaude's."

"Not staying for the performance?" Julien decided he might as well make conversation, since there was nothing else worthwhile backstage.

"Lawks, no! I wouldn't sit through that disaster again for a feast of mollie-boys."

Julien felt his lips twitch into something resembling a smile, although a month earlier, the amusing turn of phrase would have made him laugh aloud. "Is it that bad?"

"Atrocious," Fleming assured him. "One can tell the playwright is trying desperately to be witty, but the result is dismal. And while I enjoy melodrama as much as anyone, there is only so much one can take in a single sitting."

That settled it. If someone like Fleming thought a play too melodramatic, then it would definitely be too much for him. "Thank you for the warning. I won't waste my time."

"Why don't you join me at Madame Rimbaude's? Perhaps we'll each find something worthwhile there."

Julien hadn't been to any of the mollie-houses since he began his association with Gabriel. While he didn't care much for the sort of encounter that usually took place at Madame Rimbaude's, perhaps some faceless, willing body—or several—was just what he needed to take his mind off Leander. "I believe I will."

They left the theater and found a hackney to take them to Madame Rimbaude's, as did most men who frequented the establishment. No one wanted their coach seen outside a mollie-house, whether they hid their nature from Society or not. A coach recognized by the authorities was more attention than anyone wanted.

Madame Rimbaude greeted them personally and served them each a glass of port. When several pale, thin young men in elaborately frilled dresses caught Fleming's eye, Julien waved him off to mingle with them and took a seat on one of the garishly upholstered settees.

Many young men cast looks in his direction, likely attracted to the scent of wealth. A bold few even sauntered over to him, but left again when he didn't respond, going back to the house's more attentive patrons.

When Madame Rimbaude brought him his fourth glass of port, along with the bottle, she took a seat next to him. "Ees zair no one 'oo catches your eye, milord?" Her French accent was a well-known facade. Angry moments revealed a very pronounced Cockney cadence. The real mystery about her was whether the husky voice belonged to an actual woman.

"Not at the moment."

"Are you searching for anyzing in particulaire?"

Intelligent blue eyes. An earnest American voice. A shy nature and aversion to crowds. "Not really."

"You 'aven't been 'ere for some time, but I remembaire zee sort you enjoy. 'As zat changed?"

"No. I believe I prefer to merely look tonight."

"Ah!" Understanding lit the heavily painted features. "I can arrange zat. Zair are two very 'andsome men 'oo would be 'appy to—"

"That's not what I meant," Julien said. Realizing she didn't make any profit from a man sitting and drinking her liquor, he fished a guinea from his pocket and pressed it casually into her hand. "I'd prefer to just sit here, if you don't mind."

"But of course." Madame Rimbaude smiled benignly, her fingers closing easily around the coin. "I am always 'appy to 'ave you, milord. If zair eez anyzing else you require, tell me so at once," she said and then got up to see to her other patrons.

When he was nearly finished with his bottle of port, Julien beckoned to the extraordinarily handsome young man who had been glancing in his direction much of the night. The man walked over and sat down.

"What's your name?" Julien asked, looking into eyes that were more green than blue. *That might be a good thing*, he told himself.

"Will," he replied. He didn't seem nervous, so obviously he wasn't new, but he also lacked the calculating glint in his eye that so many of Madame Rimbaude's employees had. "Can I get you some more port, my lord?"

Julien was somewhat surprised that Will would suggest that instead of going immediately to the transaction, but the young man seemed content to just sit with him. Either he was one of those rare men who worked at a mollie-house for reasons other than money or he was a better actor than Gabriel could have hoped to be. "No, but get yourself a glass if you like."

"No, thank you."

The handsome face was framed by dark chestnut—almost black— curls and Julien's hand moved to toy with them almost of its own volition. "Have you a room here, Will?"

"Do I live here, you mean?" Will smiled slightly. "I do not. I have my own lodgings elsewhere."

So he didn't work for Madame Rimbaude. Julien finished his last glass. "I believe I will have more port. In fact, have another bottle sent to an available room. All on my bill, of course."

"That's very generous of you. I'll see to it at once."

Julien watched as Will rose and moved across the room to speak to Madame Rimbaude. He obviously had some education; his speech alone made that evident. Three months ago Julien would have been very pleased to encounter him.

He saw Will waiting by the stairs and stood up to follow. Will led him into one of the house's nicer rooms on the first floor. These rooms were often used by men who were simply looking for a place to be together. The mollie-boys who worked and lived in the house had rooms on the second and third floors.

There was only a bed and table in the room, but both were clean and of good quality. Julien sat on the bed and, when Will set the bottle down, immediately refilled his glass.

"May I?" Will indicated the spot next to him on the bed.

"Of course," Julien replied, glad that Will wasn't rushing.

Half a bottle of port later, they hadn't progressed any further than a few kisses and caresses and Julien began to wonder if two entire bottles would be enough to erase Leander's memory from his mind. He finished the second bottle only to find that they weren't.

Gently, and with some regret, he pushed Will away. At one time he would have moved such a beautiful, well-mannered young man into the house on Windmill Street before the next day was out.

But that was before he'd met Leander.

"I'm afraid I've wasted your time," he said. Setting his empty glass aside, he fished in his waistcoat pocket until he felt a note. He pulled it out and saw it was five pounds, so he handed it to Will. "For your trouble."

Will drew back with a frown. "That's not necessary, my lord."

"Not to worry." Julien pushed the money into Will's hand. "I have plenty to pay for the room."

"Very well," Will said, standing. "Let's have Madame arrange a hack for you."

"Excellent notion." As he stood and made his way back downstairs it occurred to Julien that he hadn't drank so much in years. Nor was he

holding it as well as he used to, judging by the looks he received along the way. He found more money in his waistcoat and paid Madame Rimbaude before allowing Will to escort him to the waiting hackney. "You're a fine, clever lad, Will," he said, pausing with one foot on the tiny step. "Pretty too. If it wasn't for that bloody American I'd have taken you home with me."

"Yes, my lord," Will said patiently. "Good night, sir."

Julien *did* have the presence of mind to tell the driver to take him to the Haymarket Theatre instead of giving the directions to his home. His coach was still waiting, as he'd known it would be, and he heard the footman assure the driver he would be paid just as soon as his lordship was made comfortable.

Julien collapsed onto the velvet seat and allowed blackness to overtake him, secure in the knowledge that he would be well looked after by his staff, as always.

"JULIEN? How ill is he? Has Hudson called for the doctor?"

Bloody hell. What was Cordelia doing in his bedchamber?

"What do you mean 'not exactly ill'? Is he or isn't he?"

Haranguing my staff, apparently.

"Imbibed? You mean *drunk*?"

Julien heard the indignation in her voice and knew he was in for a lecture. He would have covered his ears with a pillow, but that would require moving and Julien was certain if he did, his head would fall off.

"Julien!" She was right next to his bed now. "Get up at once!"

Perhaps it would be better if his head did fall off. "Have a care, Aunt." He had to force the words past his parched tongue. "I'm not a well man."

"That's your own fault. Now get up at once. I have to speak to you about a most urgent matter."

Julien opened his eyes and his head was immediately assaulted with shards of pain. "I'm not about to get up with you in the room."

"Very well. I'll wait in your study. But if you aren't there in ten minutes, I'm coming back."

The slamming of the door reverberated through his teeth.

"Forgive me, my lord." Kay's voice was—thankfully—quiet and apologetic. "I couldn't stop her."

"No one can when her mind is made up," Julien assured him with a groan. "Get my dressing gown and have Hudson fetch some very strong coffee."

Kay stayed only long enough to help Julien with his dressing gown before taking himself off to find the butler. Slowly, Julien made his way to the study.

"What possessed you to drink to such excess?" Cordelia demanded once he'd dropped into a chair opposite her.

"Foolishness," Julien replied, holding up his head with one hand.

"Then...." Cordelia hesitated. "Then it wasn't because of the rumors?"

"Rumors?"

"About Dearborne."

Julien wondered if he was still a bit drunk. Cordelia already knew about him and Leander; surely no one knew about their argument. Unless Fleming had— "What rumors?"

"Oh, Julien." Cordelia looked truly upset. "It's all anyone could talk about at the ball. Dearborne is nowhere to be found. Lord Archer called on him at Afton Manor, but he never arrived there."

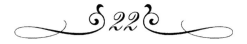

Julien refused to let himself become excited, either by the rumors, or by learning, once again, that Leander might *not* be ignoring his letters. "Perhaps he traveled to his other estate after all."

"You need to discover if that is the case," Cordelia said. "Lord Tracy had it from Mayfield himself that you and Dearborne quarreled the morning before he left."

Hudson arriving with the coffee was a welcome reprieve and Julien unclenched his teeth in order to take a long sip of the strong brew.

"Julien, if you know where Dearborne is—"

"I do not."

"Oh, Julien." Cordelia rose and began pacing. "If Dearborne is not heard from…. Julien, Tobias Norville is being mentioned."

This was getting stranger by the moment. "I can assure you that Tobias Norville could not possibly be involved in this matter."

"Do try to clear your head, Julien!" Cordelia stopped pacing long enough to glare at him. "People are comparing Dearborne's disappearance to Norville's."

Oh. The cup rattled in its saucer as Julien set it down. "Ridiculous," he said with a surety he didn't feel. "It is not even certain that Lean— that Dearborne is missing."

"Someone needs to find him and inform him of this situation, then, so he can let it be known that he is alive and well."

Part of Julien longed to leave for Somerset at once in search of Leander, but not for the same reason as Cordelia wanted it. "Perhaps I'll send a letter to his estate."

"Mayfield claims he sent a letter already, but hasn't had a reply."

"I believe I'd prefer to send my own letter."

"You'd best do it soon." Cordelia began pacing again. "The rumors last night were most unpleasant. There are saying that whatever happened to Norville has happened to Dearborne. They are bringing up the old rumors that you... did away with Norville."

Rumors that Leander never believed, even when most of Society did. "I can assure you that is not the case."

"I know that. I never once thought—but Julien, two young men whose names were linked with yours. Both disappeared. More than the ton might take an interest in this."

Julien refilled his cup. He needed to think about this when his head was clear. "Would you like some coffee, Aunt?" he asked, wanting this conversation finished.

Cordelia looked incredulous. "Have you heard a single word I've said?"

"Are you afraid I'll hang?"

"Aren't you?"

"They rarely hang men for sodomy these days." Perhaps if he was brutally blunt, his aunt would abandon the subject. In any case, his head was pounding too much for tact.

He should have known it wouldn't be enough to deter her. "They *do* hang men for murder. Tobias Norville might not have caused much notice, but Dearborne is an earl, for all that he is American."

"Again, no one can even say for certain that Dearborne has vanished," Julien countered. "I will send a letter today, and but by messenger. This way we will have our answer in a day or two."

STANDING stoically near the door to the card room, Julien wondered how much longer he'd have to endure Lady Rockingham's ball before Cordelia and Penelope deemed his ordeal over.

More than a week had passed since Cordelia had barged into his bedchamber; more than a week without anyone hearing from or about

Leander. Although Julien had refused to allow himself to worry when Cordelia first told him about the rumors, once word came that Leander was not at Eversley Park in Somerset, it was impossible not to be concerned.

It could have been his concern for Leander that kept Julien from realizing just how much the American Earl's disappearance was being discussed. After five days of waiting at home for a reply, Julien had gone to White's, partly to get out of the house, but mostly to discover if there was any word about Leander. No one in the club would speak to him or even meet his eyes, although there were plenty of whispers whenever his back was turned. Trying to behave as though he didn't notice the looks or mutterings, Julien had wandered over to the club's betting book and studied it so he wouldn't have to notice all the men ignoring him.

> *Lord P wagers Lord T that it will be discovered that a certain foreign earl fled back to his homeland in order to escape the attentions of a certain sodomite earl.*

> *Lord W wagers Lord F that the corpse of a certain colonial will turn up in the Thames with his trousers around his ankles.*

Bile had risen in the back of Julien's throat and he'd slammed the book shut. When he'd cast his glare around the room, every man in the club had suddenly become absorbed in his newspaper or conversation. He'd stalked out of the club and gone to Jupiter's where the patrons prided themselves on being more serious-minded, or at the very least, more open-minded than those who frequented White's. Once inside, however, his reception had been nearly identical. Even the gossipy Vance had pretended not to see him.

After that, Julien hadn't been eager to venture into Society again unless it was absolutely necessary. A few days later, Bertram had arrived in London with his family to take up residence in Rupert Street. It had been a distraction, if not exactly a welcome one. Then the rumors about Julien had reached Augusta and Julien had been able to watch as she tried to use his title to advance her social position even while she tried to distance herself from him. It had been amusing for a few days, at least.

Then he'd mentioned to Seaforth that he was considering going to Shadowcross and remaining there indefinitely. The very next day, both

Cordelia and Penelope had descended on him, insisting that he remain in London, as going to the country would only increase speculation.

None of his friends had ever asked if Mayfield's story about his quarrel with Leander was true or whether Julien had any idea what had happened to Tobias Norville. Either they believed in him wholeheartedly or they simply didn't want to know the answers. Julien hoped it was the former, but was beginning to dread it was actually the latter.

Whatever else they thought, Cordelia and Penelope had decided that in order to dispel the rumors, Julien needed to appear in Society regularly instead of hiding away as if he'd done something wrong.

Which was why he currently found himself at Lady Rockingham's ball. He'd had his choice of soirees to attend, as always. A little thing like suspicion of murder wasn't enough to keep him off the best guest lists; in fact, it only increased his cachet, making his presence a coup for any hostess. Julien had finally agreed to attend Lady Rockingham's ball because she was one of the few hostesses not motivated by the desire for notoriety—at least not entirely.

At one time he might have amused himself by striking up conversations with the most sanctimonious gossips, watching them squirm while he made roundabout threats, but he couldn't see the humor in this situation, not when Leander was still missing. The more time passed without a word from Leander, the more Julien regretted the demands he'd made that last morning.

For all he knew, Lord P was correct in his wager and Leander had left London to get away from him. Now that Leander had a fortune, most of the troubles that had plagued him in America no longer existed. Leander might prefer the solid ground of the farmland he'd known all his life to the treacherous waters of London Society.

Then there was the fact that the night before their quarrel had been Leander's first time. Although Julien didn't recall seeing any signs of discomfort the next morning, he had been too angry to truly notice. The thought that he might have hurt Leander only tightened the knot in Julien's stomach. He had *known* Leander was ill that night, despite the younger man's insistence to the contrary. He should have simply seen to it that Leander arrived at his own home safely. If he had, then perhaps none of this would have happened. But no, he had only been concerned

with satisfying his own lusts. Tobias might not be entirely his fault, but Leander was.

"You look dreadfully bored, Blackstone. Why don't we go in and have a hand or two of commerce?"

"Did your sister send you over to speak to me?" Julien asked, knowing Archer was one of the few people present who actually *would* talk to him voluntarily.

"She did not. You're in a cheerful mood this evening."

"It wasn't my decision to attend, as you must well know."

"The evening will pass more quickly over a game of cards," Archer pointed out.

"Is there a difference between enduring stares in the card room or out here?"

Archer didn't hesitate. "In there you'll have to concentrate on your cards or I'll win a packet off you."

Julien smiled reluctantly. Archer was nothing if not tenacious, but with a sister like Penelope, that was probably to be expected. Before he could agree, however, a shrill voice sounded from his right.

"New prey already, Blackstone? I suppose my brother should be grateful you waited so long after finishing with him before you went after poor Dearborne."

"Miss Norville." Archer was quick to jump in, likely hoping to prevent the inevitable scene. "I can assure that Blackstone is not—"

"I can assure *you*, Lord Archer, that I am quite familiar with the manner in which Blackstone operates."

"Lavinia," Julien said firmly. "This is not the time or place to have this discussion."

Lavinia's pretty face was now set in bitter lines. "No doubt you'd prefer never to have it."

All conversation around them had ceased, which was likely what prompted Archer to sacrifice himself. "Miss Norville, would you be so kind as to honor me with a dance?"

At one time, Lavinia would have been thrilled to dance with the son of a marquis—even a younger son—but now the invitation barely gave her pause. "You are most generous to try to help Blackstone, Lord Archer, but he is not deserving of it."

Julien lowered his voice to a deliberately threatening tone he hadn't been inclined to use for months. "Lavinia, cease this at once. Think of your father."

Wariness flashed across Lavinia's features, but was gone in the next instant. "Nothing could be worse for father than losing Tobias was."

"Do you truly want to discuss what happened to Tobias?"

"Then you admit you know!" Lavinia exclaimed triumphantly.

Julien cursed himself for allowing her to lead him into a verbal trap. By now people were openly hanging on every word of their conversation. Julien was tempted to blurt out the entire story, but Lavinia only knew half of it and would likely deny the rest. There was no guarantee people would believe the truth over Lavinia's version, and it would only cause more pain and humiliation to Sir Francis. "I admit nothing."

Cordelia saw disaster looming and made her way through the crowd. "Miss Norville, what a lovely surprise." Her voice was pleasant, but no one could miss the icy undertone. "I don't recall seeing you on the guest list."

Lavinia glanced around, realizing the tables were about to turn on her. "I arrived with friends."

"Is that so? I'd love to meet them, dear."

Now Lavinia was looking decidedly uneasy. No one in the crowd stepped forward to identify themselves as her escort. No doubt they were well aware that they would be stricken from any future guest lists that Lady Carysfort and Lady Rockingham had the ability to influence, and their influence was considerable.

Julien knew that Cordelia was only trying to protect him, but if he was going to hide, he preferred to do so behind the walls of his home and not his aunt's skirts.

This was a bad idea from the start and he never should have agreed to it. Fortunately, it was fairly simple to correct his mistake. Without another word to anyone, he stalked across the ballroom and toward the front door. The crowd parted before him as if by magic.

Once outside, he quickly found his coach, glad he'd insisted on arriving in his own equipage. "Home," he said shortly, climbing inside. He didn't know if his aunt or friends had followed him out of the house and didn't look back to find out.

JULIEN had to fight not to squirm like a nine-year-old child. He'd always thought nothing could make him more uncomfortable than one of his aunt's guilt-inducing lectures, but an apologetic and concerned Cordelia was ten times worse.

"I never should have nagged you to go," she said for the fifth time. "Neither Lady Rockingham or I had any idea that Lavinia Norville would have the nerve to—"

"I know, Aunt," Julien assured her.

"When I discover who had the bad taste to bring her, I'll—"

"That seems unlikely."

Cordelia sighed. "Oh, Julien, if I'd had any notion how upset you were about Dearborne, I never would have—"

"I beg your pardon?"

"You've been very different since we heard about his disappearance. Not yourself at all."

"What are you suggesting?" Julien asked, and then braced himself.

"I knew you were fond of Dearborne," she said, patting his hand. "But I didn't realize how fond."

Relieved though he was, part of Julien almost wished that Cordelia had been referring to suspicion. That might have been easier to endure.

"I beg your pardon, my lord." Julien was so grateful to Hudson for

the interruption that he vowed to give the butler a bonus, then changed his mind when he heard the man's next words. "Lord Seaforth and Lady Penelope are here to see you."

Good God. Julien prayed Penelope was here to give some of her tart opinions about his actions at the ball. Anything but more sympathy. "Show them in, Hudson."

Julien rose when the couple entered, Penelope rushing in ahead of her fiancé. "Julien, we have the most—oh, Lady Carysfort. I'm so glad to see you here as well."

Cordelia rose when she saw how excited Penelope was. "What is it, my dear?"

"Dearborne has returned."

If he were the romantic sort, Julien would have attributed the sudden brightening of the room to her statement. Being a man of logic, however, he knew it was simply that the surprise of her news had made him more alert. "How do you know?" he asked when he regained the ability to speak.

"We saw a coach outside his house when we passed. Footmen were carrying trunks in. I wanted to call on him at once, but—"

"But I managed to convince her to tell you first," Seaforth finished.

"Seaforth's coach is waiting outside. We could leave at once."

"I see no reason to rush." Now that he knew Leander was safe at home, Julien's annoyance with the American returned, sharper than ever.

"Julien, don't be ridiculous." Cordelia took his hand and tugged him along. "We'd be happy to ride with you and Lord Seaforth, thank you."

The short ride to Leander's home was passed in a lively discussion about who should call. Penelope saw no reason why they shouldn't all go to the door, but Cordelia was adamant that only she and Julien go in—at least initially. Cordelia won, in the end. Even Penelope didn't have a chance when Cordelia's mind was made up.

Julien handed her down from the coach and then followed her up the steps to Leander's door. She knocked sharply and when the butler answered, said, "Lord Blackstone and Lady Carysfort to see Lord

Dearborne."

Powell, strangely enough, looked flustered. "Lady Carysfort, Lord Blackstone.... I... that is...."

"Is the earl at home or not?" Cordelia frowned.

"He is, but—"

"Who is it, Powell?" asked a decidedly American voice.

For a split second Julien thought the young man who appeared was Leander. Although there was a strong resemblance, this man was taller and had an almost rakish appearance.

"The Earl of Blackstone and Viscountess Carysfort to see Lord Dearborne, sir," Powell managed.

Sharp blue eyes, several shades darker than Leander's, flicked over them. "I'll get Kit. I'm sure he'll want to speak to them."

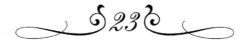

$\mathcal{K}$it," Julien said blankly, staring at the man who came to the door. The resemblance between all three brothers was strong, with Kit's features being slightly more patrician.

"I have proof of my identity," he replied mildly, as if he'd been asked before.

Julien was unable to reply, but Cordelia managed to speak as if there was nothing unusual about the situation. "Completely unnecessary. You are quite the image of your father and grandfather."

"You knew my father?" Kit looked surprised.

"Only a little. His cousin, the daughter of the late earl, was married to my brother."

Kit nodded slowly. "And you are…?"

"The Viscountess Carysfort. This is my nephew, the Earl of Blackstone."

Something flickered across the strong, even features, but it was gone too quickly to identify. "This is my brother, Chauncey Mayfield."

"Chance Mayfield," Chance corrected at once.

From what little he'd heard about the second Mayfield brother, Julien wasn't terribly surprised by his preferred moniker.

"Please come in." Kit gestured toward the drawing room. "I apologize for the mess," he added, nodding toward the trunks and boxes littering the foyer. "We only arrived last night and the majority of our things were delivered this morning."

Julien didn't move from the doorway, and noticed Cordelia hadn't, either. "We've no wish to impose." He wanted to get out of the house immediately and digest this unbelievable turn of events.

"In truth," Cordelia explained, "we called because we thought

Dearborne had returned. I beg your pardon, I mean Mr. Mayfield," she corrected, then looked in Chance's direction and added, "Mr. Leander Mayfield."

"You know Lee?" Kit asked, his tone unusually casual.

"Yes. He's an excellent young man." Cordelia smiled. "We haven't seen for some weeks and were beginning to worry."

"We were surprised that he was not here when we arrived," Kit admitted.

"But we'll track him down soon enough," Chance said firmly.

To Julien the words sounded ominous. He looked at Chance only to find the dark blue eyes fastened on him with some enmity.

"We'll be on our way, then," Cordelia said. "I hope we will see you again once Mr. Mayfield has returned."

"Yes, I'm sure my wife will look forward to meeting you, Lady Carysfort," Kit said, either not noticing or ignoring the sharp look Chance gave him.

"Lady Dearborne?" Cordelia smiled cheerfully. "I will be very happy to meet her."

Julien could tell how flustered his aunt was, but doubted anyone else could. She had failed to notice the way Kit—Julien couldn't think of him as *Dearborne*—had deliberately left his name out of the future meeting.

While they were saying their goodbyes, Cordelia took his arm and even leaned on him slightly as he escorted her out of the house and helped her into the coach. Julien told the driver to return to his house and could hear Seaforth and Penelope bombarding Cordelia with questions.

"Julien, what in God's name is happening?" Seaforth demanded the moment Julien was inside. He glanced at Penelope, who was patting Cordelia's hand in an effort to calm the older woman. "What's all this about Dearborne not being Dearborne? Not being the earl?"

"It's true," Julien said, keeping his voice cool in an effort to hide the turmoil of his own thoughts. "His eldest brother is the Earl of Dearborne."

"I can't believe he would tell such a lie." Cordelia was quite upset.

"He didn't," Julien assured her. "Dearborne's—that is, Leander's, two older brothers were lost at sea, so he thought. They had been gone for over a year before he learned of the earldom." Julien believed that. No one seeing Leander's grief could have possibly thought otherwise.

"Do they know where Dearb—where Mr. Mayfield is?" Penelope asked.

"They do not," Cordelia said.

"Surely once he hears his brothers are in London he'll return at once," Penelope said with a game attempt at certainty.

MORLEIGH MAYFIELD glared at the slim form lying still on the low bed. *Damnable, troublesome Americans!* He'd waited patiently for years to inherit the Dearborne title and fortune, only to have some colonial come along and claim it. From the moment he'd met the young man at the docks, he'd been planning to reclaim what was rightfully his.

That wasn't entirely true. When he first set eyes on Leander Mayfield, looking so lost and helpless, he'd forgotten about the Dearborne fortune and instead began considering other possibilities for such a handsome young man. Leander was a little older than Morleigh usually liked his partners, but his beauty more than made up for that. He changed his plans with the intention of wringing every bit of pleasure he could get from the pretty interloper before finishing him. Leander's reclusive nature certainly helped. He was reluctant to venture into Society, and therefore Society would barely notice that there had ever been an American heir to the earldom.

Unfortunately, the meddlesome Lady Carysfort decided to take an interest in the colonial and before long her sodomite nephew did the same. Morleigh could hardly blame Blackstone for having the same designs on the pretty American that he'd had, but it did make things more difficult—especially when Leander seemed to return his interest. When he first saw Blackstone speaking to Leander at the theater, Morleigh arranged to end Leander's life that very night. His attempt had been too hurried, and clumsy at best; he knew that now. He'd sent Leander's coach home, intending the young earl to take a hackney,

which could be waylaid. Leander had actually played right into his hands, wandering off onto the darker streets and making the job much easier for the London cutthroat he'd hired during the performance.

Blackstone, damn him, had been riding by just in time to save the colonial, ruining Morleigh's plan and cementing an attachment between he and Leander. By taking Leander under his wing—and into his bed, of that Morleigh had no doubt—Blackstone made it impossible for the American Earl to simply disappear without questions arising. Morleigh's second attempt—planned when his spy told him Leander was attending a house party at Shadowcross Manor—had been better thought out, but still not successful. It had only resulted in Leander taking a fall from his horse, not any permanent injuries.

After that, Morleigh began to plan more carefully, and realized he might be able to use the attachment between Blackstone and the colonial to his advantage. He didn't know what had happened that last morning when he called on Leander, but the young man had been visibly upset about something and was quick to agree when Morleigh suggested that they travel to Afton Manor. Still suffering from his injured ribs and the chill he'd caught days before, Leander had been no match for the antimony mixture Morleigh put in his negus upon their arrival.

The apothecary who had prepared the poison had assured Morleigh that, given in small doses, the poison would mimic the symptoms of consumption. Morleigh had waited for years already, and was willing to wait another month or two for his reward. The poison, along with large doses of laudanum, kept Leander weak and feverish. Morleigh was once again tempted to amuse himself with the helpless young man, but knew that marks on the body would raise suspicion should they ever be seen, and settled for his usual fare of young men and women from London's hells.

The small staff at Afton Manor was well paid to ignore Leander's presence except for administering his "medicine." Morleigh amused himself occasionally by listening to Leander's delirious mumblings. There were numerous apologies to "Julien" and Leander often called for "Kit" or sometimes for "Chance." It was all very entertaining until he received word from his London spy that the Earl of Dearborne had returned. He'd rushed back to the city only to find two more Americans

standing in the way of *his* title. Americans who were far less malleable than Leander had been. The eldest, Christopher Mayfield, or *Kit*, as his brother and wife called him, had documents proving his identity and had already engaged an attorney to look after any problems.

It was truly fortunate that Morleigh had been so patient. It became obvious as soon as he'd met the brothers that they were determined to find their youngest sibling. It was only a matter of time before they decided to search the estates for him. The rumors were still circulating about Blackstone, but that was no guarantee that the finger would be pointed at him. With some thought, Morleigh came up with another plan—by far the best one yet—and immediately put it into action. He relayed all the gossip about Blackstone to the brothers and then returned to Afton Manor to pay off the staff and move Leander.

His man-of-affairs—who was very resourceful, even acting as his procurer when necessary—found a tiny cottage, little more than a shed, on the land bordering Blackstone's and rented it from Lord Marling. The building's cellar was perfect for his needs, with earthen walls that assured no one would hear if Leander ever summoned the strength to call for help.

"When they do find you wasted away," he said, even though he doubted Leander could hear, "it will be so close to Blackstone's land that there will be only one conclusion."

Leander moaned, but didn't move.

Perhaps he could hear after all, but that was of little matter. "Not that I truly have anything against Blackstone. He just happened to make himself very, very convenient."

Now all he had to do was wait until the time was right to finally finish the young American. A time when he could be sure all suspicion was completely focused on Blackstone. He moved closer and held up the lantern as a new thought struck him. Now that Blackstone was to be blamed, the body would not have to remain unmarked. If fact, it might be better if there was some damage done. Perhaps he would have the chance to enjoy the pretty American after all.

Perhaps not, Morleigh decided as he studied the motionless figure. It wasn't terribly entertaining unless his playmates were awake enough

to be afraid.

FOR about a week, Society busied itself with gossiping about whether Leander Mayfield—the False Earl, as he was now being called—had truly tried to steal the title from his brother and whether he'd fled to escape being exposed as an imposter.

After the ton tired of that, it was as if Leander Mayfield had never existed. Who cared about a shy, bookish American when the *true* Earl of Dearborne was handsome, had beautiful manners, and was willing to attend far more balls and assemblies? The mamas with eligible daughters were disappointed to find he was already married, but the rest of Society was more than satisfied by the extraordinarily beautiful Countess of Dearborne. There was almost no discussion about her character, but character was of little matter if one possessed an abundance of golden curls, thickly lashed turquoise eyes, and perfect cupid's-bow lips. When it became known that the Countess usually went by "Daisy" instead of Margaret, everyone began referring to her as the "American Flower" and making all manner of floral references to describe her beauty.

And then there was Chance. Although the ton normally wouldn't concern itself with an untitled American, Chance Mayfield was the brother of an earl, ridiculously handsome, impressively dashing, extremely charming, and had an exciting story about being lost at sea to his credit. Mothers could warn their daughters away as much as they liked, but to no avail. Women, both young and old, constantly tried to catch his eye. Chance seemed to enjoy the attention, but spent the majority of his time in the company of Morleigh Mayfield.

Whereas Kit's main purpose in moving through Society seemed to be finding his youngest brother, Chance only seemed interested in having a good time and indulging his every whim, at least as far as Julien had been able to observe.

Julien couldn't help wondering if gossip about he and Leander had reached Kit's ears, and was constantly on guard for a confrontation, but none developed. It was strange and a bit unnerving, because even if Kit hadn't been told about the nature of Julien's relationship with Leander,

he surely would have heard that they were acquainted, and that Leander had attended a house party at Shadowcross Manor. Perhaps Kit, like so many others, suspected him, in which case he might expect a challenge any day now. Whenever they happened to be at the same function, Kit completely ignored him and Julien was sure that if he made any attempt at conversation, he would receive a cut direct. Still, Julien felt no animosity toward the new earl; he couldn't when the man was so obviously determined to find Leander.

That was more than anyone could say for Chance, who, like the rest of the ton, seemed to have forgotten Leander ever existed. In addition to disgust, Julien felt strangely disappointed by that. From what Leander had said about Chance, Julien had pictured a slightly wilder brother, but he'd assumed Chance would have the same core of strength and integrity he'd seen in Leander and that he'd sensed in Kit from their first meeting. Instead, he'd already heard plenty of rumors about Chance visiting all manner of gambling dens and brothels before moving on to some of the worst hells in the city. The fact that he constantly did so in the company of Morleigh Mayfield made Julien wonder if the middle brother might share some of his cousin's cruel tastes.

It was really none of his concern, though. Julien only wanted to find Leander alive and well. Never for a moment did he believe that Leander had disappeared to avoid seeing his brothers, although he suspected even Seaforth and Penelope were beginning to have their doubts. Julien was certain that if Leander knew Kit, Chance, and Margaret were in London, he would move heaven and earth to return. The fact that he hadn't boded ill. Thus far, Julien had exhausted every lead he could think of in his search, but still continued to seek out new answers and was certain Kit was doing the same. That was the only thing that mattered. If Chance Mayfield decided to drink himself to death or catch the pox, Julien could have cared less.

"My lord, there is a Mr. Gibson here to see you." The butler's voice held a note of disapproval that caught Julien's attention.

"I don't know anyone by that name," Julien said, annoyed to have his brooding interrupted. "Send him away."

"Yes, my lord." Hudson retreated again, leaving Julien alone with his thoughts and his brandy.

Julien set the glass aside. It was rather early in the day to be drinking. If Cordelia called to check on his well-being—something she was doing very often of late—he'd receive yet another lecture.

"I beg your pardon, my lord," Hudson returned. "But Mr. Gibson asked me to inform you that he was the Earl of Dearborne's—that is, Mr. Leander Mayfield's—valet. He says he has information for you."

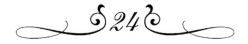

*J*ulien was on his feet immediately. "Show him in." While he waited, he tried to recall what Leander's valet looked like, but without success.

"Mr. John Gibson, my lord." Hudson ushered in a man who was vaguely familiar, but who looked far too unkempt and seedy to be the valet of an earl.

"Thank you, Hudson." When the butler left, closing the door behind him, Julien turned toward Gibson, who stood with his hat in his hands, looking miserable. "What is it, Gibson? You told my butler you have information for me."

"Lord Blackstone, I came to you, m'lord, because… because I know what went on… between you and Lord Dearborne."

Julien gritted his teeth. "If you've come here thinking to bleed me for money, I—"

"No! No, m'lord." Gibson ducked his head. "I've already had money for what I've done, damn every farthing of it."

"What have you done?" Julien demanded.

"I was paid, m'lord, to keep account and report his lordship's whereabouts at all times."

It took a moment for Julien to find his voice. "By whom?"

"By Mr. Morleigh Mayfield, sir."

What had been merely a suspicion was now a certainty, but Julien only felt worse for it. "When did he begin paying you?"

"He engaged me days before his lordship arrived in London. I was to watch his lordship until—"

"Was Mayfield at Shadowcross Manor when Dearborne visited?"

"He stayed at an inn in the village."

"And you informed him when Dearborne and I toured my estate."

"I did, sir." Gibson's head hung down.

That explained the poacher, although it was doubtful Morleigh did the shooting himself. More likely he'd hired someone to do the dirty work for him. "He wanted the title." Julien nearly choked on the words as despair overtook him. If that was the case, then Leander was likely dead already. He looked at the valet and his fury began to build. "And he paid you off when the job was done."

"He paid me when his lordship arrived at Afton Manor."

"I happen to know Lord Dearborne never arrived at Afton Manor," Julien snarled. "What the devil do you mean by coming here with this now?"

"Please, m'lord!" Gibson's hat was twisted beyond repair. "It was all well and good when I thought his lordship was like any other swell; makes no difference to me who has a title. But his lordship, he wasn't like any of the fancy I've met. Not him likin' the lads—he wouldn't be the first like that—but the way he spoke to us what was in service. He even knew the names of the scullery maids. He was a good soul, and I didn't want to spy, but Morleigh Mayfield is not the sort to cross."

Julien's throat tightened when Gibson spoke of Leander. How very like the young American to know the names of his entire staff, even those he wasn't supposed to acknowledge existed.

"I thought his lordship was done for sure when I left Afton Manor," Gibson continued. "I ain't thought of nothing since—been fairly sick with it. But yesterday I met up with Clifton. He was the butler what Mayfield hired at Afton Manor. Mayfield paid them off just after them other Americans got to London. That's when he took his lordship away."

"Took him away? He's alive?" Julien wanted to shake the skinny man until the truth fell out of him. Why hadn't he said so in the first place? "Dearborne is alive?"

"He was then, Clifton said, but very ill."

"Where did Mayfield take him?"

"Clifton didn't say, sir."

"I will call for my coach. You will take me to this Clifton at once." Julien reached for the bellpull only to be stopped by Gibson's words.

"He's off to Scotland, m'lord. All the staff was to travel to Scotland when Mayfield discharged them. Paid extra for that, he did. I'm supposed to be there as well."

Julien decided he needed to speak to Kit at once, preferably without Chance being present. He didn't trust anyone who spent so much time with Morleigh Mayfield and certainly didn't want Mayfield to get wind of his suspicions. "You have lodgings in Town?"

"At a lodging house. Busby Street, near St. Matthew's in Bethnal Green."

"Go," Julien ordered, drawing the bellpull. "Stay there until I come for you. Do you need funds?"

"No. I don't want anything."

"Very well. Hudson," Julien said when the butler entered. "Please show Mr. Gibson out and have my horse saddled."

"At once, my lord." Hudson stood aside to let Gibson pass.

Julien tossed back the rest of his brandy and tried to slow his racing thoughts. What he wanted to do was search the city until he found Mayfield and then twist the man's expensive linen cravat until he choked out the truth about Leander. What he *did* do was walk calmly upstairs to change clothes and plan what he was going to say to Kit.

"PLEASE inform the Earl of Dearborne that the Earl of Blackstone is here and it is imperative I speak to him at once."

Powell broke custom by opening the door fully and allowing Julien to enter. "I shall tell Lord Dearborne you're here, sir."

Julien took some solace in the butler's actions. Either Kit finally wanted to see him and had told Powell to admit him if he called, or at the very least, Powell believed he wanted to help Leander and based his

actions on that. Julien never thought he'd concern himself with any servant's opinion of him. Leander's influence, no doubt.

Moments later, Powell reappeared. "This way, please, my lord."

The butler led him into the drawing room where Kit was standing by the mantel. In contrast to Leander's face, Kit's was set in stoic, solemn lines that revealed nothing.

"Dearborne." Julien didn't bother with the formality of bowing.

"Blackstone. What brings you to my door today?" If Leander had often seemed younger than his twenty-two years, Kit seemed much older than his twenty-seven.

"I have some information about Leander that is very important."

A muscle in Kit's jaw worked and Julien realized belatedly that he'd called Leander by his given name. "What is it?" Kit's words sounded as though they came through gritted teeth.

"His valet, John Gibson, called on me a short while ago."

"Lee's valet?" Kit repeated with a slight frown.

"He was hired by Morleigh Mayfield to spy on Lea—your brother. Mayfield wanted him out of the way in order to inherit. According to Gibson, Leander was alive when you and your brother Chance arrived in London and Mayfield moved him after that."

"Why would Lee's valet go to you with this?" Kit demanded.

Julien knew he had to tread carefully here. "He knew—he'd accompanied your brother to a house party I gave."

"And where was he when Leander disappeared?"

"He didn't say. Only that Mayfield paid him off immediately after."

"More likely sent him packing after Lee went missing," Kit replied. "This Gibson's story sounds rather farfetched. Most likely it is the lie of an employee unhappy to have been sacked."

It hadn't occurred to Julien that Kit wouldn't believe him. "I'm certain Gibson is sincere. Most of the facts support what he is saying."

"Or he adapted his story to suit what he knew. You are accusing my

cousin of murder."

Julien was amazed that Mayfield had made a good enough impression for Kit to defend him. "I urge you to learn more about Mayfield."

"I know all I need to about Morleigh. He has been kind enough to show Chance around London and Chance speaks very well of him."

No doubt. "Your brother is mistaken."

Kit's posture stiffened. "Am I to take your word over that of my brother?"

"If you look closely at his activities, you will find they are not very… wholesome."

"That's an odd accusation coming from you."

It took all of Julien's control not to flinch at the icy tone. "It is no secret that Mayfield fully expected to inherit until the discovery of Leander's existence."

"That is no longer a possibility."

"No. Should anything happened to you, Chance would inherit," Julien said, a little more harshly than he'd intended.

Kit's voice lowered dangerously. "Now you accuse my brother of wanting me dead?"

Julien shifted uncomfortably, something else he rarely did. "No, of course not, but Mayfield is not above using someone to further his means. If your brother is unfamiliar with—"

"Now you claim my brother is too foolish to know if he's being manipulated?"

"No." Julien hoped to dig himself out of the mess he was creating. "I just—"

"Since arriving in London, I've heard your name in connection with Leander's far more than I would like and in ways I find disturbing." Kit's lip curled slightly as he spoke. "Now you come to me with a tale told by a servant who was sacked accusing my cousin and my *brother* of wanting to kill me and Leander in order to inherit a title."

This was going much worse than Julien had ever imagined. "My only concern is Leander's well-being," he said, drawing on every bit of dignity in his possession. "I assure you that I want to find Leander as much as—"

"*Stop.*" Kit's seething voice held such a note of command that Julien, who was not accustomed to following anyone's orders, fell silent immediately. "Stop referring to my brother in such a familiar manner before I lose my temper." Although his expression could have been carved from stone, there was a fury in Kit's eyes that promised violence.

Julien found the man's protectiveness of his brothers admirable— even if one brother wasn't deserving of it—but he knew it wouldn't be wise to say so aloud. He would have to find some way to pursue the matter on his own, but had no intention of saying *that*, either. "Obviously we have nothing more to discuss," he said, and his voice was as even and detached as if he'd been discussing the weather. "I'll be on my way."

Kit didn't deign to reply.

Julien left without waiting for Powell to show him out. As he rode home, he shook off the unsettling meeting. He couldn't recall the last time anyone had managed to rattle him the way Kit Mayfield had.

If he had to proceed on his own, so be it.

The door that connected the drawing room to a smaller sitting room opened, making Kit turn. "You heard?"

"I heard." Chance scowled, folding his arms in front of his chest as he leaned against the jamb. "I don't like him."

"Perhaps Morleigh needs to know about this."

Chance nodded. "I'll tell him."

JULIEN tried to find a comfortable position on the poorly padded seat in the coach he'd hired. He'd arrived home the previous night only to be reminded by Kay that he was bidden to his aunt's for dinner. Had it been

anyone else, Julien would have cried off, but he knew that Cordelia would come to fetch him herself if he did. He'd had the time to summon his man-of-affairs and give him orders to learn about any holdings Mayfield had, beginning in London and moving outward.

Cordelia, no doubt trying to help take his mind off Leander, had also invited Seaforth, Penelope, and Lady Rockingham. Then, just in case that wasn't enough to amuse him, she'd also invited Bertram and Augusta to annoy him. To Cordelia's credit, Augusta had been far more successful at distraction by annoying him than any of his friends and their scholarly discussions. She had been eager to regale everyone with tales of the invitations and the compliments she'd been receiving since her arrival.

Julien shifted again and then resigned himself to jolting of the ill-sprung vehicle. His coach, with its coat of arms on the door, would have been too conspicuous in Bethnal Green. Any expensive equipage would have attracted attention in the area.

Although Bethnal Green was not as dangerous as some areas of London, Julien thought it better to be cautious. He was using his own coachman and footman, but they were dressed in nondescript clothing rather than their usual livery. Julien didn't want anyone wondering what the Earl of Blackstone was doing in one of the poorest parts of the city.

The coach was unable to stop directly in front of the lodging house, which was blocked by a large wooden handcart. Julien was out of the coach before his footman could climb down and open the door for him. "Wait here for me."

"Yes, sir."

Several people were peering into the handcart and it seemed as though nearly all of the lodging house's residents were assembled in front of it. Julien saw a booted foot hanging off the end of the cart and realized it was actually an ambulance, sometimes used to transport the ill or injured, but usually reserved for moving the dead.

It was likely a fairly common sight in some parts of London, but Julien was unaccustomed to such things and he couldn't help but look inside.

The dead gaze of John Gibson stared back at him.

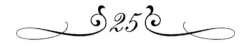

$\mathcal{F}$ive pounds likely would have been enough to satisfy the owner of Lady Perdition, but Julien paid the man ten to assure his silence. The owner didn't seem to think anything strange about Julien's request; he merely leered as if he knew what Julien was about. That puzzled Julien somewhat as he took a seat behind one of the fire screens. He would have expected such a reaction from a brothel owner, but not from the keeper of a gaming hell.

Perhaps the man had heard of the Earl of Blackstone's preference, but did he truly believe Julien got satisfaction from peeping at desperate men as they lost fortunes on the turn of a card?

Whatever the keeper thought, it was of no matter to Julien as long as it meant he was allowed to use the same concealed nooks as the hell's employees did to keep an eye on the gamblers for possible cheats. Now all he had to do was wait for Morleigh and Chance to arrive.

If they arrived at all. Julien only had the passing information that Archer had chanced to overhear about their plans for the evening. He'd decided it was better to wait on the possibility of them visiting the hell than attempt to follow the pair and risk being noticed. If not tonight, then another night and another hell, of that Julien was certain. His only worry was that Leander's time would run out before he learned anything useful.

After two hours behind the fire screen nursing the same tumbler of gin, Julien was almost ready to leave for the night when he heard the voice he'd been waiting for.

"Let's join a game of faro," Morleigh was suggesting to his companion. "You'll never learn if you don't play it."

"I hate losing," came an American voice. "I especially hate losing money."

"Nonsense," Morleigh scoffed. "A gentleman knows how to lose money gracefully. Surely your brother will cover any debts you might

incur."

"He probably would, but I'd rather not have to ask," Chance said. "I have my own money, of course, but not enough to lose so often at a game of chance."

"And here I thought you received a fortune from that ship you and your brother rescued."

There was a note of avarice in Morleigh's voice, which didn't surprise Julien in the least. His man-of-affairs had discovered that not only was Mayfield *not* renting any other properties, but he was behind on the rent for his house in Dorset Square and had several large debts with various tradesmen.

"Most of the money invested in that ship was Leander's," Chance explained. "Kit is holding it until his return."

"What if he doesn't return?"

"Then Kit will hold it for him until he is found."

"That hardly seems fair." Morleigh's tone became commiserating. "You and Christopher were the ones who risked your lives locating the ship."

There was a long silence before Chance spoke again. "That's what I told Kit. And even once Leander does get it, all he's going to do is throw it away on stacks of books."

"And if it should transpire that Leander is… has passed?" Morleigh pressed.

Chance's silence was even longer. "Kit has the Dearborne fortune, so I suppose I'd get it. Not that it does me much good now." He let out a contemptuous snort. "When he was younger, he was always on the verge of dying and now…." There was another pause, so long that Julien thought Chance might change the subject. "Now that it would actually be useful to someone, he's disappeared instead."

Julien's grip tightened until the tumbler in his hand threatened to crack. It took all of his restraint not to knock over the fire screen and go for Chance's throat. Instead he had to wait more than an hour, listening to the pair discuss various people in Society. Julien paid attention just in

case he was one of the names mentioned, but the conversation remained limited to which men in the ton were the easiest to beat at cards and which women were the easiest to coax into bed.

Then Morleigh suggested that if Chance was not in the mood for cards, there were other amusements they could indulge in. He named one of the most notorious hells in the city, insisting that Chance would enjoy himself there.

Finally they left, and Julien was able to leave Lady Perdition and find a hackney to take him home. Although he'd gained new information about both men, none of it was particularly helpful to finding Leander. Even worse, most of the information boded very ill for Leander's survival.

If Leander was to have any hope at all, Julien knew he needed to keep a closer, constant watch on both Morleigh and Chance.

"COFFEE," was all Chance Mayfield said as he strode past Powell without pausing to give the man his hat or gloves. "Strong, strong coffee."

"Yes, sir." Powell barely had time to answer before the sitting room door closed.

Chance paced the length of his room, tossing his hat onto a delicately carved chair, his coat onto the silk-covered settee, and his gloves on a table intricately inlaid with a marble mosaic. At one time any single piece of such elegant furniture would have given him pause, but now he barely noticed it.

He thought about pouring himself a glass of brandy, but decided to wait for the coffee instead. By no means was he a teetotaler, but the last thing he wanted now was more drink to remind him of the evening's activities. He had shrugged out of his frockcoat and was unfastening his cravat when Kit walked in, also without a topcoat or cravat and with a book under his arm. The door had barely closed behind him before opening again to admit Daisy, who was in her dressing gown. Kit looked at his wife in surprise.

To Chance the situation was so obvious he didn't even need to comment on it. Kit had spent the night waiting for him, most likely in the library with the books Leander had purchased and had insisted Daisy go upstairs to get some sleep. Daisy would have humored her husband by going upstairs, but had been waiting up as well, listening for the sound of the front door.

"Well?" was all Daisy said. Chance merely looked at her without replying.

"It's nearly four in the morning," Kit pointed out. "Where have you been?"

"Trust me when I say you don't want to know."

Powell walked in at that moment, saving Chance from having to explain any further.

Kit frowned as the butler set the tray of coffee down. "Powell, I thought I told you to get some sleep."

"You did, my lord. And I have." Powell bowed and left the room.

Chance immediately poured himself a cup of coffee, inhaling deeply to dispel the scents of sweat and smoke and terror from his nostrils.

"Have you found out where Lee is?" Kit asked.

Chance was tired, and such a ridiculous question only irritated him further. "If I knew where Lee was, do you think I'd be here without him? Do you think I'd have let that evil bastard—beg pardon, Daisy—go home to a comfortable bed? I'd have beaten him into the ground."

"You learned nothing helpful then?" As always, Kit ignored most of Chance's ire and got right to the heart of the matter.

"I'm almost certain that Lee is still alive," Chance said, calming somewhat after a large swallow of coffee. "Why Morleigh is keeping him alive is beyond me." That was an outright lie. After seeing what Morleigh considered entertainment, he had some idea of why the man might keep Leander alive, but he couldn't bear to dwell on that possibility for too long.

"Well, I don't know that it matters *why* he's kept alive," Kit said, absently taking the cup of coffee Daisy handed him. "So long as he is."

"It might have something to do with money," Chance added, hoping what he said was true. "Nearly everything that damnable—beg pardon, Daisy—snake does seems to have something to do with money. Tonight he kept asking me about Lee's money from the ship, about what would happen to the money if Lee was never found, or if he was dead."

"What did you tell him?"

"That you were holding it for him until he was found, and that if he died the money would probably come to me."

"Are you out of your mind?" Kit's voice rose. "What are you thinking?! Leander is as good as dead."

"He believes that if Leander dies, *I* get the money. For all that he's being friendly to me, he doesn't want that. Not when there's a chance he can get *his* hands on it."

"But he hasn't said that he knows where Lee is."

"Not yet, but he's stopped claiming that Blackstone had anything to do with Lee's disappearance." Chance's lip curled. "He's becoming more assured of my intentions. It shouldn't be too much longer before he's convinced he can confide in me." Especially not after the places they'd gone tonight. Although he hadn't had to participate in any of Morleigh's games, it had been all Chance could do not to let his horror show when he'd realized what Morleigh had planned for the terrified girl he'd rented. Every instinct had screamed at him to put a stop to it, but he'd done his damnedest to appear intrigued, telling himself the entire time that gaining Morleigh's trust was the only chance to find his brother. It was a choice that he knew would haunt him the rest of his days, but that didn't deter him from his course.

"Have you encountered Blackstone at all?" Kit asked.

"No. For all his warnings to you, he hasn't been around. So much for any real concern he had for Lee."

"Are you convinced Blackstone is not involved in Lee's disappearance?" Kit persisted.

"Yes. Aren't you?"

"I don't like the man."

"Neither do I," Chance admitted. "For all that he claimed to be worried about Lee, he seems to have forgotten about him quickly enough."

"That's for the best," Kit said.

"You'd have no complaint about him if Blackstone's name hadn't been linked to Leander's the way it was." Daisy frowned at her husband. "If not for that, you'd think his interest in Lee's well-being very admirable."

Chance looked at Kit's clenched jaw and wondered if Daisy wasn't right. He had heard whispers about such men while in college—they both had—but had never thought much about it before. He didn't want to think about it now, either, and certainly not in regards to his younger brother. Since he'd begun moving through London's underground with Morleigh Mayfield, however, he'd seen things much worse than two men together. Suddenly, a very repugnant thought occurred to him. "You don't think… what with Morleigh and I being in each other's company nearly all the time… that people might think he and I are…."

"That's hardly important now." Kit scowled.

"I doubt it," Daisy tried to reassure him. "From what I've heard, Blackstone never made a secret of… of his… well," her face flushed. "That's why there's all the talk about he and Leander."

"All the better for Blackstone to keep his distance from Lee after we find him."

For a moment, Chance considered asking Kit what he would do if it turned out that Leander was similarly inclined, but remained silent. As long as Lee was alive, Chance was certain he could bear anything else and he hoped Kit felt the same. There'd be enough time to deal with that after they'd got Lee back.

"How much longer do you think it will take before Morleigh trusts you enough to tell you about Leander?" Daisy asked.

"Not much longer. Telling him about John Gibson went a long way toward convincing him." Chance wasn't about to tell them that when he'd told Morleigh, he'd made certain to imply that he knew Gibson had something to do with Leander's disappearance, something that had gone

even further toward convincing the man. Unlike the girl in the brothel, Chance had no guilt for what happened to Gibson. The valet had betrayed Leander and only tried to help after the fact. Kit was already worried about this plan and if he knew how far Chance was going to win Morleigh's trust, he'd call the whole thing off. "If I keep talking the way I have been about Lee, and especially about the money, he'll come around."

"I hope so." Daisy sighed. "It would be awful if we got Leander back only to lose you."

Chance gave her his best smile, one that had gotten him out of trouble with his professors and had gotten many a young lady in trouble with her parents. "Don't worry about me. I know enough to keep an eye on Morleigh."

Daisy, however, had known him since they both were ten and was as immune as Chance's brothers to that smile. "I'm not talking about Morleigh himself. I'm talking about the things you must have to do to make him believe you."

Chance now felt Kit's eyes on him as well, his older brother's attention finally diverted from Leander. Not for the first time, Chance wished that Daisy wasn't *quite* so clever.

"Chance?" Kit's voice held a new note of concern.

"Don't worry about me," Chance said again, more firmly. "You said yourself; finding Lee is more important than anything else."

"Chance—"

"It's nothing I can't handle," Chance said, and hoped he was telling the truth.

THE door closed, leaving him in darkness again. It was the only indication he had as to how much time had passed and it was a poor indicator at best. A man—someone who worked for Morleigh Mayfield, no doubt—would come in to force broth or gruel down his throat before leaving again. He didn't know how often it was happening, but it was at

least often enough to keep him alive. Sometimes, times like now, when his feverish mind cleared enough for him to follow a thought, he would wonder why Morleigh was trying to keep him alive at all. Was the man hoping the illness would finish him off?

If he was, then he was going to be disappointed. Leander had spent his entire childhood and much of his adulthood hanging on between life and death. This situation was hardly new or frightening for him. He knew how to hold off the Grim Reaper—how to avoid the clutches of those bony hands—indefinitely.

The Valley of the Shadow didn't fill him with the despair it might have someone else in his circumstances, which only hastened their demise. To Leander, that Valley was as familiar as his tiny bedroom in Pelham. A year ago, he might have been tempted to travel through the Valley to meet his parents and brothers again, but now he dug in his heels with all the strength he had left. More than anything, he wanted to see Julien again. He wanted to be with Julien again, but would settle for the chance to apologize for not believing his warning about Morleigh.

It made Leander heartsick whenever he thought about it, so he didn't think about it often.

At the moment he didn't have the strength to lift his head. Not that it mattered; he was surrounded by impenetrable darkness that was only broken by weak lantern light whenever the man fed him. The scent of earthen walls told Leander all he needed to know about his surroundings, in any case: he was underground.

That might have pushed some people even closer to despair and death, but Leander made himself think of their cellar on the farm, which had never frightened him.

It was all he could do to keep awake, so he dug his heels even deeper, hoping it would be enough to anchor himself when he drifted off to sleep again.

26

"Why don't you come out to Seabrooke for a while?" Seaforth asked as he took a chair across from Julien.

"I was under the impression that your fiancée and my aunt had decided that I should remain in London." Julien glanced at the clock. There were still several hours before he had to meet Tooley and Beeton. "I thought my leaving London would bring too much speculation, that I was to continue appearing in Society as if nothing unusual had happened."

Seaforth looked exasperated, which hardly surprised Julien, since he'd been expertly avoiding any real conversation with his friend. "You know as well as I do that the gossip about young Mayfield has all but ceased since the arrival of his brothers."

Julien kept his expression neutral despite the surge of anger that went through him. "I'm well aware of that."

"So the reasons for you to remain in London are no more. Even if they weren't, you only appear briefly at a single ball a night and not even those we usually attend."

Julien remained silent, not wanting to discuss the reasons for his recent actions.

"You need a change of air and scenery," Seaforth continued. "Penelope and Lady Carysfort are becoming quite concerned."

And this is becoming quite tiresome, Julien wanted to say. While he didn't like worrying his aunt or Penelope, at the moment he had more important things on his mind. "There's no need."

"I must say, I'm becoming concerned as well."

That got Julien's full attention. If Seaforth had ever been concerned about his activities, he'd never shown any sign of it before, let alone spoken of it aloud.

"The places you've been frequenting lately… you know I've never said a word about you visiting the…er, mollie-houses." Seaforth shifted in his chair. "I understand that you… well." He cleared his throat. "But the places I've heard you've been visiting lately, the hells… if it were only the gambling hells, it wouldn't be quite so bad, but some of the brothels…."

Apparently, he hadn't been as cautious as he'd thought. Julien could think of no explanation for his recent actions except the truth, and he didn't want to tell Seaforth what he was actually doing. Seaforth would either try to talk him out of it or want to help, and at the moment, Julien didn't want either. Morleigh Mayfield had proven just how dangerous he was when he killed John Gibson; the Bow Street Runners Julien had hired had learned that a man matching Morleigh's description had visited Gibson's lodging house not long before the valet's drunken fall down the stairs. Since then, Julien had managed to eavesdrop on a few more conversations between Morleigh and Chance, but had learned nothing useful about Leander. He continued to employ the Runners to follow the men, certain that at some point, one of them would lead the way to Leander. Steering Seaforth in another direction, he asked, "And what do you think visiting Seabrooke will accomplish?"

"The country air would do you some good. You haven't been looking well."

"Thank you," Julien said, letting amusement creep into his voice.

Seaforth sighed. "Julien…."

Julien automatically tensed. Despite knowing one another for years, rarely did they address each other by their Christian names. It meant Seaforth wasn't about to drop the subject.

"The attachment between you and Leander Mayfield—"

"I don't want to discuss Leander Mayfield," Julien interrupted sharply.

"It's since his disappearance that you've been acting so differently. We've all noticed it. You didn't act this way when Tobias Norville disappeared and I can't help thinking—"

"That some of the rumors may be true after all?" Julien finished for

him.

"You know better than that," Seaforth said sternly.

"You trust me, then, when I say I did no harm to either of them?"

"Good Lord, Julien!" Seaforth looked appalled. "Of course, I do."

"Then trust me when I say I know what I'm about."

Seaforth's eyes narrowed. "What *are* you about?"

"That, I can't say."

Seaforth studied him a moment more. "I hope it doesn't go on too much longer," he sighed, rising.

"So do I," Julien said sincerely, standing to bid his friend goodbye.

HIS plan was unfolding even more beautifully than he'd anticipated.

Morleigh thought he'd have to trick Chance Mayfield in order for the man to be of any help to him, but now he knew that would not be necessary. Judging by the way Chance spoke of his younger brother, there was no love lost between them, and Chance seemed especially angered that the majority of the money from their shipping venture was being held for Leander. There had to be some way to utilize that to his advantage.

Even though he would have preferred to hire someone to do the job for him, Morleigh had had to do away with John Gibson personally after Chance told him about Gibson going to Blackstone. Time had been of the essence. If Leander turned up dead now, a closer look might be taken at his valet's "accident," particularly if Blackstone started to make noise about it. Better to have someone else finish Leander for him so that even if Blackstone wasn't blamed, the death would not lead back to Morleigh Mayfield.

But who? His man-of-affairs, who was checking on Leander every few days, wasn't foolish enough to risk his own neck in such a manner. And as his employer, Morleigh knew attention would immediately focus on him. Hiring someone also meant the risk of that person giving him up

if they were caught. Trying to convince Chance to do the deed would be...

Perfect.

A whole new realm of possibilities opened up before Morleigh. Chance Mayfield might be the key, not only to finishing Leander, but also to inheriting the title and fortune that were rightfully his. So many possibilities, and all of them to his advantage.

Once Chance had Leander's blood on his hands, Morleigh would have that to hold over his head. He could threaten to go to Kit with what he knew—no, threats would likely make that hothead turn on him. He could tell Chance that Kit had found out he'd killed Leander, which would likely force Chance to rid himself of his other brother.

Morleigh would see to it that Chance hung for his crime. It would be a tragic, sordid tale that would make Morleigh, as the new Earl of Dearborne, even more sought after.

He'd have to take Chance out to the old cottage to show him where Leander was, but he also wanted to make certain he was seen in London whenever Leander was murdered. How to convince Chance to go back to do the deed alone?

Still, if he couldn't, if it came down to it, he could always claim he wasn't there, and likely find some others to create a suitable alibi for him. In many ways, Chance would prove to be an even better dupe than Blackstone would have been. After all, no one in court was going to believe a colonial over an Englishman.

WHEN the footman set the tea tray down, Julien took the pot at once. He hoped that waiting on his aunt would please her enough to distract her from the true purpose of her call, which was no doubt some sort of discussion of his current well-being. A slight arch of her eyebrows was the only indication of Cordelia's surprise as she accepted the cup.

"Thank you, Julien. I don't recall the last time you were so attentive."

Julien congratulated himself as he sat back with his own cup.

"In fact," Cordelia continued, "I don't recall you *ever* being so attentive. It makes one wonder at these sudden changes."

Damnation. He'd gone too far and aroused her suspicion. All he could do now was try to maintain his composure.

"Not to mention all the balls you've been attending lately—and without anyone prodding you to do so."

That wasn't necessarily so, but he couldn't tell her that. He'd started going to balls out of sheer necessity. The Bow Street Runners he'd hired were doing their job, but some places they simply could not follow. The glittering balls were off limits to the Runners, but were often the starting point for Chance and Morleigh's evenings of revelry. Julien would learn of their plans and then follow.

Tooley and Beeton each followed one of the men during the day. Julien had told them to especially watch Morleigh, hoping he might reveal some clue as to Leander's whereabouts. Thus far, however, nothing useful had come of it.

"I would be quite pleased by this change if not for the other new habits I've been hearing about," Cordelia said.

It seemed like ages since he'd been able to speak honestly with his aunt, when he didn't have to watch his every word for fear of revealing too much. "What new habits?"

"Don't start that with me, young man. I'll no longer tolerate it. What are you about, frequenting such places?"

"I thought that ladies didn't acknowledge *such places* even existed."

"I wish I didn't have to acknowledge them," Cordelia sniffed. "But when my nephew insists on worrying me by visiting hells nearly every night, I have no choice."

"There's nothing for you to worry about, Aunt."

"There most certainly is. You've become a completely different person since Dearborne—that is, Leander—disappeared."

Julien said nothing, as there was no way to deny Cordelia's observations.

"I can't help but think back to when Tobias Norville disappeared."

Chilled, Julien set his cup aside and stood. "Have all the rumors finally changed your mind, Aunt?"

"That's not what I meant, as you ought to know perfectly well by now," Cordelia replied, an edge to her voice. "If you would just stop being so secretive about Norville, you wouldn't have to suspect everyone of suspecting you."

There was definitely some truth to that—more than Julien cared to admit. "Is that the true reason for your visit, then? To find out what happened to Tobias Norville?"

Cordelia set her cup back in its saucer with a small crash. "No, you foolish boy! I am here because you have been behaving in a most worrisome manner. It's not just the hells that concern me; you've become thinner. You look as though you haven't slept well in weeks."

"I've been busy," Julien offered, but knew it was a weak excuse.

"So I've heard," Cordelia retorted dryly. "At places you've never been known to frequent before." Her voice softened. "Your attachment to Leander is even deeper than I originally thought, isn't it?"

Not trusting his voice, Julien kept his gaze focused on the view from his drawing room window. He heard Cordelia sigh and then the rustle of fabric as she stood.

"Julien…," she began and then let out another sigh. "I suppose I should go, then."

Julien decided things couldn't go on like this any longer. He took a deep breath. "Tobias left England by choice," he said without turning.

A heavy silence descended, broken only by Cordelia's footsteps as she moved closer to him. She didn't speak, which somehow made it easier for Julien to continue.

"Tobias wanted to keep our attachment as quiet as possible, which I understood; the consequences for him would have been more severe than for me. He got it into his head that the best way for us to continue together would be for me to marry Lavinia."

"You never intended to marry."

"No. And I certainly wasn't going to marry anyone with the intention of being unfaithful. I told Tobias so."

"What happened?" Cordelia's voice had dropped to a near-whisper.

"He refused to see me for several weeks, and then I got a note inviting me to his home. When I arrived, Tobias told me to wait upstairs in a bedchamber I *thought* was his. Instead, I found Lavinia in only her nightgown." The pain of Tobias's betrayal hadn't faded much over time—not until he met Leander. Now it was as sharp as ever. "I thought I had made a mistake until I heard Tobias berating their parlor maid for not getting a message to his father. I went back down to confront him and he admitted he'd intended his father to find Lavinia and me in a compromising position."

"He tried to *force* you to marry her?"

"I wouldn't have, of course, and I told him that. He apologized and begged for another chance. He was trying to… er… convince me when Sir Francis finally came home."

"Oh, my."

"Indeed." Julien felt a rueful smile tug at his lips. "Sir Francis didn't say a word, even after Tobias ran out of the house. I went after Tobias and found him at a house that was rented by an Italian count. I'd met the man once or twice—we had similar inclinations. And similar tastes, it seems. I went back the next morning to call and was told by the servant that the count and his companion had left for the Continent. That was the last I ever heard of Tobias."

"Oh, Julien—"

"I never spoke to Sir Francis again, but I heard he was a broken man after that."

"That wasn't your fault," Cordelia insisted. "Tobias betrayed your trust and then didn't have the courage to face his father. If anyone is to blame, he is."

Julien didn't say anything. He'd often wondered what he could have done differently, but never thought of anything he was willing to change about his actions. His real regret was trusting Tobias with his heart and ignoring the weakness of character he'd occasionally observed under the

breezy confidence Tobias had always displayed.

"And Leander?"

"I don't know what happened to him." That wasn't a lie. Not *exactly*.

"It's different with him, isn't it?"

"Yes." There was no point in trying to elaborate how vastly different the two men were. Whereas Leander was uncertain about many superficial things, he had a core of strength and loyalty that was unwavering. Leander would never have dreamed of asking of him what Tobias had. Leander would never have asked what Julien had asked of him. Despite the fact that such stubborn loyalty was likely what had led to this trouble, Julien couldn't bring himself to wish for Leander to be any different.

Cordelia seemed to realize he wasn't going to look at her. "I'll be on my way," she said with a light touch on his arm.

Julien waited until he heard the front door close behind her before tearing his gaze from the window.

JULIEN was just stepping out of the hackney he'd hired when he heard an angry, distinctly American voice swearing at someone or something. So he hadn't missed them. Good. He'd watched them leave the ball, but had been unable to extricate himself from the conversation with Lady Tremayne without arousing too much suspicion. It had taken him nearly three-quarters of an hour to get himself to the Faro's Tomb and apparently the men had already been inside. Instead of getting into a hackney, however, they had walked into an alley. That was unusual enough for Julien to risk getting closer in order to hear what they were saying.

Quickly, he paid the driver and moved into the shadows to listen. The darkness that hid him also prevented him from seeing the men, but by now he easily recognized the voices of Chance and Morleigh Mayfield.

"Calm yourself." Morleigh sounded more amused than anything.

"Calm myself?" Chance practically snarled. "That money was all I had left. It was supposed to last me until—"

"Until?"

"Until I could get the money from the *Atlantic Maiden*." Chance's voice was so low, Julien had to strain to hear it.

"You won't have that money until your brother is proven dead. Ask Dearborne for the blunt to pay off your vowels."

"I can't do that. Kit is already up in arms about my playing cards. If he finds out how much I owe—damnation!"

"What if I told you I could arrange for you to get that shipping fortune?" Morleigh's voice was far too casual.

There was a long silence.

"You just finished saying yourself that the only way I could get it is if—" Chance stopped. "What do you mean?" he finally asked, sounding cautious.

"I can show you how to solve all your problems."

"How?" Chance whispered.

"It will take several days to set things in motion," Morleigh warned. "To do what has to be done."

That must mean Leander is alive. Julien's heart began to race.

"The sooner we can start, the better," Chance said. "I need that money."

"We could leave now." Morleigh was also beginning to sound eager. "We have a fair amount of traveling to do. I know of a place on this street where we can hire a coach and they will ask no questions."

"Perfect."

Julien moved further into the shadows as Morleigh and Chance walked up the street. Morleigh intended to take Chance to Leander. Tonight. Now. It left Julien with neither the time nor the means to contact the Runners to assist him.

He only hoped the place Morleigh spoke of could also hire him a decent horse.

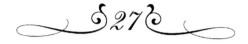

The sun was going to rise soon and Morleigh still hadn't given any indication as to their destination. They had been riding for at least five hours, and as the time went on, Morleigh spoke more and more blatantly about the purpose of their journey, albeit without actually mentioning Leander's name. Chance was hard-pressed to maintain his facade, knowing that soon he would find his little brother. When that finally happened, Morleigh was in for a thrashing like he'd never known.

"Where are we going?" Chance finally asked. "One of the Dearborne estates?"

"Of course not," Morleigh snorted. "That would be far too great a risk. We're near Shadowcross Manor, although not actually on the property."

Shadowcross. Chance had heard the place mentioned a few times and knew that Leander had visited it. "Blackstone's estate."

"Indeed." Morleigh looked smug. "This close to Shadowcross, the investigation will inevitably focus on Blackstone. I intend him to be blamed."

Chance told himself he shouldn't have been surprised by such ruthlessness. "Why Blackstone?"

"Their names were already connected. It seemed only natural." Morleigh's voice was matter-of-fact. "It's doubtful he would hang for it, though," he added with disappointment.

Not for the first time since climbing into the hired coach, Chance wished he'd brought a pistol—wished he *had* a pistol. He should have purchased one the moment he began spending time in Morleigh's company. It would have been reassuring, even if he'd never actually fired one. He was, after all, a good shot when hunting with his father's rifle.

Chance had been caught off-guard tonight. He hadn't expected to find out about Leander's whereabouts so suddenly, which, considering that getting Morleigh to lead him to Leander had always been his aim, was utter stupidity on his part. He should have been ready for it at any time and have planned for a way to get word to Kit when it finally happened. Instead, here he was being taken to Leander, but no one knew about it, and all he had was the knife in his boot to assure his and his brother's safety.

And he *did* have the knife in his boot, Chance told himself firmly. There was no need to reach down and check for it. The knife was there. It was the same knife he'd worn since the day he and Kit set sail in search of the *Atlantic Maiden*. That knife had been with him through the shipwreck off Cape Agulhas, their survival, their rescue, and even the eventual recovery of the *Maiden*. Chance always wore it, albeit more for luck than actual protection. He *knew* it was there.

"Do you have a pistol?" Morleigh's voice made Chance freeze.

For a moment Chance wondered wildly whether he had said something aloud about his knife, and then, insanely, whether Morleigh could have somehow read his thoughts. Finally, reason returned, and Chance accepted that it was a perfectly natural question. He was grateful for the darkness that hid his brief panic from the other man. "I've never owned one. And I never thought to buy one."

"Fortunately I have," Morleigh replied. "I trust you know how."

"Know how?" Chance caught himself immediately. "To shoot? Of course." Just in case Morleigh was starting to doubt him, he added, "I did bring a knife."

"Did you?" Morleigh approved. "Then you'll have your choice, won't you? You'd be less likely to get any… thing on your clothing with the gun, but perhaps you'd prefer your knife. I imagine you must be accustomed to butchering animals back on your farm."

The amusement in Morleigh's voice sickened him. Chance had never killed anyone in his life, never come close to it—not even during the desperate weeks after the shipwreck. Although he possessed a quicker temper than either of his brothers, he had never actually contemplated the reality of taking another's life. Now he found himself

contemplating whether he wanted the pleasure of sticking Morleigh like the vile pig he was or the irony of shooting the man with his own gun.

DAWN was beginning to paint the sky with streaks of dusty rose before Julien finally allowed his mount to slow to an easy canter and gave the animal's neck an appreciative pat. He'd been dubious when the groom had led out the unimpressive gelding, but the horse was, as promised, "a real goer," gamely keeping pace with Mayfield's coach throughout the night.

Julien settled himself more comfortably in the saddle, which eased his aching muscles slightly. For the entire ride his focus had been narrowed to keeping the coach-lantern in sight while staying far enough back that he wasn't seen or heard. Now that he no longer had to worry about losing the coach to the inky darkness, he was able to take note of his surroundings. Early on, he'd vaguely registered the fact that they were heading into Hampshire, but was shocked at how familiar his current surroundings were. They were less than an hour's ride from Shadowcross Manor.

God help him, had Mayfield been holding Leander near Shadowcross the entire time? If only he hadn't listened to Cordelia and Penelope and traveled to Shadowcross weeks ago instead of staying in London to salvage a reputation he barely cared about, perhaps he would have noticed—

No. This isn't the time to wonder about what could have been. Julien knew he had to remain focused on the task at hand. If Leander was to have a chance, Julien had to successfully take on two men with only a single pistol.

When he noticed the coach heading for a turn, Julien drew back on the reins, bringing his mount to a complete halt. The road the coach was on would take them onto Lord Marling's property, near where it bordered Julien's. That couldn't be a coincidence, Julien thought, gritting his teeth. Why hadn't the Bow Street Runners turned up any connection between Marling and Mayfield? If only they had discovered one, then perhaps—

Stop it. Again, Julien forced himself to concentrate and took another look at his surroundings. One of the few advantages he now had was that he knew the area so well. Nudging his horse into motion again, he guided the animal off the road and into the small wood that ran along it. From the shadows of the trees he could follow more closely without being seen or heard.

Julien allowed the horse to pick his way carefully through the trees, keeping his eyes on the coach. When the vehicle halted, Julien dismounted and moved closer on foot, slipping one hand into the pocket of his greatcoat to grip his pistol. For a moment, he considered rushing forward and confronting the men, but the driver would make the odds three-to-one. Hired coachmen tended to overlook a great deal that was going on around them, especially if the price was right, but an armed man bursting from a copse of trees would provoke a reaction from even the drunkest reprobate. Instead, he waited and watched as the pair disembarked. When they disappeared down a slight slope, Julien hurried toward the coach, being careful to keep himself hidden behind the vehicle.

Doubtful he could sneak past the coachman unobserved, Julien reached into his pocket and found a five-pound note. "You didn't see me," he hissed, thrusting the bill up at the coachman.

"See who?" the coachman asked, as if he encountered this situation every day. Considering where he'd been hired from, Julien wasn't terribly surprised.

Extracting another note, Julien risked a question. "What did you hear them say?"

"The old cove was talkin' about a cottage." The coachman readily snatched up the second bill.

Julien had the vague memory of an abandoned tenant's cottage in the area. He peered around the coach, then up at the driver, who ignored him and pulled out a flask. Seeing no sign of either Morleigh or Chance, he took out his pistol and started down the slope.

HE couldn't do it.

Chance stared down at the motionless form of Morleigh Mayfield, his fist still clenched around the barrel of the pistol Morleigh had handed him before bending to open the cellar door. It had been the perfect opportunity, but at the last minute Chance found himself unable to actually kill the man. Instead, he used the butt of the pistol to render Morleigh unconscious.

He *wanted* to be able to kill Morleigh, and wanted to be able to take pleasure in the killing, but hadn't been able to do it. It was enough, Chance told himself as he tucked the pistol into the waistband of his trousers, that he'd found his brother. In the end, Morleigh's life or death didn't matter nearly as much as finding Leander and bringing him back to London.

There was a lantern in the corner and Chance lit it before opening the cellar door. He peered down into the darkness, then swallowed hard and started slowly down the steps. Morleigh had kept Leander in God knew *what* kind of conditions and Lee had never been that strong. Chance was suddenly frightened of what he would find. Lee might not have survived his imprisonment, or if he had, the effects could still carry him off weeks later. Even if he recovered, there was no telling what Morleigh had done to him while holding him prisoner, no telling what effect the imprisonment would have on Leander's mind.

Maybe he *would* kill Morleigh after all, Chance decided.

But not until he found his brother.

"Lee?" he called softly when he reached the dirt floor. Stale air, thick with the scent of sickness and waste, assaulted him, increasing his fear. "Leander?" He held up the lantern to better illuminate the tiny space and what he saw robbed him of his voice.

The weak light cast stark shadows over Leander's drawn face, his black hair was filthy and matted, and there were frightening hollows in his cheeks, but all Chance cared about in that moment were his brother's eyes. They were sunken and cloudy with sickness, but open and calm and *aware*.

"Chance...." The word was little more than a sigh. "You came for me."

Chance fell to his knees next to the sagging rope bed and started to put the lantern on the floor so he could pull his brother into his arms. At the last minute, he stopped and merely laid a hand on Leander's shoulder, not wanting to risk causing pain by moving him unnecessarily. "Of course I did," he said in the most reassuring manner he could. How odd that Leander didn't seem the least bit surprised to see him. "Are you ready to go?"

"I suppose it's past time, isn't it?" Leander looked wistful. "I would have liked to stay a bit longer, but it will be good to see Kit and Father again. Is Mother there as well?"

Chance was about to shrug Leander's words off as fevered nonsense until he realized the implication of them. "No, Lee. Lee, I'm here to take you back to London." He tightened his grip on Leander's shoulder for emphasis. "You're going to be fine," he added, sending up a silent prayer that he was telling the truth.

"Don't you know?" Leander's voice was rusty with disuse, but gentle. With a feebleness that was painful to watch, Leander reached up to put his hand over Chance's. "You were lost at sea, Chance. You and Kit both. You're dead now."

A chuckle escaped past the lump in Chance's throat. Leander was trying to reassure *him*? "No, Lee, listen to me. Our ship was wrecked, but we survived—we both did. We got back to Pelham and heard that you had sailed for London. We've been looking for you ever since." He twisted his hand to grip Leander's thin one. "Kit is waiting for us in London. Daisy too. Kit married her before we sailed."

Leander blinked slowly and Chance wondered if his words even made it through.

"I tricked Morleigh into leading me to—" Chance stopped when Leander's eyes widened and, impossibly, his waxen skin grew even paler.

"Chance?" The blue eyes filled with tears, "No, this is... no. I don't... how...?"

"It's all right, Lee." Chance brushed dirty hair off Leander's forehead. "It will be fine, I promise you. I'll take you home and we'll get you warm and well and Kit will explain—" The sound of something

moving on the floor above them brought Chance's rambling assurances to a halt. This was an abandoned cottage, so it could have been an animal, but Chance doubted it. Morleigh was coming around.

"Chance?"

"Hush, Lee," Chance ordered in a whisper, and his brother immediately fell silent. "I'll be back for you," he promised, rising. "Just be still."

Thank God he'd held onto the pistol. Now he pulled it out and crept back up the rickety steps. When his eyes drew level with the cottage floor, the first thing he saw was Morleigh's motionless form, still laying where he'd left it. Chance's shoulders slumped in relief. It had only been an animal, after all.

"Put that pistol on the floor and finish climbing up here," ordered a deadly voice.

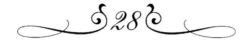

*J*ulien didn't know what might have prompted Morleigh and Chance to turn on each other, and didn't care. The important thing was that he only had to take on one man instead of two to ensure Leander's safety.

If there was any hope left for Leander. When he saw Chance rising from the cellar, Julien suspected he was too late. He allowed rage to overtake him; rage was much easier to deal with than despair.

Chance set the pistol down as instructed. "I can explain why I'm here. Something—"

"I know why you're here. And God help you if he's dead."

The younger man climbed fully out of the cellar and turned to face him. "Blackstone?"

"Mayfield," Julien returned with icy formality.

"What in God's name are you doing here?" Chance asked, looking more bewildered than worried. "You live nearby, don't you? How did you know—?"

"Is he alive?" Julien demanded, seeing no point in giving Chance the opportunity to talk himself out of the situation.

Chance's eyes flicked toward Morleigh. "Yes. I found I couldn't do it, as much as he deserves it."

His words only added more fuel to Julien's fury. "Deserved it? You vile—I ought to shoot you where you stand."

"Over *him*?" Chance asked incredulously. "Blackstone, you have no idea. Do you believe he's a friend of yours? Trust me, he's not. He wanted to—"

Julien didn't wait to hear another word. All he wanted was to see Leander with his own eyes. With another snarl at Chance, he started for

the cellar door.

Almost immediately, Chance began moving as well. "Are you mad?" he hissed, grabbing for the pistol and shoving it upward.

What does he hope to accomplish by killing me? Julien wondered as they struggled for the weapon. *He'll never be able to explain three dead bodies.* "Give up, man!"

"Put the gun down!" Chance growled.

Julien only tightened his grip. Chance didn't look like a typical farm boy any more than Leander did, but he definitely had the strength attributed to one. This had to end soon, or it wouldn't end well. "You don't have a prayer of getting away with this."

"Getting away with—wait, Blackstone—"

"Give up now." Julien thought he felt Chance's grip loosen slightly. "You can't possibly win this situation."

"How true," said another voice, making both men freeze.

CHANCE stepped away from Blackstone, and his only thought was that he deserved to be shot for sheer stupidity. Not only had he *not* killed Morleigh when he had the chance, but he'd set down the pistol within the man's reach. In the blink of an eye, he'd gone from rescuing his brother to having two pistols pointed at him, held by two men who wanted him dead.

"I admit that I underestimated you," Morleigh said.

Chance didn't know which one of them he was speaking to, but he did know where Leander's only hope of rescue lay. "Blackstone—" he began, and immediately stopped. Anything he said would sound like lies to save his own neck. He'd been too convincing in his attempt to win over Morleigh.

"For God's sake, Blackstone, what are you waiting for?" Morleigh growled. "Shoot, damn you!"

Chance looked at the cellar door, trying to judge whether he could

make a leap for it and save his neck as well as Leander's. If Blackstone shot him, then Morleigh would be able to shoot Blackstone and kill Leander. He started for the door when a shot shattered the still morning air.

Immediately, Chance dropped to his knees, and it wasn't until the echo had stopped that he realized he wasn't the one who had been hit. Morleigh was on the floor again, this time with a red stain blossoming over the front of his waistcoat. Warily, Chance looked at Blackstone.

"He told me to shoot," Blackstone said dryly.

Not sure how to reply, Chance took the pistol from Morleigh's hand and slipped it back into the waist of his trousers. Much to his surprise, Blackstone didn't object.

"You've been acting this entire time," Blackstone said. "To draw Mayfield in."

"Yes," Chance said, finally relaxing a bit.

"Bravo. Your excellent acting almost got you killed."

Chance laughed weakly. "How did you know?"

"When you looked at the cellar door, I could see it wasn't your own life you were concerned for."

"Yes. Lee." *Dear God. Lee. If he heard the shot he must be terrified.* Without another word, Chance rushed downcellar, practically ignoring the stairs in his hurry. "Lee?" He could see Leander moving in the lantern light, trying unsuccessfully to push himself up. "No, Lee! Don't try to move."

Leander collapsed back on the bed. "I—I can't—" Then he froze, his eyes looking past Chance's shoulder. "*Julien....*"

The way Leander said Blackstone's name made Chance swallow hard. He didn't know how much of the rumors were true, but there was definitely a deep connection between the two men.

"Shadowcross Manor is but five miles from here." Blackstone's voice was rough. "He could be made comfortable there."

Chance was tempted to agree, but he knew that Kit would be furious and insist on taking Leander back to London. Moving Leander twice

wouldn't help his strength. "Thank you, but Kit has been waiting to see him for a long time."

"Of course," Blackstone acquiesced immediately.

"Kit," Leander murmured. Chance began to wonder if he had truly grasped what was happening. "But... I don't—" Leander looked to Blackstone again, obviously searching for answers.

"You were entirely correct about your brother." Blackstone's tone was conversational, but there was a slight shakiness to his voice. "He is doing quite well as the new Earl of Dearborne."

Finally, Leander tore his eyes from Blackstone to look at Chance again. "You're alive. *Alive*..." he breathed and his eyes filled. "Oh, God...."

"Ssshh, Lee, it will all be fine." Chance glanced over his shoulder. "Will you help me get him to the coach?"

"Of course," Blackstone said again, never taking his eyes from Leander's face.

Leander kept looking from Chance to Blackstone when they lifted him from the bed, but as they maneuvered him up from the cellar, his eyes slid shut and his head fell back against Chance's shoulder. Chance was surprised that his strength had lasted as long as it did.

Blackstone's attention was focused on Leander with an intensity that Chance didn't know how to react to. "How did you happen to be out here?" he finally asked. It didn't really matter to him, but he felt as if he ought to say *something*.

"I followed you from London." Blackstone removed his greatcoat and wrapped it around Leander. "I was in the alley and overheard your conversation."

"You were at the hell?" Chance had a sudden chill, one that had nothing to do with the morning air. "What were you doing there?"

"Following you. I followed you to the hell when I heard you mention it at Lady Tremayne's ball. As I have been for days."

"You've been following us for days?"

"Weeks," Blackstone corrected, pulling his coat more snugly around

Leander's shoulders. "I've never liked or trusted Morleigh Mayfield."

"Yes, I know." Chance recalled Blackstone's visit with Kit. "And by extension, you didn't trust me."

Blackstone tore his gaze from Leander's face long enough to give Chance a sharp look. "I did not. You played your part well."

As they approached the coach, the driver watched them from his perch with little interest. Apparently, the man didn't consider opening the coach door part of his duties, nor was he moved by any spirit of kindness to help them.

Before he climbed into the coach, Chance took off his greatcoat to cover Leander with it as well. Blackstone helped settle Leander as comfortably as possible and then got down from the coach.

"Where are you going?" Chance asked.

"My horse is tied among the trees."

"You ought to be able to tie him to the back of the coach," Chance said. Kit wouldn't be happy when Blackstone arrived with them, but the man had saved his life and had been trying to save Leander's. To Chance, that meant more than any rumors about Blackstone's interest in other men.

"I'll ride back." Blackstone's voice was impassive. "Someone has to inform the magistrate about Mayfield and the body has to be removed from Marling's property. I'll speak to them about the situation, but someone will likely call on you to discuss it as well."

"Oh." Chance had never given Morleigh another thought once he was no longer a threat. Before he could say anything more, Blackstone shut the coach door. Chance heard the earl speaking to the driver and then the coach began moving.

Early on in the journey, all of Chance's attention was taken up by his unconscious brother. Holding Leander securely against the jolting of the coach and making certain that he was warm and his breathing was steady were his only concerns. Once he'd reassured himself that Leander was as comfortable as possible, Chance's thoughts turned back to Blackstone.

Strange that Blackstone had chosen not to ride with them. Chance had been certain he would, and had even resigned himself to Blackstone sitting across from them and watching Leander for the entire ride.

At one time, not very long ago, Chance would have been appalled and thoroughly disgusted by the possibility that a *man* had designs on his brother or that Leander might return any such feeling. Although he wasn't comfortable with the situation, he didn't feel the need to damage anything—or anyone—over it.

Perhaps it was the wealth of emotion in Leander's voice when he'd said Blackstone's name; this was obviously someone Leander trusted and cared deeply for. Chance knew that his younger brother would not give his affections so completely to anyone undeserving. That they were both men didn't bother Chance nearly as much as the things he'd seen while in Morleigh's company. After watching men who gained pleasure from inflicting as much pain and terror as possible on both men and women, the notion of two men being loving with each other seemed relatively harmless. Chance didn't want to think about what might happen between his brother and Blackstone when they were alone, but he was certain it involved genuine affection and not pain.

It probably involved a great deal more than *affection.* Chance thought back to the way the earl looked at his brother, not as if Leander was the most important thing in the world, but as if Leander was the *only* thing in his world.

eander was completely oblivious to the initial uproar caused by his return and Morleigh's death. While he laid in bed, feverish and often insensible, Kit, Daisy, and Chance dealt with questions from the authorities and dozens upon dozens of callers.

The country magistrate wasn't difficult to appease. The words of an earl and another earl's brother easily satisfied him. The callers, however, were determined to wring as much gossip and scandal from Morleigh's death and Leander's near-death as possible. Under the thinnest guise of concern, they asked all manner of intrusive questions, trying Kit's patience, testing Chance's temper, and causing Daisy to insist more than once that the offenders leave her house. Word spread very quickly that the lovely new Countess of Dearborne possessed a razor-sharp tongue capable of flaying the skin from someone's back and that she had no qualms about using it. After that, the curious were more careful about calling.

Even after Leander was well on his way to recovery, conscious and coherent once again, he gave little thought to the world outside his room. His brothers were alive and well and *here*. He was part of a family again, comforted and protected. What more could he ask for?

He still hadn't dared to voice the answer to that question.

For once, Leander had no use for books during his convalescence. Instead, nearly every waking moment was spent with either one or both of his brothers. They, too, seemed eager to spend as much time as possible with him and for the first time, they had neither school nor chores to keep them from it. The story his brothers had to tell about their loss at sea was comparable to anything Leander had ever read in his books. As if surviving the shipwreck off the southern tip of Africa wasn't adventure enough, Kit and Chance had also survived months on a small island where they found the remains and cargo of the *Atlantic Maiden* and several other ships. Along with a handful of other survivors,

they managed to hold out and finally signal a ship that brought them to a Dutch port on the mainland. From there, they hired another ship to bring all the recovered cargo back to Boston. The resulting profit, Leander learned, didn't make him as wealthy as the Dearborne earldom had, but it was enough for him to live comfortably amidst a multitude of books, if he wanted.

What Leander enjoyed most was when both brothers tried to tell the story together. Chance's attempts at embellishment irritated Kit to no end, while Kit's straightforward manner of relaying facts was far too boring for Chance.

To Leander's surprise, Kit and Chance had just as many questions for him about his life during their time apart. As far as Leander was concerned, plays and books could hardly compare to shipwrecks and deserted islands, but he told them everything he'd done since arriving in England.

Almost.

He was careful to mention Julien as little as possible, especially in front of Kit. When Chance told of how Julien had helped in Leander's rescue and how he had been following Morleigh in his search for Leander, Kit's fury had been palpable. Leander didn't know how much his brothers knew about his feelings for Julien, but Kit's reaction made him reluctant to tell them anything. It was easy enough to avoid the subject of Julien, since the man hadn't called a single time to inquire after Leander's health.

Once Daisy had driven off the less-than-sincere, a handful of people continued to call. They were the people Leander's family eventually allowed to visit him. The first to see Leander—even before he was able to leave his bed—were Lord and Lady Carysfort. Leander could tell immediately that Lady Carysfort and Daisy were going to be the best of friends. Also permitted into his chambers were Penelope and Seaforth. None of them mentioned Julien, and whenever Leander attempted to, they would change the subject.

After several weeks in bed, Leander was finally able to convince his brothers that he wasn't going to drop dead if they allowed him up and about. The tiny circle of callers was expanded to include Lord Archer and several members of the Arthurian League. Leander was amused to

see that Lady Helena Colchester, who called with her older sister Flora, was far more interested in seeing Chance than seeing him.

Still, there was nothing from Julien: no call, no note, no word.

He didn't like to suspect his brothers, but Leander began to wonder if perhaps his family wasn't allowing Julien to see him. He eventually dismissed the thought. If Julien had been trying to contact him, but was being put off, surely Lady Carysfort would have said *something* about it. Instead, it was as if Julien didn't exist. And while Kit made no secret of his dislike for the Earl of Blackstone, Chance didn't appear to have any real animosity toward him. At one point, Leander recalled, Kit became all the more infuriated when Chance seemed to be defending Julien. Neither of them had ever acknowledged that there could possibly be anything between their youngest brother and another man, although *Julien's* preferences had been alluded to, vaguely but crudely, and always by Kit. That was something of a surprise to Leander, for Kit had always been calm and even-tempered while Chance had been hotheaded and apt to speak without thinking.

Both his brothers had changed since they were last together so long ago, but those changes were much more visible in Chance. Kit was much as he'd always been, only more so: responsible, authoritative, and overprotective of his family, especially his sickly youngest brother. Chance had always been brasher than either of his brothers, often doing or saying what Leander wished he had the nerve to do or say.

At one time, the prospect of becoming a wealthy member of the English aristocracy would have filled Chance with boundless enthusiasm. He would have already explored all the Dearborne estates, visited every shop on Bond Street, met all manner of people and collected the hearts of several young ladies, all the while endlessly teasing Kit about being "his lordship." Instead, although Chance readily told Leander everything that had happened to him and Kit while they were "lost at sea," he barely spoke of his time in London thus far. Exactly *how* Chance had managed to get Morleigh to lead him to the cottage in Hampshire was something he had refused to discuss with Leander, but whatever it was had left him quieter and much more serious.

Leander knew he had changed a great deal as well, although his

brothers hadn't let on that they'd noticed anything. He'd learned things about himself that he hadn't even known were possible months before, accepted those things and admitted them to others.

Just not his brothers.

At least not yet.

But he knew he would have to tell them if he ever intended to see Julien again, and he definitely intended to see Julien again, if only to apologize and thank him for saving his life. If, after that, Julien didn't want to see him again, then he would just have to find the strength to accept that as well.

"... asks after you each time we call. Of course, we put him off, as you asked, but—"

Julien tossed Cordelia's letter aside and poured himself another glass of port. No doubt his aunt could lecture as well on paper as she could in person and that was the last thing he wanted at the moment. He walked over to the window and looked out over the immaculate lawns of Shadowcross Manor as he sipped his drink.

The only reason he'd opened Cordelia's letter in the first place was to see if she had any news about how Leander's recovery was progressing. He knew what Cordelia would say to that; that if he'd remained in London, he would be able to check on Leander's progress in person, which was probably true. Kit would likely refuse him entry if he called, but Julien was fairly certain Chance would allow him in.

But even if Chance was grateful to him for his assistance in saving Leander, that was no guarantee that he would accept an attachment between his younger brother and another man. It was the reason Julien had retired to the country in the first place—to spare Leander the distress of making such a choice.

Julien quickly drained his glass of port in a vain attempt to silence the tiny but persistent voice that insisted he had retired to the country in order to spare himself the pain of not being Leander's choice.

As he turned to refill his glass once more, his eye fell on Cordelia's letter again. Unable to resist, he picked it up. The next few lines were dedicated to his aunt's disapproval of his "insistence on becoming a hermit," so Julien merely skimmed the letter until Leander's name caught his eye.

"... for anything that may have occurred between Leander and Mayfield, do you? Naturally, I cannot ask Leander such a thing, but I am certain he would not have willingly—"

Julien clenched his fist, crumpling the letter before he threw it into the fire. Then he hurled his drink after it with such force that the heavy crystal shattered.

Did Cordelia actually believe that he would hold Leander responsible for anything that might have happened while he was in Mayfield's clutches? Julien desperately swallowed the bile rising in his throat. The thought of Morleigh Mayfield touching Leander, *forcing* him, made Julien sick with rage, but it wouldn't have kept him from the younger man.

If anything, the opposite was true. What Leander may have suffered at Morleigh's hands could have left him unwilling or unable to endure another man's touch, and he didn't need Julien's presence reminding him of past intimacies between them.

Returning to the sideboard, Julien poured himself another drink, quickly tossing it back to kill the sour taste in his mouth. As he refilled his glass for the fifth time, he could easily imagine what Cordelia would have to say about him drinking so much so early in the day.

A few more drinks ought to take care of all that.

"WHEN you are well enough, I hope you will accept an invitation to a dinner party I intend to give. Normally, it would be a ball, but I know how you feel about those."

Leander smiled at Lady Carysfort's pronouncement. "I will be glad to accept, but I don't know when I'll be able."

"Kit—that is, Dearborne." Although Daisy had adapted with surprising ease to her new position as Countess of Dearborne, she still had difficulty remembering that referring to one's husband by his nickname simply wasn't done in front of others. "Feels that Leander still isn't well enough to leave the house. He is even reluctant to let him go out for a carriage ride."

"Not even a carriage ride?" Lord Carysfort said skeptically. "Dearborne is very cautious. You look fit enough to me."

Leander didn't say that he felt perfectly fine; that he felt well enough to attend a dinner party or two, even a ball if he had to; that certainly he was well enough for a carriage ride. All he said was, "Kit doesn't like to take risks." It hadn't occurred to him to contradict his eldest brother's decision, despite the fact that he'd been itching to leave the house for the past several days.

"Well, if Lord Dearborne doesn't object, perhaps you could give a ball, Lady Dearborne," Lady Carysfort suggested. "I'm certain it would be the most sought-after invitation of the Season."

"A ball?" Daisy looked flustered, but intrigued. "I wouldn't have the slightest notion where to begin, or whom to invite, although I suppose Lee would have some idea about that part." She glanced at him before turning back to Lady Carysfort. "Perhaps if you could guide me in the planning—"

"My dear, I'd be delighted!"

As Lady Carysfort leaned forward enthusiastically, Leander exchanged a resigned look with Lord Carysfort. The viscount shifted slightly, likely making himself more comfortable for a much-longer-than-anticipated call.

"The guest list is the first thing, of course, but you could begin preparing the house." Lady Carysfort paused, frowning slightly. "I can't recall the last time there was a ball here at Esmond House. It's been some years—five years at the very least. We should inspect the ballroom to discover if any work needs to be done."

"We'll have plenty of time to see to it," Daisy assured her. "Ki— Dearborne won't want to have a houseful of people until he feels Leander is strong enough."

"I declare, Leander," Lady Carysfort had been given leave to call Leander by name, as had her husband, on their first visit to Leander's sickroom. "Your brother is trying to make you into as much of a hermit as Julien." The moment the name left her lips, Lady Carysfort clasped her gloved hand over her mouth.

A tense silence fell over the parlor. Leander could feel everyone's eyes on him. "I was always under the impression that you refused to allow Blackstone to become a hermit." He felt proud of his casual tone, of sounding as though his heart *hadn't* lurched at the mention of Julien's name.

Lady Carysfort lowered her hand. Her lips were pursed, although her eyes regarded Leander warmly. "That's much more difficult since he's taken himself off to Shadowcross."

"Julien is at—?"

Before Leander could finish his question, Lord Carysfort sprang up from the sofa. "My dear, if we don't take our leave now, we will miss the appointment with your modiste." He took his wife's hand and drew her to her feet. "I trust you'll excuse us," he said as he propelled Lady Carysfort out of the parlor before Daisy could protest.

Daisy didn't know Lord Carysfort well enough to realize just how transparent his excuse was, but Leander knew that Carysfort never had the slightest idea about his wife's schedule; he simply escorted her wherever she wished to go.

Leander wasn't about to call Lord Carysfort on the lie, however. Nor did he waste time wondering about the real reason for it. He had more important things to do while Daisy saw the couple to the door.

He had to prepare for a trip to Shadowcross Manor.

He found it odd that Daisy didn't follow him up to his room once she had seen Lord and Lady Carysfort on their way, but he didn't let it concern him. After telling Powell to have Rand prepare the coach for a journey to Hampshire and to find him a small trunk, he went upstairs. Then came the search through all the dressers and wardrobes in his room since he had no real notion where his things were kept. He tried to recall where he'd seen Gibson retrieve various items of clothing, but his mind had usually been otherwise occupied, first by his strange new situation,

then by the books he'd discovered, and then by Julien. Gibson had been so quiet that it had been easy for Leander to lose himself in his thoughts.

Gibson. Leander paused in his search to reflect on his valet. The man had apparently been reporting to Morleigh about him all along, but seemed to have had a change of heart at some point—one that had proved fatal. No one had spoken to him about Gibson, but Leander had been able to piece together the story from bits of conversation here and there when he'd hovered between waking and sleeping. It was the same way he had learned that the man who would occasionally check on him in the cellar—Morleigh's man-of-affairs, Basil Clement—had put a bullet through his head.

It wasn't a monumental task, Leander told himself, dismissing the footman who delivered a suitable trunk. There were only so many places his things could be. He began his search with the largest wardrobe, where he discovered his coats. As he retrieved his favorite blue one, the door to his room opened. He turned, expecting to see Daisy or one of the servants, but it was Kit.

"What are you doing?"

When he saw Chance and Daisy behind Kit, Leander resigned himself to a battle. "I'm packing some things." He was tempted to leave it at that and force Kit to keep asking questions, but decided there was no point in drawing it out. Taking a deep breath, he braced himself to challenge his eldest brother for the first time in his life. "I'm traveling to Hampshire."

"Hampshire." Kit's face could have been carved from stone.

"I'm not certain how long I'll be away."

"You aren't going."

"I assure you, I'm well enough to travel."

Kit paused momentarily in the face of Leander's calm contradiction of his order. "I don't want to play with words, Leander. Daisy told me about the call."

"I didn't tell you so you could rail at him like this," Daisy spoke up.

Kit glanced at her, briefly thrown, and then gathered himself again.

"Blackstone's estate is in Hampshire."

"Yes. Shadowcross." Leander found his shirts and folded them into the trunk, not letting himself think about where this conversation would inevitably lead. If he did, he would only lose his nerve.

"What if Blackstone refuses to see you?" Chance asked.

My heart will very likely break, Leander thought, but knew that wasn't what Chance meant. "There's an inn not far from Shadowcross. I can stay there."

"If you like, I can go with you."

As much as Leander appreciated Chance's offer and the acceptance it implied, this was a trip he had to make alone. Before he could say anything, however, Kit, with as much firmness as Leander had ever heard from him, announced, "No one is going anywhere."

Leander thought it best not to contradict him aloud again, and so he merely kept packing.

"Master Leander," Powell appeared in the doorway. "The coach is ready, sir."

"Thank you, Powell." Leander rolled up several pairs of fine woolen stockings and tucked them in next to his shirts. "I'll be down soon."

"The Dearborne coach?" Kit said.

"Yes."

"I won't allow you to use it."

"Kit!" Daisy frowned at her husband. "Of course you may use the coach if you truly want to make this trip," she said, moving closer to Leander. "But are you certain this is the best time for you to travel? You haven't even left the house since your return."

"I'll be fine," Leander assured her. "And I can hire a coach. It's simple enough to do." Silence fell over the room, but Leander did his best to ignore it and continued packing. He added several pairs of trousers to the trunk. Now if he could just find his waistcoats, he could be on his way. Opening another drawer, he found his nightshirts and added one, along with his dressing robe.

"Leander, stop this," Kit commanded. "You aren't going anywhere."

"I am. I'm going to Shadowcross."

"Why? Why this need to see Blackstone?"

Leander swallowed hard and was about to reply when Kit's hand came up.

"No! I don't want to hear any of the lies Blackstone has fed you." Kit made an obvious effort to calm himself. "Lee, he took advantage of you. It's not your fault—"

Suddenly Leander realized this wasn't a choice between his family and Julien. Even if he never saw Julien again, it wouldn't change what he was, and Kit needed to know that. He closed and fastened his trunk before turning to face his brother. Hoping his voice wouldn't shake, he looked Kit in the eye. "It's *not* Julien's fault. All he did was—"

"*What* did he do?" Kit hissed through gritted teeth.

"He—it's because of Julien that I learned that what I'd felt all my life wasn't something that was wrong with *me*. That there were other men—other people—in the world like me."

"No," Kit said flatly. "Leander, what you're saying is—"

"I love him." Leander swallowed hard when Kit's lip curled. "But even if I didn't, it wouldn't change what I am." His voice was shaking, but he forced himself to continue. "You can refuse to see me ever again, you can report me to the authorities and have me arrested—even hung— but none of it will change what I am."

Kit stared at him with a frozen expression that Leander had seen before, but had never been the recipient of.

Leander couldn't hold that icy gaze. Before this, Kit had never regarded him with anything except approval and respect. He turned to Chance who, much to his relief, looked discomfited but not furious or disgusted.

"There are worse things you could be," Chance said with a hint of a smile that vanished when Kit growled something unintelligible. "It's true. Morleigh Mayfield is proof enough of that."

Without another word, Kit stalked out of the room.

Leander blinked desperately and didn't notice Daisy's approach until he felt her hand on his arm. "You won't be disowned or arrested, I promise you." She kissed his cheek and then followed her husband from the room.

"Kit will come around." Chance hoisted Leander's trunk onto his shoulder. "He just hates that this all happened without his permission." He paused and peered more closely at Leander. "Are you truly well enough to make this journey?"

"Yes, I—" His voice was hoarse and Leander cleared his throat. "Yes. I'd best go arrange to hire a coach." He headed for the stairs, and found himself unable to express his gratitude when Chance followed behind as if this trip was the most natural thing in the world.

They arrived in the front hall to find Kit staring out one of the windows, Daisy beside him. She turned to look at them, but Kit didn't move. Powell was by the door, holding Leander's hat and gloves.

"Charles!" the butler barked when they arrived, startling everyone. When a footman appeared, Powell nodded toward Chance and Charles hurried forward to take the trunk from him. "Put Master Leander's trunk in—"

"Wait," Leander interrupted. The footman stopped in his tracks. "I'll be hiring a vehicle. So someone needs to tell Rand that—"

"Take the coach."

Leander looked at Kit, who hadn't turned from the window when he spoke. Daisy met his eyes, giving him a small smile. "Thank you," Leander said as Charles continued outside with his trunk.

"Have a good trip." Chance clapped him on the shoulder as he took his hat and gloves from Powell.

"Write."

The word was a command and Kit *still* hadn't taken his gaze from the window, but Leander felt one of the knots in his stomach begin to loosen. "I will," he promised, then stepped outside where Charles was holding the door to the coach open for him.

Leander was glad to climb into the familiar vehicle despite the long journey he knew lay ahead. The seven-hour drive gave him plenty of time to reflect on everything that had just happened. It had been worse than he'd hoped for, but much better than he'd feared. If nothing else, he had a family to return to if Julien never wanted to see him again.

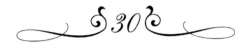

30

*A*t one time Alexander Banbury's newest book about the final days of the Roman Empire would have kept Julien enthralled for hours. At the very least, it would have held his attention for more than twenty minutes, but this evening he could barely get through a page without his mind wandering. He might as well be trying to read one of the dusty Arthurian tomes that surrounded him for all the interest the Romans currently held.

Setting the book aside, he rose and walked to the desk that was still buried under piles of papers. Perhaps an exceedingly dry essay on a subject that didn't interest him was just what he needed to help him fall asleep. Nothing else he'd tried thus far had been very successful.

When he'd first arrived at Shadowcross, drink had seemed like the simplest solution. Julien had consumed innumerable bottles of port in an effort to close his eyes without seeing Leander, but had given it up after a week, unwilling to endure the dulling of his mind on a regular basis. Next he'd tried exhausting himself with long rides, sometimes going through three horses a day. The results were somewhat better, providing he stayed away from the Blackrock Folly.

He shuffled the essays, looking for one that was suitably dull, when his eyes fell on the one about Arthur and Lancelot that had so fascinated Leander. It was ridiculous, really. Leander had only visited Shadowcross a single time and yet everywhere Julien turned, there was something to remind him of the young American. Cursing quietly, he shoved the offending essay aside, and then sighed in frustration as his actions caused an entire stack of books and paper to slide to the floor.

The entrance of his butler was a welcome distraction. "What is it, Lennox?"

"My lord, are you home to Mr. Leander Mayfield?"

Julien knew he couldn't possibly have heard correctly. He'd

obviously been brooding over Leander so much that his mind had broken. "I beg your pardon?"

"Mr. Mayfield wishes to see you," Lennox clarified.

"Mr. Mayfield. Leander Mayfield? Mr. Leander Mayfield." Julien was vaguely aware that he sounded like a fool, but hoped that repeating it would help him believe it.

"Yes, sir."

Julien stood. Leander was here. In his house. Leander had come to Shadowcross to see him.

"Shall I show him in, sir?" Lennox asked patiently.

Normally that would be a ridiculous question, but Julien supposed it was reasonable at the moment, considering he had yet to say an intelligent word. "Yes." Julien cleared his throat. "Of course."

After Lennox left the room, Julien tried desperately to gather his wits and his nerves, to summon that implacable exterior he was always known for.

The door opened again and Lennox stood aside to let Leander pass before closing it behind him.

Leander was pale and drawn, and had shadows under his eyes. It was obvious he wasn't completely recovered from his ordeal. He was gnawing on his lower lip as his gaze darted around the room. He looked painfully uncertain, nervous, and not entirely well.

Julien couldn't tear his eyes away.

He had to say something, though. "Hello." The greeting came out colder than he intended, but it was the only way he could keep his voice steady.

Leander gave him a hesitant smile. "I almost asked Lennox to tell you I was someone else. I didn't know if I'd find you at home." When Julien remained quiet, unable to form a reply, Leander plunged on, speaking quickly. "I was going to have him say I was someone Lady Carysfort sent to catalog the library."

"*Did* she send you?"

"I'm not sure." Leander tilted his head, a slight frown creasing his brow. "She may have."

Hardly surprising. "Well, if that's the case," Julien gestured grandly around him, "don't let me keep you from your task."

"Julien…."

The familiar note of exasperation demolished what little control Julien had left. In three strides, he was across the library, running his hands over Leander's neck, shoulders, and arms, reassuring himself that Leander was alive, that he was whole, that he was *here*.

Leander stood still, watching Julien's hands with a soft smile.

After a moment, Julien came to his senses and withdrew. He was the one who had left; his actions now were presumptuous, not to mention uninvited. "Forgive me. I forgot myself."

Shaking his head, Leander wrapped his arms around Julien and leaned against him.

Stifling a groan, Julien crushed Leander to him, shivering when he felt Leander's face press against his neck. He had no idea how long they remained like that, but had no intention of breaking the embrace. Fortunately, he didn't have to in order to satisfy his curiosity. "Lady Carysfort told you I was here at Shadowcross?"

"I still don't know if it was intentional or not." Leander's voice was slightly muffled, and Julien could feel his warm breath as he spoke. "She acted like it was a mistake, but… not that I mean to doubt Lady Carysfort…."

Chuckling, Julien buried his face in the soft black hair. "One can never be certain with Aunt Cordelia. She made no mention of it in her last letter, though."

"That would have been impossible. Her call was only this afternoon."

This afternoon? Julien pulled away and took Leander's face in his hands. "You only learned where I was this afternoon?" That certainly explained why he'd arrived at such an odd hour. "You must have left London at once. Why not wait until morning to travel?"

"I wanted to see you," Leander replied with that disarming honesty that was so typical of him.

It never failed to devastate Julien. Unable to find a suitable reply, he brought his mouth down on Leander's.

The response was immediate. Leander parted his lips and wound his arms around Julien's neck. Julien let his lips roam over Leander's nose, eyes, and forehead, then down along his cheeks and jaw. Leander returned as many kisses as he could, running his fingers through Julien's hair constantly. He only removed them to assist when Julien pushed his coat off his shoulders.

Julien had unbuttoned Leander's waistcoat and almost had his cravat off before he realized Leander was pushing *against* him, mumbling something between kisses.

"Wait," Leander panted, taking hold of Julien's arms. "Wait, Julien."

Horrified, Julien stepped away. How could he have forgotten that Leander had been in Mayfield's clutches for weeks? "Forgive me, Leander. I should have been more careful. I should have noticed the moment you became uncomfortable."

"What?"

Carefully, gently, Julien put his hands on Leander's shoulders. "We don't have to do anything you don't wish to." He brushed Leander's cheek with the backs of his fingers. "If you need some time to put what Mayfield did behind you, I understand perfectly." When Leander still looked puzzled, he continued, "I know what kind of a man Mayfield was. I've heard much about his tastes."

"Yes," Leander nodded. "You tried to warn me. One of the reasons I came here was to apologize for not believing you."

"Dear God, don't apologize."

"But—"

"Leander, however Mayfield forced himself on you while he had you prisoner—"

"Forced himself?!" Leander's eyes were wide. "You mean you think

he...? No! There was no... he didn't. Most of the time it was the other man—Clement—who would check that I was still alive."

Julien felt a huge weight lift from his shoulders. "Then why did you call a halt to what we were doing?"

"Before we got carried away," color stained Leander's cheeks, "I wanted to be sure arrangements were made for Rand."

"Rand?"

"My coachman. Well, Kit's coachman, now. I don't want him to have to drive all the way back to London tonight. There is room here for him and the horses, isn't there?"

Mirth was bubbling in his chest and Julien had to bite his tongue to keep it from escaping. Of course. *Of course* Leander was concerned with the well-being of his staff. It was so typical of him. That, combined with relief that Mayfield hadn't laid his foul hands on Leander, made Julien almost giddy. "Did you have a specific guestroom in mind?" he grinned. "Or shall I just give up my room and sleep in the parlor?"

"Julien, that's—"

Unable to hold back any longer, Julien burst into laughter, pulling Leander close again.

"Julien, are you quite well?" Leander asked, even as he returned the embrace.

"I believe I'm supposed to ask that of you." Julien drew back just enough to give him a quick kiss on the forehead and then the lips. "I assure you that my staff will see that Rand is provided every comfort." He stepped back and began retying Leander's cravat. "Let us go and see to that now. Have you any luggage?"

"One trunk," Leander replied. Taking his cue from Julien, he began buttoning his waistcoat.

"I'll have it brought to the room next to mine." Julien kissed away the slight frown that appeared on Leander's face. "You can't possibly believe that's where you'll be sleeping, can you?"

Leander's flush deepened, but he returned the kiss.

Julien kept his hand on Leander's back as they left the library.

Lennox was at his usual post in the front hall. "Lennox, see to it that Mr. Mayfield's horses are stabled and that his coachman is given a good meal and a comfortable place for the night."

"Yes, sir."

"Kay?" Julien called, guiding Leander toward, then up, the stairs.

The valet appeared on the staircase. "Yes, my lord?"

"See that Mr. Mayfield's trunk is unpacked in the room next to mine. After that, you will not be required again this evening."

"Yes, sir," Kay said, nodding respectfully to Leander as he passed them on the stairs.

When they were finally alone in his bedchamber, Julien was dismayed to see that Leander looked even more nervous that he had when he'd arrived. Was he a bit paler or was that just the room's light? "Leander?" The long trip would have tired him, perhaps too much. "If you want to stay in the guestroom, you only have to say the word. I completely understand that you aren't yet well enough—"

That was as far as Julien got before Leander grabbed his lapels, pulling him down for a hard kiss before toppling them both back onto the bed. Julien's laughter was half-smothered by Leander's demanding lips. He'd forgotten what kind of a reaction remarks about Leander's health could provoke. Quickly, he made short work of Leander's waistcoat, cravat and shirt, reveling in the way Leander gasped and shuddered at his touch.

There was a hint of desperation in Leander's movements as he tried to shove Julien's coat off, but he wasn't making much progress in their current position. Julien gathered himself and then quickly rolled them so he was on top. Straddling the slim hips, he tore off his own coat and shirt, equally eager to be skin to skin. Staring down at Leander, Julien still had difficulty believing what he was seeing, believing that Leander was in his bed once again. Leander was thinner, but just as beautiful as ever, *more* beautiful than ever, if that was possible. "God, I missed you," he breathed, bending to press kisses to Leander's chest.

"Why didn't you come to see me?" There was a plaintive note in Leander's voice.

"Because I'm a fool." Julien skimmed his teeth over a nipple.

With a moan, Leander arched against him and then flailed his legs slightly. Confused, Julien turned his head and saw that Leander was kicking off his boots. He pressed his lips between Leander's collarbones briefly before he rose so they could finish shedding their clothes. When he was able to press the full length of his body against Leander's, a groan of pure joy escaped him.

"Julien." Leander ran his hands up and down Julien's ribs. "I want," he let out a gasp and tried to continue. "I want…."

"Anything you want." Julien nuzzled into Leander's neck and behind his ear. "You only have to say the word."

"You… in—inside me."

Julien's face was pressed against Leander's and he felt it grow warmer. Leander was blushing at his own boldness, naturally. He turned his head to kiss the reddened cheek. "Your wish is my command, and my pleasure."

After Leander's first visit to Shadowcross, Julien, in a rare moment of optimism, had a tiny jar of oil placed on his bedside table. In his later moments of pessimism, he left it there to remind himself of what he'd lost. Now he finally was able to use it, and his hand shook as he reached for it.

He let his hand glide up and down the back of Leander's thighs, stopping to squeeze the round cheeks whenever he encountered them. Leander's eyes slid shut and he lifted his knees to allow Julien more access. Julien covered the fingers of one hand with oil, carefully slipping them into the dark cleft until he found the tight opening.

Leander was definitely more relaxed this time, and Julien had little difficulty getting two fingers inside to find the spot he was looking for. He knew he'd found it when Leander made a choked sound, but continued to move his fingers in and out until Leander's head was thrashing on the pillow.

"Julien… Julien, *please*…."

Feeling somewhat desperate, Julien coated himself with oil and sank into the welcoming body with one thrust. Leander's breath caught and

Julien held still until he felt the younger man relax.

"Yes, Julien. Oh God, yes." Leander's legs came up and wrapped around his waist.

Julien lost himself in the sensation of Leander surrounding him, and began plunging mindlessly over and over. He was almost frightened to let himself go completely for fear of finding this was all a dream. Only when he felt Leander's release spreading over his stomach did Julien allow himself to follow.

It was almost a surprise to come to his senses and find that instead of being alone in bed, cold and messy, he was sweaty and messy, limbs tangled with those of a beautiful young man. He withdrew carefully and the only response from Leander was a slight sigh. He placed kisses on Leander's face and neck as he cleaned them both off, basking in the sleepy, contented smile his actions prompted.

When he lay back down, Leander automatically nestled close. For the first time since Leander's disappearance, Julien slid easily into sleep.

LEANDER awoke cocooned in warmth with fingers carding through his hair. He sighed happily and opened his mouth to comment on how good he felt, but what came out was, "Why did you leave?"

The fingers stopped and Leander opened his eyes to see Julien propped on one arm, looking down at him. "I didn't want to make you choose between me and your brothers."

He was an idiot to have asked that and probably an even bigger idiot for saying what he was about to say. "That wasn't your decision to make. You only have to decide whether you want to be with me."

"I believe we've established the answer to that," Julien replied.

The last few knots inside Leander dissolved and he lifted his head to give Julien a kiss. "I'm glad," he said and let his head fall back.

Julien began stroking his hair again. "How did your family respond to your choice?"

"Well, part of it isn't really a choice at all, is it?" Leander waited until Julien nodded his understanding before he continued. "And I told them so. Chance took it better than I thought he would. He said there were worse things in the world. Kit... I don't know if Kit is more upset about the way I am or that I've chosen to be with you in particular." He risked a glance at Julien's face and was relieved to see a wry smile. "Daisy said he would come around." He felt Julien's lips press against his temple and closed his eyes in contentment.

"And what will you do now?" Julien murmured against his skin. "I understand you have a comfortable fortune of your own."

"I do." Leander smiled. "We all do. Kit inherited the Dearborne fortune and turned his share of the shipping profits over to Chance, but my share is more than both of theirs put together. I wanted to split half with Chance, but he said we both have more than we'll ever need, so it doesn't really matter."

"So you can be a gentleman of leisure." Julien's voice took on a teasing note that Leander knew well.

"I suppose." He tried to respond in kind. "I could take a house in London and live a life of idleness and dissipation."

"And would that suit you?" Julien sounded amused by his efforts.

"Not in the least," Leander replied seriously, accepting that he would never be as good at such light-hearted banter as Julien was. "I'll never go to college, but I still want to continue my studies."

"Mmm... and remind me what it is you study."

Leander laughed. "I study the legends of King Arthur."

"Is that so? Well, it happens that I've inherited a large collection of Arthurian literature that is in need of cataloguing."

"Perhaps I could do that in exchange for room and board."

"Perhaps you could." They exchanged several deep kisses. "Do you see that wardrobe?" Julien asked when they broke apart, nodding across the room.

Leander turned to look in the direction Julien indicated, wondering where this was leading. "Yes."

"Behind it is a door that is no longer in use. Do you know where that door leads?"

Leander knew immediately. "To a guestroom with my trunk in it?"

"What a clever young man," Julien said approvingly. "You're hired."

Laughing, Leander drew Julien down again. "Is there a wardrobe on the other side as well?"

"I believe the door is covered by a wall hanging. It used to be a suite of rooms, but Algernon had no use for such luxury and changed it into a guestroom. When I inherited I never saw any real reason to change things."

"Until now." Leander couldn't stop smiling.

"Until now."

"I won't be spending too much time in that room, though, will I?" Leander felt a little daring and willed himself not to blush. "I'll be spending my days in the library and my nights here."

That earned him another kiss. "But not right away. Not the days in the library, at least."

"What?"

"You aren't completely recovered yet, Leander. That's plain enough to see. You likely shouldn't have made the trip to Shadowcross."

Leander's light-heartedness evaporated. "You sound like Kit."

"I doubt that." Julien's tone was dry. "All I mean is that a few days' rest would be best."

"You want me to remain bed-ridden." Leander sighed in exasperation. "You know how I feel about that."

"I do." Julien's eyes gleamed in the candlelight. "I was hoping to convince you, however."

"How?"

"By staying in bed with you."

A wealth of new possibilities opened up in Leander's imagination.

"Days...?"

Then Julien's lips came down on his and Leander suspected that if Julien had any say in the matter, he'd never associate staying in bed with illness again.

V.B. KILDAIRE is a Canadian prairie girl from Manitoba who has worked at a national park, a radio station, and a family-owned store. She has an unhealthy obsession with mad monarchs and unexplained history. She is also servant to a very spoiled cat.

Visit V.B. Kildaire's blog at http://vbkildaire.livejournal.com/

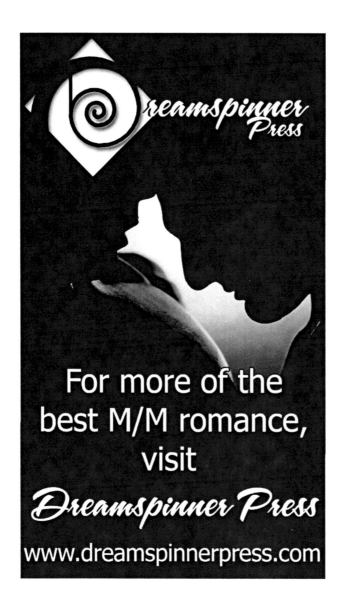

Printed in the United States
148813LV00003B/45/P

9 781615 810093